H

"Rarely has an author painted the great American West in strokes so bold, vivid, and true."
—Ralph Compton

OUTFOXED

Leaving their ponies in the thicket, they crept forward until they reached a point some thirty yards from the pine shelter. There they split up on either side of the trail in order to set up a cross fire. Yellow Hand hoped to catch his enemy as he walked out of his shelter, so he waited until the sun had risen over the ridges to the east. Still, Joe Fox did not come out. Too impatient to wait longer, he inched a few yards closer, then gave Red Sky the signal to shoot, and both warriors opened fire with their repeating rifles, pumping round after round into the makeshift shelter, sending pine limbs flying and filling the ravine with thunderous echoes.

After both men emptied the magazines of their rifles, they charged up to the shelter to peer inside. Stunned, they stood gaping into an empty hut. "Up here," Joe Fox said, and they both turned toward the sound, looking up into the glare of the sun as it framed a dark image against a background of young pines. In the blinding light, it appeared to the two assassins that the image stood in a flaming arch, and in the next instant fiery missiles reached out to strike down both of them.

THE BLACKFOOT TRAIL

Charles G. West

A SIGNET BOOK

SIGNET
Published by New American Library, a division of
Penguin Group (USA) Inc., 375 Hudson Street,
New York, New York 10014, USA
Penguin Group (Canada), 90 Eglinton Avenue East, Suite 700, Toronto,
Ontario M4P 2Y3, Canada (a division of Pearson Penguin Canada Inc.)
Penguin Books Ltd., 80 Strand, London WC2R 0RL, England
Penguin Ireland, 25 St. Stephen's Green, Dublin 2,
Ireland (a division of Penguin Books Ltd.)
Penguin Group (Australia), 250 Camberwell Road, Camberwell, Victoria 3124,
Australia (a division of Pearson Australia Group Pty. Ltd.)
Penguin Books India Pvt. Ltd., 11 Community Centre, Panchsheel Park,
New Delhi - 110 017, India
Penguin Group (NZ), 67 Apollo Drive, Rosedale, North Shore 0632,
New Zealand (a division of Pearson New Zealand Ltd.)
Penguin Books (South Africa) (Pty.) Ltd., 24 Sturdee Avenue,
Rosebank, Johannesburg 2196, South Africa

Penguin Books Ltd., Registered Offices:
80 Strand, London WC2R 0RL, England

First published by Signet, an imprint of New American Library,
a division of Penguin Group (USA) Inc.

First Printing, December 2009
10 9 8 7 6 5 4 3 2 1

For Ronda

Chapter 1

"Joe Fox!"

The call rang out again and again, echoing off the face of the rocky cliff that stood like a castle wall before the two nearly exhausted men. "Joe Fox!" Malcolm Lindstrom called again while looking about him nervously. It had been a long, hard climb up to the base of the cliff, through thick forests of firs and pines that seemed to be put there by God solely for the purpose of keeping strangers from scaling the majestic peak.

"I don't know about this," Pete Watson complained. "It gives me a worrisome feeling." He turned away from the wall and peered down the narrow game trail they had followed to this point, half expecting to see a Blackfoot war party emerge from the forest behind them. "Smack-dab in the heart of Blackfoot country, just the two of us, lookin' for a man that some say don't even exist." He turned back to Malcolm. "How do we know this Joe Fox feller ain't just a legend the Indians dreamed up? Hell, that feller down by the river sent us up here and he probably ain't ever really seen him, just that the Injuns said this is where *they've* seen him." Frowning, he scanned the dark forest behind him. "I

hate to say this, but that feller mighta just been settin'
us up to get jumped by some of his Blackfoot friends. I
never trusted a Frenchman, anyway."

"You worry too much," Malcolm said, although he
was entertaining some of the same thoughts expressed
by his brother-in-law. The fact of the matter was they
were where they were. It was too late to consider whether
the Frenchman at the trading post on the river below
was a scoundrel, bent upon sending a party of warriors to ambush them. As far as the real or imagined existence of the man the Blackfoot called Joe Fox, Father
Paul claimed to have known him as a boy, before the
legend was created. And it was the priest's conviction
that Joe Fox, if he could be found, was the best bet to
find Malcolm's brother and the rest of the party that
set out to follow a northern route to Oregon.

Malcolm was not a man to take unnecessary risks,
and he had advised his brother against joining a party
of seven families determined to join an earlier group
that had made the journey by wagon the year before.
Because of a late start, and the fact that there had been
reports of Sioux war parties along the South Pass route,
they had decided to cross farther north through the
mountains, hoping to strike the Mullan Road. The road,
blazed by an army captain named John Mullan, was
reported to be the first wagon road across the Rockies,
running from Fort Benton on the Missouri to Fort Walla
Walla in Washington.

Reports they had heard told of poor conditions on the
road, so they decided their chances were better if they
traveled by mule train instead of trying to cross with
wagons. They were led by a man named Skinner, who
claimed to know a route to the Mullan Road that was
safe and short. He claimed that he would have them
safely in the Willamette Valley before August. It was
now late September, and already some snow had fallen
in the mountains, with no sign of the pilgrims. His

brother, Bradley, had promised to telegraph him as soon as they had safely reached Fort Walla Walla, and there had been no word.

Malcolm feared the worst. Everyone he had talked to who had any knowledge of the Rocky Mountains had told him the undertaking was a fool's mission this late in the season. But he was determined to do all he could to find the missing party. Accompanied by his brother-in-law, he had followed the route of the mule train as far as Helena, where the trail disappeared. Asking around several businesses in Helena, they came upon some store owners who remembered the mule train and told them it had moved on toward the west. Malcolm and Pete had met with no luck in picking up their trail.

Coming upon a mission run by a Jesuit priest named Father Paul, he and Pete had sought help there. Father Paul had advised them to search for Joe Fox, stating his belief that Fox was their best chance of finding the party of settlers. "No one knows the mountains better than Joe Fox," Father Paul had claimed, after first questioning the wisdom of the undertaking. "And he can travel through the Blackfoot country without fear of harm by the Indians."

"Beggin' your pardon, Father," Malcolm had questioned, "but how in the world would we ever find Joe Fox? If nobody but Injuns has ever seen him, what chance have we got? We could wander around in those mountains for fifty years and never lay eyes on him, especially if what they say about him not wantin' to be found is true."

"That's probably pretty much the truth," Father Paul had confessed. "But the only reason I'm suggesting it is because one of my congregation, Sam Black Crow, told me just yesterday that he was sure he had sighted Joe Fox on the east slope of Blackjack Mountain, up near the cliff." Seeing their puzzled expressions, he had told them that he could explain how to find Black-jack Mountain. "I'm told that he often camps in these parts this time of the year. You may think it too dangerous to seek him out, but I think it's your only chance of finding your brother and the others." So now they stood, staring at a blank stone wall, with no idea where to go from this point.

"You know, your sister's gonna be mad as hell at you if anything happens to me," Pete joked halfheartedly.

"Hell," Malcolm replied, "she'd most likely hug my neck." Beginning to feel a bit stupid for climbing up a mountain in hopes of finding a single soul in this vast wilderness, he nevertheless gave one last call. "Joe Fox!"

"What do you want?"

Both men jumped, startled by the soft voice right behind them, where there had been no one moments before. Like a ghost, the tall figure seemed to have materialized from nowhere to stand before them, dressed in animal skins, holding a rifle ready to fire. Struck dumb and stunned, Pete, without thinking, started to lift his rifle from the ground.

"Don't do that," the ominous figure cautioned.

Realizing then, Pete dropped the rifle to the ground. "I wasn't gonna . . . ," he stammered. Malcolm, noting the serious warning in the man's eyes, carefully laid his rifle upon the ground as well.

"Why do you call my name?"

Sensing no immediate threat, Malcolm asked, "Are you Joe Fox?" When he was answered with a simple nod, he continued. "We were hoping you would help us find a party of white families that musta got lost somewhere in these mountains on their way west."

"Who told you to come to me?" Joe asked, his face expressionless, his eyes gazing unblinking at the two white men who had somehow stumbled into his domain.

"Father Paul, at the mission," Malcolm quickly responded, hoping that would influence the emotionless man. Studying him carefully, Malcolm was not certain whether Joe Fox was Indian or white. It was hard to tell, dressed as he was in skins, clean shaven, and wearing his dark hair in two long braids. He was tall—taller than either Malcolm or Pete. The Blackfeet were a tall people, but Joe Fox was taller still. Under his soft cow-skin shirt he wore an unadorned breechcloth and leggings that reached to his thighs. A belt held a knife sheath and a small pouch. In addition to an early-model Winchester, he had a bow strapped to his back and a weasel-skin quiver of arrows. Malcolm had never seen a more fitting image of a Blackfoot warrior, and yet this magnificent specimen of raw power was possessed of fine, chiseled facial features more suggestive of a white man. Malcolm decided that Joe Fox was a half-breed.

It was obvious to the two strangers that the mention of Father Paul caused the man to pause. In truth, Joe had not thought about the man who had tried to teach him the ways of Christianity for quite some time. "Why would Father Paul send you to me?" he asked, his words slow and deliberate, suggesting a lack of recent use of English.

"Like I said," Malcolm replied, "we're lookin' for some folks that mighta got lost in these mountains. The army wouldn't help us—said they didn't have the troops to spare. Father Paul sent us to find you—said there wasn't nobody that knowed the mountains like you." He watched Joe Fox carefully, trying to gauge the stoic man's reaction as he continued to consider the two intruders in his home. In was plain to see Joe Fox's reluctance to involve himself in their plight.

Joe shifted his gaze from one of his visitors to the other, sizing them up. He could read nothing that held a hint of larceny in the face of either man. The one who did all of the talking had a look of sincerity in his eyes. The other seemed more concerned with thoughts of his personal safety. After a long pause, Joe finally spoke again. "Those folks you're looking for musta been crazy to try to cross through all the mountain ranges between here and Oregon country. You're lucky you two got up this far with your scalps still on. Many of my people have gone to the reservation, but many have not and still live as *Na'pi* meant the *Sik'-si-kau* to live. The Blackfeet don't like the white man, and it is dangerous for two white men to pass through this country." He glanced again at Pete before continuing. "I saw your horses below by the stream. I thought about stealing them, but I was curious to see what fools would leave their horses alone by a stream where two game trails crossed."

The castigating remark was ignored by Malcolm as he continued to present his case. "The folks we're lookin' for are good Christian people. My brother and his wife are with 'em. They ain't out to bother the Blackfoot or any other tribe. They're just wantin' to pass through on their way to Oregon."

Joe studied the two men for a few moments more while he made up his mind. He was reluctant to have anything to do with a party of settlers, even if they were not intent upon settling in his mountains. He had to give in to a weakness for helping those who could not help themselves, however, so he finally wavered. "I know the party you speak of," he said. "I watched them as they tried to cross this mountain range. I counted thirty-six mules, all packed heavy."

"That's right," Pete interrupted. "There was eight families and each one of 'em took four mules."

Joe glanced briefly at Pete. He was not an educated man by any stretch of the imagination, but he knew that eight times four was not thirty-six. He was not interested enough to question it, however. "Mighty tempting to a Blackfoot war party," he said. "They tried to come in following the river, but they had to turn around when they got to the falls. They tried two more times before giving up and moving on."

Excited to find that Joe Fox had actually seen the party, Malcolm pressed, "Where'd they go then?"

Joe shook his head before answering. "I don't know. I was just glad they left." When he saw the disappointment in Malcolm's eyes, he added, "All I can tell you is they pushed on north of here, lookin' for another place to try, I s'pose."

"Can you find 'em?" Pete asked.

"I might if I was lookin' for 'em," Joe answered. He paused, then added, "If they're still alive."

"We don't expect you to do it for nothin'," Malcolm said. "We can pay you." He hesitated then. "How much would it take to get you to track 'em?"

Joe had to stop and think about it for a moment, for he was still making up his mind whether he would help them. He had no idea about charging a fee for guiding someone. In principle he wasn't for hire, but he had decided that Malcolm was a good man, so he said, "I never said for sure that I could find 'em, but I'll see what I can do. For my part, I'll ask for extra cartridges for my rifle and some supplies—sugar, salt, and coffee. I ain't had no coffee in four months."

"Done!" Malcolm responded eagerly, and thrust out his hand. Joe simply stared at it for a long moment before shaking. Saying nothing more, he turned abruptly and strode off toward the trees. Malcolm and Pete exchanged puzzled glances, then hurried off after him.

"We need to fetch our horses," Pete called out after their new partner. "We left 'em below by that stream."

Without turning his head, Joe said, "They're with my horses," causing them to exchange glances again. "Keep up. I expect there'll be a Blackfoot war party up here any minute now."

His words caused considerable concern for the two white men. "Damn!" Pete exclaimed. "I told you that damn Frenchman would set the Injuns on us."

"The Frenchman didn't tell anybody," Joe said without turning his head to face them. "He didn't have to. Every Blackfoot this side of the mountains could hear you yellin' my name and follow your trail up here."

Moving rapidly, although seemingly without effort, their tall, silent guide led them along a rocky ledge covered with a light dusting of snow; this carried them away from the face of the cliff and into another thick forest of firs. After a few minutes' walk, they came upon a small clearing to discover their horses tied beside two belonging to Joe Fox. Without offering any instructions, Joe went directly to a paint pony with an Indian saddle and mounted. He reached down to take the lead rope on his packhorse; then, pausing only to make sure his two partners were following suit, he turned the paint's head toward a small game trail that led down the mountain. Still nervous and unsure about their contract with this silent enigma, Malcolm and Pete dutifully followed.

It was dusk, with darkness rapidly approaching, by the time they reached a narrow river at the base of the mountain. "Make camp here" were the first words spoken by their somber guide since leaving the cliff. He slid gracefully off the back of his horse and led it to the water to drink. "We'll cook some of that salt pork in your packs tonight. Maybe in the mornin' I'll find some fresh meat."

It was not lost on Malcolm that Joe Fox had evidently looked through their packs when he first found their horses. He could see no point in commenting on it, however. "Where does this river lead?" he asked, thinking it looked to be a possible passage through the solid mountain range before them.

"It leads to some waterfalls about halfway up the mountain on the other side of this one we're lookin' at," Joe answered. "Your friends thought the same thing you're thinkin'. They followed it till they had to turn back at the falls. There's a way around the falls, but I reckon they couldn't find it." He shrugged his shoulders. "Wouldn'ta done 'em much good if they had. They'da probably got lost. Those mules woulda had to have wings to get over the mountains on the other side of the falls."

Malcolm nodded, then asked, "So they headed north from here, along the base of these mountains?"

"After they tried a couple more places," Joe replied, "both of 'em box canyons."

Almost surprised that their tight-lipped guide could actually talk beyond a few short words, Pete asked, "Think you can track 'em?"

"Maybe," Joe replied, "but it ain't likely. It's been two months since then. I doubt there'll be any tracks to follow."

Confused by his answer, Pete sputtered, "Then how the hell are you gonna . . . ?"

Joe shrugged his shoulders again, his expression never changing. "All I can do is show you the way to get through the mountains. I can take you to a couple of trails the Kutenai and Flatheads use to get to the buffalo country over on this side. If your friends were lucky, they mighta took one of those."

Obviously dismayed by the news, Pete looked at Malcolm and commented, "I was thinkin' he might be able to track 'em. They coulda wandered off anywhere in them mountains, and we might never find 'em."

"Maybe you changed your mind about goin' with me," Joe said, seeing his dismay.

"No, no," Malcolm was quick to reply. "We ain't got a chance in hell on our own."

It was settled then, and they went about making their camp by the river. Pete sliced some of the salt pork they had brought while Malcolm filled the coffeepot with water and set it on the fire Joe had built. There was little conversation after their supper, and all three were soon in their blankets. Malcolm lay awake for a while after he first heard Pete's lusty snoring. As when fully awake, their new partner was silent in his slumber, but Malcolm speculated that he would be alert at the slightest sound. Malcolm thought about the happenings of the day as he lay there staring up at a moonless sky, wondering about the strange man he and Pete had taken on as a guide.

Malcolm was not the first person to wonder about Joe Fox. No one really knew where he came from, not even Joe Fox, and there was some uncertainty about his exact age. He was two or three, or maybe four when he was found by an old Blackfoot woman named Crying Woman. The boy was sitting beside the body of his mother on the bank of Gray Fox Creek. His dead mother looked to be Piegan, and Crying Woman speculated that she was possibly a casualty of the bloody war between the Piegans and the Gros Ventre. But the boy looked more white than Piegan, causing Crying Woman to further speculate upon the heritage of the father.

Childless, Crying Woman took the boy home to her village, where she and her husband endeavored to rear him as a Blackfoot warrior. At first the child would not speak beyond a single word. Whenever he was addressed by either his adoptive mother or father, he would respond with the word *Joe*. Crying Woman decided that it was his name that he repeated. When it was time to give him a proper name, his new father decided to call the boy Joe Fox because he was found beside Gray Fox Creek. The boy seemed satisfied with his name.

A gangly youngster in his early years, he was often the butt of many of the other boys' jokes. His Blackfoot father was not pleased by the development of his son, but Crying Woman never lost faith in Joe's promise. She saw a quiet courage in the youngster that she believed would one day reveal itself. By the time he reached the age of thirteen or fourteen, the gangly youth had disappeared, justifying his mother's faith. A leader among his peers in the village, he was soon allowed to accompany war parties into Crow country, an honor for a boy of his age.

It was about this time in his life that a Jesuit priest built a mission on the Teton River. Along with some of the other boys who were curious about the white man, Joe visited the mission and became friends with the priest. Realizing Joe had a latent knowledge of English from his early childhood, the priest encouraged him to practice it. Thinking it a game, Joe participated in the lessons until he decided the priest was too focused on saving his soul.

The visits to the mission ceased when Joe was around eighteen years of age. While he was visiting the priest, a Crow war party, seeking revenge for an attack on a Crow hunting party, raided the Blackfoot village, killing many, among them Joe's adoptive mother and father. Consumed by grief and guilt, he blamed his parents' death on himself. He had not been there to protect them. He knew their deaths called for retaliation on his part, so he rode with a war party that caught up to the Crows near the same creek where he had been found by Crying Woman. A fierce battle ensued with warriors killed on both sides. Joe accounted for two of the Crow dead.

After the battle, there was much singing and dancing about the Blackfoot victory, but Joe could not eradicate his feeling of guilt for the loss of his parents. Seeking help, he went to an old medicine man named Hears Thunder. The old man listened while Joe recounted the turmoil with his inner demons of guilt. Then he told him he must go to the mountains, fast for three days, and ask Na'pi to send a vision. "You must stay and meditate until Man Above visits you and shows you your path," Hears Thunder had said.

Joe's fast lasted for four and a half days before he fell, exhausted and weak, into a deep sleep. Many unrelated things flew haphazardly through his mind, but upon awakening, one vision remained in his memory. A man came to him, a white man. He did not say so, but Joe felt certain it was his father. *Neither white nor red are you, but a man alone*, the vision said. *You must go your own way and follow the voices of the trees and rocks.*

The young man was certain then that he was neither Blackfoot nor white. He abandoned thoughts of going in search of his white father, as well as returning to the village of his adoptive parents. Many years had passed since then, but Joe remained in the mountains. In time, he became a legend, talked about by the young men of the tribe when they sat around their campfires, telling of finding sign of the tall warrior on this mountain or that river. But few could boast of actually seeing the lone warrior with their own eyes. In fact, Joe was not totally aware of his image as a phantom until visiting the trading post to trade some hides. The Frenchman who ran the store had been surprised to find that the legend called Joe Fox was, in fact, a real man. By that time, Joe was resigned to remain in his beloved mountains, accustomed to his solitary existence, content to live without the company of other men, and unconcerned what image his brothers had created for him. And now, upon the arrival of Malcolm and Pete, he found it hard to explain why he had not avoided these two white men. He could have, easily.

Morning found Malcolm tangled in his blanket, and nearly as tired as when he had turned in the night before. He had tossed and turned, sleeping in fits, hearing noises in the night, noises in addition to Pete's snoring. Finally wide-awake, he sat up to look around him, and noticed at once that Joe Fox was gone. His first thought was to look toward the bank where the horses had been tied, and was immediately relieved to see his and Pete's horse right where they had left them. He reached over and gave Pete a kick on the leg. "You awake?" Pete answered with a grunt, but remained wrapped in his blanket. "Looks like Joe Fox decided not to help us after all."

Pete sat up, and just as Malcolm had, looked to see if the horses were still there. When it was apparent that they had not been robbed, he blinked away the sleep and continued to stare toward the river. After a moment, he said, "Well, if that's so, he left his pack-horse."

"Damn . . ." Malcolm sighed contritely, embarrassed by his initial suspicions. "I reckon I spoke too soon." No more than a moment after he said it, they both turned at the sound of a horse climbing up from the river. Uncomfortable with having been caught still in their blankets, both men scrambled up out of bed.

"I was lucky," Joe remarked as he rode into camp with a small deer draped across the paint in front of his saddle. "Caught this little doe coming outta the river." Malcolm was about to remark that he had not heard the gun shot when he noticed the arrow still embedded just behind the deer's front leg.

After a breakfast that was a welcome departure from the salt pork and beans that had sustained Pete and Malcolm for several weeks, they broke camp and Joe led them north along the base of the mountains. Unknown to them, the missing party they sought to find was camped less than forty miles away as the hawk flies.

Chapter 2

"We're gonna have to decide what we're gonna do," Jake Simmons insisted. "That son of a bitch don't have no idea where the hell we are, and we're gonna be settin' here in the middle of these mountains all winter."

Bradley Lindstrom nodded his head solemnly, knowing what Jake said was probably true. They had been encamped there for three days, resting the mules and waiting while their guide purportedly scouted the cuts and valleys, searching for the trail he claimed to be there. That it had probably been covered up by a hard winter was what he had offered as an excuse for the delay, one of many such delays on this ill-fated journey.

Bradley felt responsible for their troubles. He had accepted the man's word when Skinner claimed to have traveled through these mountains to Walla Walla before, and the guide had been hired primarily upon Bradley's judgment. *I should have listened to Malcolm and waited until next spring to take the old wagon route to the west*, he thought.

There were other factors to consider, however. The old wagon trail led through country that was still threatened with Sioux and Cheyenne war parties. Bradley had deemed it safer to avoid that area altogether. Making their way up to Bismarck in Dakota Territory, the small party of settlers had embarked on a more northerly route to the west. Glancing up now at the worried gaze of Jake Simmons, he said, "I reckon you're right. We've got to do somethin' to protect our women and children. We can't sit here in this valley all winter."

"Maybe we oughta think about tryin' to build some kind of shelters," the third member of the discussion, Raymond Chadwick, suggested. "Bad weather's gonna be here before you know it, and there ain't nothin' but more of these damn mountains every way you look."

"Hell," Jake snorted. "We can't stay here. We'd freeze to death in these mountains, if we didn't starve to death first." During the last few days, when they had been lightly blanketed by an early-spring snow, there had been several mentions of the legendary Donner party. And that had not helped the general morale of the party of settlers.

"Jake's right," Bradley said. "We can't stay here. One thing I think we're all agreed on, though, we'll be better off without Skinner leadin' us. I'm the one who hired him. I reckon it's up to me to fire him."

"Don't go puttin' too much of the blame on yourself," Raymond said. "We'll back you up. Won't we, Jake?"

"Yes, sir," Jake replied, "the three of us will tell him we're done with him." He gave Bradley a reassuring nod of the head, then added, "If he ever shows up again."

A few minutes before dusk, Skinner appeared, emerging from the trees to the south of the camp. Unlike the majority of the train he led, Skinner rode a dark brown Morgan. He always sat slightly slumped in the saddle as if constantly tired, wearing a surly expression, except when forcing a belligerent smile. Nancy Lindstrom said Skinner looked like he was measuring everyone he met, and found them all lacking. Cora Simmons said he looked like a weasel with always an eye on the women on the train, especially her daughter, Callie. At any rate, his popularity with the eight families had begun a diminishing spiral from the first day he addressed the group and announced that he knew the way West better than any living man. As the weeks piled one upon another, confidence in his ability waned, but by then the die had been cast. So they felt they must tolerate him since not one of them knew the way, and he still maintained that he would lead them to the Willamette Valley, where their friends and relatives waited. Now, after this evening's discussion between the three unappointed but accepted leaders of the group, it seemed the time had come to rid themselves of Skinner and his surly attitude.

"Maybe we oughta talk this over with the rest of the train to make sure ever'body's thinkin' the same as we are," Raymond Chadwick said as he watched Skinner approach. "There's been some talk about turnin' back while we still got the chance."

"They've already said whatever we think is best," Bradley said. "We've been goin' around in circles so long, I ain't sure anybody knows the way back to Three Forks, includin' Skinner. It's time to face up to him. He don't know where we're at any more than we do. We've already throwed away good money on him. It don't make sense to pay him to wander around these mountains hopin' to find a way out. I reckon we can do that for ourselves."

"Bradley's right," Jake said, "ain't no use in puttin' it off."

The three settlers climbed slowly to their feet as Skinner drew his horse up before them. "Damned if I ain't 'bout to starve," he announced as he dismounted. "I hope you got some coffee left in that pot." When no one answered and no cup was offered, he paused to cast a suspicious eye upon the three. "What the hell's wrong with you fellers? You look like you smell a fart."

"We've been talkin' over some things," Bradley spoke up.

Knowing at once that he didn't like the sound of that, Skinner shot back, "What kinda things?"

"Well," Bradley replied, looking at Jake for support, "for one thing, we was wonderin' where you've been all day."

Certain now that he didn't like the way the three were looking at him, he became immediately suspicious. His reaction was one of anger. "What the hell do you think I been doin'?" he barked. "Wearin' my horse out scoutin' for that trail outta this valley. That's what I been doin', by God. Tryin' to lead you and your families to Oregon."

"Did you find the trail you've been talkin' about?" Jake asked.

"I found a couple of trails that might be it," Skinner lied. When Jake and Bradley exchanged doubting glances, Skinner fumed, "It ain't no fault of mine if the trails was covered by a bad winter." Again, there was no response to his claims. "But I know the way to go," he insisted. "Tomorrow mornin' we'll pack up and follow the river."

"I don't see how that's gonna do much good for us," Bradley said. "Looks pretty much like this river runs north and south. I never claimed to be much of a guide, but I don't see how followin' this river north is ever gonna get us west—which is what we paid you to do."

Understanding clearly now what was in the offing, Skinner began to rankle. The heavy brows lowered like two black veils, casting a dark cloud over his eyes, and he spoke slowly in a voice more closely resembling a growl. "Just what are you gettin' at, Lindstrom?"

Bradley looked toward his two compatriots for support, but there was no indication of help from that quarter, so he pressed on. "There ain't no polite way of sayin' it, so I'll just out with it. We've decided it best to try to find our way outta here ourselves. We don't think you know where we are, or how to get us where we wanna go." He paused a moment for Skinner's response, but for the moment the irate man was speechless, never figuring the meek pilgrims had the grit to fire him. "We paid you half the money before we started out. We don't figure you earned it, but we're willin' to forget it and part, no hard feelin's." He cast a quick glance in Jake's direction. There had been no discussion regarding the recovery of money already paid to Skinner. Jake never even blinked, so Bradley went on. "We think that's more'n fair for both sides."

Skinner's reaction was what Bradley had feared. The deep eyebrow-knotted scowl warned of the volcanic rumblings inside his wiry body, and Bradley braced for the eruption that was bound to follow. Instead, Skinner's stormy features relaxed to form his familiar contemptuous sneer. "Well, ain't that a fine howdy-do?" he snarled, glancing back and forth between the three leaders of the party. "Just decided to fire me, didja? And while I'm out riskin' my neck to keep you from gettin' slaughtered by Injuns." He glared at Bradley Lindstrom then. "We'll just part company, and no hard feelin's," he mocked. The storm returned to his face and he pointed a bony finger at Bradley. "Well, that ain't the way it works. We shook hands on it. Two hundred and fifty dollars when we left Bismarck, and two hundred and fifty when we get to the Willamette Valley—a deal's a deal. Now, after I took you more'n halfway, riskin' my neck, you wanna back outta the deal. Well, you can back out if that's what you wanna do, but I'll have the rest of the money you owe me—and then we'll part company with no hard feelin's."

Bradley could not respond at once, and while he stood flustered for a moment, Jake Simmons finally made some effort to back him. "Listen, Skinner," he said, "all you did was get us good and lost. We don't owe you nothin'. Thanks to you, we're likely to get caught here by winter storms. You oughta give us back the money we already gave you."

Skinner's brows lowered again to form the sneer so prevalent in his features. "You and your bellyaching bunch of pilgrims can go to hell for all I care, the whole lot of ya." He dropped his hand to rest on the handle of his pistol, daring any one of them to protest.

Alarmed by the gesture, Bradley quickly attempted to defuse the situation before it led to actual violence. "There ain't no call to get testy about this. We just wanna part ways in peace and no hard feelin's."

"You can kiss my ass," Skinner retorted, finally accepting defeat and knowing that he could not openly fight the whole mule train. "So be it," he spat and stepped back up in the saddle. "You damn fools will perish without me, and it serves you right." He pulled the Morgan's head around, and just before kicking it hard with his heels, left them with one last warning. "This won't be the last you'll see of me."

Cora Simmons came out of her tent when she heard the sound of Skinner's horse galloping out of camp. Joining the three men by the fire, she asked, "Now where's he going?"

"Who knows and who cares?" Jake replied at once. "We just fired him."

Only mildly surprised, Cora said, "So now we don't have a guide."

"Hell, we didn't have one before," Jake snorted.

"The question is what do we do now?" Raymond Chadwick reminded them.

"I don't see that we've got much choice," Bradley said. "We can't stay here, so I say we follow the river north in the mornin'." He shrugged his shoulders when it struck him that this was what Skinner had suggested. "Maybe we'll find a pass that'll take us through the mountains."

Joe Fox knelt at the crossing of two game trails and examined the droppings that he was now sure were left by the long mule train. By his estimation, some of the droppings were several days older than others. He was further puzzled by the fact that the party seemed to have taken both trails, in effect going in two different directions. He was baffled for only a moment, however, when he realized that the mule train he was tracking was going in circles, doubling back on itself. He decided to follow the fresher droppings. "They're lost all right," he said as he stepped up in the saddle and turned the paint's head up the game trail.

Malcolm and Pete filed in behind him. Those four words were the first he had spoken since earlier in the morning when he had discovered a distinct track that told him the party had veered off toward a narrow mountain pass to the west. Finding solid sign at the end of a canyon, Joe led them up through a series of game trails that sidled the mountain before them, eventually bringing them to the far side and descending toward a narrow valley below. Crossing a small stream in the valley, he had simply pointed to fresh tracks, only a few days old, left in the soft sand by the water, leaving Malcolm and Pete to come to their own conclusions.

Now, leaving the point where the two trails had crossed, Joe abruptly raised his hand, bringing them to a stop. He slid off his horse again and stooped to examine the ground. After a few moments, he got up and turned to the two men waiting for his explanation. "Trouble maybe," was all he said, and started to mount again. In need of more information than that, Malcolm finally pressed, "Wait a minute. Whaddaya mean, trouble? What kinda trouble?"

Realizing then that he credited his two companions with more experience than they had acquired, he explained. "See here," he said, pointing to some disturbed pine needles on the high side of the trail. "Riders," he continued. "Maybe Blackfoot, maybe Flathead, maybe Gros Ventre, but Indian—unshod ponies. Whoever it was musta come from up there." He pointed toward a rocky ledge above the trail. "They struck this trail, and now they're following the same tracks we are."

"Damn," Pete murmured, then asked, "Can you tell how many there were?"

"Hard to say," Joe replied. "I'd guess at six or eight, but that's only a guess."

"How long ago?" This from Malcolm.

"Two days, maybe three."

There was no need for discussion. The only thing for them was to make the best time possible and hope to catch up in time to help their friends. Malcolm worried about his brother and his sister-in-law. He was not sure how Bradley would handle adversity in the form of an Indian war party. His brother was not a man to welcome confrontation on a physical front, seeking to make peace through diplomacy whenever possible. Malcolm had never seen Bradley in a face-off with anyone. He feared Bradley might make the mistake of trying to negotiate with a Blackfoot war party. Nancy was the fighter in his brother's house. There was nothing to do but ride hard and hope.

Seth Skinner pressed his horse relentlessly, grumbling to himself as he backtracked down the mountainside, the same one he had led the settlers up days before. Still angry over his abrupt dismissal, he considered the situation he now found himself in. He had money in his pocket. That much was true—more money, in fact, than he had ever had at one time. He could not, however, stop thinking about the equal sum he would have received had he been able to finish the journey. The fact that everything he had told Bradley Lindstrom about his knowledge of the Rocky Mountains was an outright lie did not trouble his conscience. Men like Bradley Lindstrom were fair game for double-dealers like Skinner.

Taking advantage of his master's inattention, the big Morgan that Skinner rode gradually slowed its pace until finding one more to its liking. So absorbed in his thoughts of scheming to somehow get his hands on the rest of the money that Lindstrom had promised, he wasn't aware that the horse had slowed to a leisurely walk until he glanced up to see the Indian warrior sitting his pony in the middle of the trail, watching him. Realizing at that instant that he had let his survival senses doze, he jerked his horse to an abrupt halt. Not really sure what to do, Skinner turned to look behind him only to find several more Indians blocking the narrow trail in that direction. Feeling his heart beating in his throat, he returned his eyes to the Indian before him and raised his hand in a nervous greeting. "Me friend," he offered in a voice quaking with fear.

With face devoid of expression, the Indian made no response to the feeble overture, but continued to stare with unblinking eyes set beneath a wide forehead, measuring the white man with the same disdain one would show a coyote. When he finally spoke, his words were delivered in a sharp, guttural tone, heavy with contempt. "No white man is my friend," he stated emphatically.

Seeing a slender ray of hope when the savage spoke to him in English, Skinner forced a smile across his ferretlike face. "I'm a friend, sure 'nough," he insisted anxiously, casting nervous glances around him when the warriors behind him moved closer. Hoping to save his hair by offering a prize, he said, "I can lead you to a bunch of white men that *are* your enemies, and we can share their supplies and guns." He jumped nervously when a broad-shouldered warrior pulled his pony up beside him and yanked his rifle from the scabbard. Afraid to protest, he watched as the warrior examined the rifle, then said something to his friends that caused them to erupt with war cries. "Hell, I'll just take the money," Skinner said. "You boys can have everything else." He looked to either side of him as the Indians moved in closer around him. Near panic at this point, he blurted, "I've always been a friend of the Blackfoot!"

His desperate statement caused an immediate chorus of growling voices, and he knew he had said the wrong thing. The broad-faced warrior in front of him responded coldly. "We are *A'aninen*," he said, using the Gros Ventre name for themselves. "The Blackfoot are our enemies. If you are their friends, then you are our enemy."

"No! No!" Skinner fairly screamed. "I didn't mean I was their friends!" The lump in his throat that was his heart threatened to choke him in his panic. "I can lead you to a rich train of whites," he pleaded, "and you can have it all."

The broad-faced warrior smiled contemptuously. "We don't need you to lead us. A blind dog can follow this trail."

Confused, for the Gros Ventre had not made the last statement in English, Skinner looked about him anxiously, searching for some sign of mercy. An instant later, he was struck by a solid blow on his back as an arrow drove through his ribs to puncture his lung. Paralyzed by the shock, he remained rigid in the saddle for a few seconds, realizing that he was about to die. The broad-shouldered Indian on his right raised his foot and shoved him off his horse, and one of the others slid off his pony and scalped him even as he was dying.

Watching the youngest member of his war party claim his first scalp, Dead Man nodded his silent approval. While others searched the white man's saddle-bags, Two Arrows nudged his pony up beside Dead Man's. He held the rifle out for Dead Man to admire. "Shoot many times," he said. Dead Man smiled and nodded. It was a rare trophy. "Maybe the tracks will lead us to more of these guns," Two Arrows said.

Again Dead Man nodded. The acquisition of such fine weapons would be a good thing. But equally important would be the opportunity to punish the white men for trespassing in his country. Dead Man hated the white man even more than the treacherous Black-foot.

Chapter 3

"You know him?" Joe asked when Malcolm and Pete caught up to him.

"Lord a' mercy," Pete gasped when they saw the body lying beside the trail. Instinctively, both he and Malcolm grasped their rifles and began to look around them expectantly.

"The ones who did this are long gone," Joe said, then repeated the question: "Is this one of your friends?"

Malcolm and Pete both dismounted and edged up to take a closer look at the half-nude body sprawled beside the game path. "It's hard to say for sure," Pete said. "I mean, with his face all hangin' loose like that. But it don't look like anybody I've ever seen."

"We didn't know any of the folks my brother and his family joined," Malcolm pointed out, relieved to see that it wasn't his brother. "He mighta been with 'em." He turned to look up at Joe. "Blackfoot?" he asked.

"Maybe," Joe answered with a shrug of his shoulders. "Can't say who did it. They didn't leave no sign." He rose to his feet. "I wonder what he was doin' up here by himself." He climbed on his horse. "Looks like those folks you're tryin' to find might be in for some trouble. This bunch that did this are most likely on a killin' spree, and they're on your folks' trail. We'd best get along." He urged the paint forward and Malcolm and Pete scrambled to jump in the saddle and follow.

They heard the shots long before they were in sight of the mule train. Reverberating up from a canyon on the far side of a snowcapped mountain before them, the gunshots told them that their friends were apparently under siege.

"Damn!" Malcolm swore in worried consternation, thinking about his brother and his family caught in such a desperate situation. "We've got to help them!" He looked at Joe in anxious anticipation. Their guide displayed no show of emotion, and no concern as far as Malcolm could determine.

With no change of expression, Joe responded in a matter-of-fact way. "We're goin'. These horses can't make much better time on these steep trails, so it'll be close to sundown by the time we get around to the other side of this mountain."

Malcolm realized that what Joe said was true, but at times he became frustrated with the man's emotionless patience. He would learn after he knew the tall child of the mountains a little longer that Joe accepted the cards that were dealt, good or bad, and never questioned the why of things he could not change. Still, Malcolm thought, it wouldn't kill him to show a little emotion now and again. He was left to follow along behind the paint pony and try not to let his imagination create a terrible scene of what was taking place on the other side of the mountain.

As Joe had predicted, the sun was dropping close to the western peaks by the time they reached a low ridge that overlooked the valley floor and the river that ran through the center. The barrage of gunshots they had heard before had tapered off to only sporadic firing. "Wait here," Joe said after leading them into a stand of fir trees that covered the ridge. Malcolm was about to protest that he wanted to go with him, but thought better of it when Joe fixed his intense gaze upon him. Reading Malcolm's thoughts, he said, "I'll see what we got to deal with; then I'll be back to get you." Malcolm nodded.

He made his way down the ridge fifty yards or so to an outcropping of rock that offered plenty of protection while allowing a wide view of the river below. Only an occasional shot rang out now, the attacking Indians thinking to conserve their ammunition for targets of greater opportunity. Crouched behind the rocks, Joe discovered several spent rifle cartridges, and he knew that the attack had started there. Several cook fires still smoking told him that the settlers must have been camped beside the river when the Indians struck, forcing them to withdraw to take cover under the riverbanks. Consequently the warriors had advanced to a stand of trees some fifty yards from the banks of the river.

Joe scanned the trees until he located the Indian ponies tied near a thicket of berry bushes. He counted eight Indian ponies plus another saddled horse, which he assumed to have belonged to the white man they had found dead on the trail. Then he watched for rifle fire, trying to spot the eight warriors. When he was certain of at least half of them, he backed away from the rocks and returned for Malcolm and Pete. "Leave the horses here," he said. "Best I can tell, we've got eight to deal with." He paused then to ask, "Can you hit what you aim at?" When they both nodded, he said, "All right, follow me and don't shoot till I tell you to—and maybe we'll save your friends—or whatever's left of 'em." Looking in turn at each man to make sure they understood, he then turned and led them down to the rocks and positioned them to his satisfaction.

Pointing to the partially hidden raiders in the trees

below, he instructed them to pick a target. "I wanna hit 'em hard the first time, so don't miss. Shoot when I give the signal. Be ready to fire again 'cause most likely you'll see where the others are when they shoot back at us. If we hit 'em hard enough, they might hightail it." Both men eagerly nodded their understanding. Joe acknowledged this with a nod of his own.

When Joe gave the signal to fire, it produced the results that he had anticipated. Their aim was true, and three warriors fell. As he had predicted, the other five were confused at first, then reversed their positions to fire back at the sudden attack. In so doing, two of the warriors revealed their hiding places, resulting in their deaths at the sure hand of Joe Fox.

While Pete and Malcolm paused a moment to appreciate the success of the assault, Joe bounded over the face of the rocks and made straight for the raiders' horses. Pumping round after round into the bushes around the horses, he charged into their midst and scattered the frightened mounts up the hillside. One warrior who threatened to cut him off was promptly dispatched by Joe's handgun. Effectively defeated, the two remaining raiders fled up the hillside after their horses.

Crouching beneath the riverbank, the besieged party of settlers was left to gape at one another in a state of confusion over the assault from the ridge and the sudden flight of their attackers. Bradley Lindstrom eased his head up to eye level, still wary that he might attract a bullet or an arrow. In the next instant, he heard his name along with a call to hold their fire. "Brad!" The call came forth again, and he recognized his brother's voice. Astonished, he clambered up the bank, shouting to the others to stop shooting.

"Malcolm?" Bradley called out, scarcely believing his eyes as his brother and another man emerged from the trees in the fading light. "It's my brother," he said to

Raymond Chadwick, who scrambled up the riverbank behind him.

"Maybe," Raymond replied, "but he looks like an angel to me."

Realizing that the danger was over, the rest of their people began to make their way back up from the river to the campsite. Some of the younger boys and girls led the mules up out of the water, where they had been since the start of the attack. Bradley ran forth to greet his brother with a hardy hug. "I didn't know I'd ever be this glad to see you," he said, laughing. He looked at Pete then. "Howdy, Pete, you're sure a sight for sore eyes." Then he looked toward the bodies sprawled near the trees. "Just the two of you?"

Before Malcolm could answer, he saw Nancy running to greet him, so he turned to receive her welcome embrace. "Thank the Lord you showed up when you did," she said. Then she looked back toward the trees. "Are they gone?"

"They're gone," Malcolm answered.

"You two did a powerful good job of shootin'," Jake Simmons said as he hurried up to join the reunion.

"Us and Joe Fox," Pete replied. "Most of it Joe Fox." When Bradley looked around at that, searching for another person, Pete explained. "He took off after them two that got away. To make sure they had run for sure, I reckon."

Bradley stepped up and shook Pete's hand. "It's good to see you again, and that's for certain. We were in a pretty bad fix, and it looked like we were gonna be pinned down in this river till after dark." He looked back toward the woods again. "Who's Joe Fox?" he asked.

Malcolm glanced at Pete and smiled before answering. "It's hard to say. He's about as close to a wild Indian as you can get, I reckon, but if it wasn't for him, we'da never found you."

Bradley was about to press for more details, but was interrupted by the rest of the folks in the mule train as they gathered around their two rescuers. He introduced his brother and Pete to everybody and stood back while the two were made welcome. Unnoticed by the jubilant congregation, Joe emerged from the dark shadows of the firs, driving three Indian ponies. After hobbling the horses, he strode over to the body of Dead Man, made a brief examination, then went on to kneel by the body of Two Arrows. Noticing finally, Malcolm misunderstood Joe's interest in the bodies, and called to him to join them. Joe looked at the men, women, and children crowding around Malcolm and Pete with more trepidation than when facing a war party of hostiles. Reluctantly, he advanced a few yards closer.

"Here's the man you wanna give thanks to," Malcolm said, introducing the guide. "This is Joe Fox, and he's gonna lead you outta these mountains."

"Well, hallelujah," one of the women exclaimed.

"Lord knows we've been prayin' for you," another sang out.

When Joe nodded as politely as he knew how, Malcolm walked over to meet him. "I saw you kneeling beside those bodies, and I know you were raised by the Blackfeet," he said. "I know that it must be eatin' at your heart to have killed some of your own people, but you done the right thing."

Malcolm's statement was met with a look of genuine astonishment. "*Atsina*," Joe responded, using the Blackfoot word for Gros Ventre. "They weren't Blackfoot. They were Gros Ventre."

"Oh," Malcolm responded. "Then it wasn't such a bad thing for you that we killed them?"

Amazed that Malcolm was so naive, Joe smiled and said, "It was a damn good thing that we killed them. What I'm tryin' to figure out is why they're so far away from their reservation at Fort Belknap. If I had to guess, I'd suspect they're part of a bigger raidin' party. I'm sorry two of 'em got away." Recalling his childhood in the Blackfoot camp, he said, "The old ones told stories about a time when the Blackfeet and the *Atsina* were friends, and then a war broke out between them over a white horse and two dead Gros Ventre. The *Atsina* blamed the Blackfeet after seeing the horse in our village. They didn't know that a party of Snakes had given the horse to the Blackfeet. They were the ones who killed the two *Atsina* warriors, but there's been bad blood between my people and the *Atsina* ever since."

"Damn!" Pete exclaimed with a wide grin. "That's the most words I've ever heard you string together at one time."

Suddenly embarrassed, Joe shrugged and turned to tend to his horses. "You said he was gonna lead us out of these infernal mountains," Jake Simmons called after him, although his words were directed toward Malcolm.

"Well, yeah," Malcolm replied. "That's what we came here for." Hearing Malcolm's response, Joe paused and looked back at him. "That's right, ain't it, Joe?" Malcolm asked.

This was an answer that everyone wanted to hear, and a silence fell over the group as Joe's reply was awaited. The hush was broken when Nancy Lindstrom asked, "Can you lead us out of here, Mr. Fox?"

Joe Fox glanced at Pete Watson, then shifted back to the gathering around Malcolm, finally settling his gaze upon the woman standing beside Bradley. There were many conflicting thoughts running through his mind as he studied the gentle face of the woman. Like a child or an injured animal, she seemed to be pleading for his help. He wished at that moment that he had refused Malcolm's request to guide them. The gathering of gentle white people made him feel uncomfortable. He had lived alone in the solitude of the mountains since he was a boy of eighteen, living by his cunning and his courage. He came to know himself as neither Indian nor white, although he felt his allegiance was owed to the Blackfoot nation. They were the only people he really knew, but he had never felt a need for any companions but his rifle and his bow. Now he found himself with more than thirty pairs of eyes, all focused upon him, awaiting reassurance in his answer. He had given his word to Malcolm, however, and had taken payment in the form of supplies and cartridges. Besides, the childlike plea in Nancy Lindstrom's gentle face played wickedly upon his conscience. In the end, he felt he could not leave them to their fate. "I reckon I can, ma'am," he said in answer to her question.

"You know the way through these mountains?" The question came from a brute of a man who had been content to listen up to that point. He stepped through the gathering, elbowing his way past Nancy Lindstrom and several standing beside her until he stood squarely before Joe. He looked Joe up and down thoroughly with obvious distrust in his gaze. "We just run one sorry scalawag off that claimed he could lead us to the Willamette Valley. Now you show up claiming to know the way outta this canyon. How do we know you even have a notion where the Willamette Valley is?"

Joe glanced over at Bradley, noticing the tired look of impatience in his face, before meeting the gaze of the belligerent man standing before him. It took no more than a few seconds to determine the bully nature of the man. Joe's first impulse was to tell the man to find his way out himself, but the image of Nancy Lindstrom's face was still in his mind. "I can take you out," he answered softly, still meeting the huge man's gaze.

"Huh," the big man snorted rudely.

"I can take you outta here to a better place to camp," Joe Fox continued. "I ain't sure you can make it past all the mountains between here and where you're talkin' about goin' before snow closes most of the mountain passes. And I don't know the Willamette Valley you spoke of, but I know how to find Oregon."

This brought an immediate ripple of dismay over the folks gathered around him. "What the hell do you mean?" the bully demanded. "We can't spend the winter in these mountains." He turned then to address those closest to him. "I don't know about the rest of you folks, but I need to get to Oregon before winter sets in. I don't care what no half-Injun says, I say we quit pussyfootin' around and strike out straight across these damn mountains."

"Hold on, Starbeau," Bradley Lindstrom interrupted. "There ain't no call to get your back up till we talk this over."

Starbeau turned to vent his rage upon Bradley then. "That's just the damn trouble we've had all along," he charged. "You and Simmons and Chadwick ain't been good for nothin' but talkin' things over between yourselves. I've held my tongue up to now, but I'll have my say on this. You hired that damn no-account, Skinner. Now you're hirin' this half-breed that just dropped down out of a tree somewhere." He turned once again to point an accusing finger at Joe. "I wanna know why the hell we can't be past the mountains before winter sets in!"

Joe stood, silently measuring the man who demanded answers, his eyes displaying no evidence of emotion. He felt no obligation to persuade the people to trust him. He would lay out the simple facts and let them decide.

Bradley Lindstrom felt it his duty to intercede. "Let's try to keep a civil tongue here, Starbeau." He looked at Joe Fox then and asked, "Is what you say our only choice? Why can't we make it through before winter?"

"You started too late in the summer," Joe answered. "You've been goin' around in circles, and you've got too far left to go. I said I could lead you outta the mountains. I never said it would be easy, and I never promised you'd make it before spring. A man can't say for sure what the winter will be. Maybe the snow will come late and the passes will stay open, but I doubt it. I've seen no sign. I can take you to Missoula Mills, where you will find some more white people. If you are wise, you'll set up your winter camp there."

Openly disappointed in Joe's answer, Bradley asked, "What will we do? We'll perish in these mountains."

"You'll perish if you try to strike out straight west like this damn fool wants to do," Joe replied evenly, ignoring the fluster in Starbeau's face. "I'll lead you north from here until we get to a valley I know. It's a little longer than the way a hawk flies, but these mules don't look much like hawks to me. And the way I will take you, there is game for food if you have to settle in for the winter."

"If we make it to that valley you mention, will we be free of the mountains?" Raymond Chadwick asked.

Joe made a concentrated effort to hide his astonishment for the naïveté of Raymond's question. "No, you will still be in the Bitterroots. There will be many days' journey beyond that."

This was disappointing news to all thirty-seven souls gathered on the bank of the river. The jubilation felt by the deliverance from the Gros Ventre raiders was squelched by the news that their journey was to end when not even halfway finished. To make the report even more discouraging, they now faced the stark possibility of having to wait out the snows in some narrow canyon somewhere. Thoughts of the Donner party returned to many of them, and some of the women went so far as to give voice to that concern.

"Don't even start that kinda talk," Bradley warned. "We ain't the Donner party. We're able-bodied men, and we can build a warm winter camp if we have to. Joe Fox, here, says he can keep us supplied with food. We've just gotta have faith in the Lord and faith in ourselves."

"And faith in Joe Fox," Starbeau added cynically.

"Ain't nobody said you had to stay with the party," Jake Simmons blurted. He'd had about as much of Starbeau's complaining as he cared for. "You wouldn't be here in the first place, but you asked to tag along after we left Bismarck."

Jake's wife, Cora, took him by the arm, and pulled him a few steps away. "Let it lay, Jake," she cautioned.

"Yeah, little man," Starbeau warned, "you'd best listen to your wife and let it lay, else you're liable to get your scrawny little back broke."

Starbeau's threat effectively silenced the noisy crowd, and all eyes turned to Bradley Lindstrom, since he was acknowledged informally as the captain of the train. In a show of support, and sensing trouble, Malcolm moved over to stand beside his brother. In the brief moments before Bradley interceded on Jake's behalf he was reminded that allowing Starbeau to accompany the mule train had been a grave mistake that now seemed to be coming back to cause trouble.

Twenty miles out from Bismarck Starbeau had suddenly appeared, riding a broad-chested dun and leading four mules with heavy packs. He said he was a pilgrim, just like the rest of the party, looking for a place to settle where he could practice his Christian beliefs. Bradley should have listened to Jake then when his wiry little friend doubted the rough man's sincerity. It had not taken long before the rest of the party had doubts about the loner in their midst. With few words for any of the others, Starbeau had kept to himself for the entire journey, never asking nor offering assistance on any matter, and preferring never to participate in the nightly prayers. It was soon apparent that the surly brute was along strictly for the safety of numbers. Now he had permitted his venomous core to emerge and again Bradley felt it his responsibility to defuse the volatile incident.

"Cora's right, Jake," he said. "It's best to calm down. We're all just a little bit touchy right now."

"Can't no man talk to me that way," Jake complained, jerking his arm out of Cora's hand and bracing himself to face Starbeau. "I'll have your apology now, by God."

"Or what?" Starbeau sneered. "Whaddaya gonna do about it, you little bantam rooster?" He looked around him, glaring at the crowd. "I'll do what I please, and I'll say what I damn well please. What are any of you Bible-thumpin' sons of bitches gonna do about it?" When no one responded, he said, "I thought so," and turned back to Jake. Dropping his hand to rest on the pistol he wore at his side, he taunted, "All right, you yellow belly, you got a gun on your belt, you ready to back up that big mouth of yours?"

Bradley Lindstrom was stunned, scarcely able to believe what his eyes were witnessing. A gunfight was about to occur in this camp of religious folk. "We need to calm down . . . ," was the only thing he could manage to say. There was no doubt in his mind that this fight amounted to suicide for Jake Simmons, but Jake was still trying to push Cora out of his way, determined to defend his pride.

"Maybe you oughta give her the gun, Simmons," Starbeau goaded. "She looks like she's got more spunk than you." With a sinister chuckle, he winked at Cora and said, "Maybe you oughta come on over to my camp. I believe I could give you a little more of what a woman like you needs. I bet you ain't gettin' it from that bantam." Seeing the fearful effect he was having upon the peaceful congregation, he threw back his head and laughed.

Standing apart, watching the confrontation with detached interest since he felt no ties to the party of pilgrims, Joe was content to let them settle their differences among themselves. When the argument advanced beyond the mere slinging of insults back and forth, he realized that the bully Starbeau was intent upon killing the smaller man. The only motive that Joe could determine was the simple fact that Starbeau would enjoy the killing. He decided it was time to act.

Making his way through the ring of horrified spectators, he stepped in front of Jake. Turning to face Starbeau, he raised his rifle and took dead aim on the bully's forehead. The crowd that had parted slightly when Starbeau had sought to call Jake out now created a wide lane between the two men. "What the hell . . . ?" Starbeau sputtered as the tall hunter held his steady aim at his head. Recovering his belligerent composure, he snarled, "This ain't none of your affair."

With his rifle still aimed at Starbeau, Joe replied, "It ain't a fair fight."

"Ain't a fair fight?" Starbeau stammered in flustered rage. "It ain't none of your business, you damn half-breed!"

"Now it is," Joe calmly replied, the rifle still aimed directly at the bully's head. Behind him, Bradley and Cora managed to pull Jake away from the fight.

Regaining a measure of his bluster, Starbeau said, "All right, mister, if you want a showdown, you can have it. You're wearin' a pistol. Put down that rifle, and we'll see who walks away from here."

"Why would I do that?" Joe replied.

Visibly disconcerted, Starbeau insisted, "For a fair

fight, dammit! It ain't a fair fight with you already holdin' a rifle on me!"

"I don't fight fair," Joe replied calmly. Being a practical man, Joe could see no sense in entering a contest with Starbeau. To him, killing was not a game. He had never seen a gunfighter, but he had heard of such men, men who practiced drawing their handguns in a quest to be faster than other men. It made no sense to him, for there was no distinction between wrong and right, or evil and good. He had no idea if Starbeau was one who practiced pulling his weapon. The one thing Joe did know for certain was that the fuming bully could not draw his pistol before he squeezed the rifle's trigger.

With the showdown effectively brought to a stand-off by the unexpected move by Joe Fox, Starbeau was left to founder in a helpless situation. There was little he could do to salvage his pride short of committing suicide. He could not remember wanting to kill a man more than at this moment, as his hand hovered over the handle of his pistol—his fingers tingling with the itch he felt to snatch the weapon free of the holster—but he could not make the move. Staring into the deadly calm eyes of the hunter, he was convinced that the man would not hesitate to kill him.

Though it was only seconds, it seemed much longer to those who witnessed the impasse between the bullish Starbeau and the mysterious man of the mountains. A low murmur wafted through the relieved crowd of spectators when Starbeau at last abruptly turned with a grunt of disgust, and started toward his tent. Joe lowered his rifle slowly, watching the sullen brute depart until Malcolm appeared at his elbow, distracting him for a second with a comment. "That was too close for comfort," Malcolm said, and was about to continue when Joe suddenly shoved him aside as the bullet from Starbeau's pistol made a loud snapping sound as it passed between them. With reflexes sharpened by a life of survival in the wild, Joe whipped his rifle up and fired before the sound of Starbeau's shot had faded away. The shot slammed into the big man's shoulder, spinning him around as he fell to the ground, his pistol landing in the sand. Joe cocked the Winchester, ready to fire again.

"Damn, I'm sorry," Malcolm uttered, apologizing for distracting Joe long enough for Starbeau to spin around and take the shot. "He coulda killed one of us if you hadn't pushed me outta the way."

Joe didn't take time to acknowledge Malcolm's apology. He went straight to the wounded man, his rifle aimed at his head. "Wait!" Bradley Lindstrom yelled and ran to intercede. He reached Starbeau just as Joe was preparing to finish the job. "There's been enough killin' without us startin' to kill each other," he exclaimed. "He's wounded, and you were right to shoot to defend yourself, but if you shoot him now, it'll be nothin' less than murder."

Joe paused briefly to give Bradley a puzzled look. "The man tried to kill me," he stated. "I don't give a man more'n one chance if I can help it."

"The Bible says, *Thou shalt not kill*," Bradley pleaded. "We are Christians, so I'm askin' you not to pull that trigger. At least let us call a council to talk this thing over."

Joe looked at the frightened face of the wounded man on the ground, then looked back at Bradley, hardly believing he had heard right. "What does your Bible say about those Gros Ventre we killed?"

Joined by Raymond Chadwick and Jake Simmons then, Bradley answered, "They were heathens," he said, "savages, no different than protectin' ourselves from a pack of wolves."

"Bradley's right," Jake spoke up. "I reckon I'm the one most to blame. I forgot my Christian duty when I got my back up over Starbeau's remarks. I think he's been punished enough. He's hurt pretty bad, looks like. I think it's best to just let him go his own way if he doesn't share our beliefs, and let the rest of us go ours."

"He's right," Raymond said. "The whole reason we're bound for Oregon is to be free to practice our religion as we see fit, doin' harm to no one."

Astonished, Joe glanced over to meet Malcolm's eye. Bradley's brother merely shrugged his shoulders, as surprised as Joe. Bradley had never mentioned to him that the real reason for setting out across the prairie was to establish a religious settlement in Oregon. Joe glanced back at Bradley. "He'll try again," he said.

"Maybe not, if we show him mercy and forgiveness," Raymond Chadwick said, "but we must be sure this whole incident is finished."

"What do you say, Starbeau?" Bradley asked. "Is it over?"

Grimacing with the pain in his shoulder, Starbeau recognized an opportunity, so he took it. "It's over and done," he grunted. "I just took leave of my senses for a spell there. I got no hard feelin's for Simmons or anybody else. And I'd appreciate it if you'd let me stay with the party."

"Praise the Lord," one of the women sang out, and Bradley turned to see a chorus of nodding heads with a few "Amens" in response.

"Good," Bradley said to Starbeau. "I think you've made a wise decision. If you give Him a chance, the Lord will show you the way. Now, let's get you over to your tent, and see if we can patch that wound up."

Unable to understand what had just taken place, Joe reluctantly eased the hammer down on his rifle and stepped back. He again questioned his wisdom when he decided to lead the party of settlers, for it was plain that a strain of lunacy ran through the whole mule train. "I reckon if that's what you folks want," he said. He then gave the wounded man a long look. "Maybe you folks are right, but a coyote's still a coyote whether he's been shot or not, and I always keep my eye on wounded coyotes." Having said his piece, he started toward his horses. "I expect we'd best get movin' first thing in the morning," he said as he departed.

Never comfortable in a crowd, Joe built his fire near his horses and apart from the main camp. He thought about the strange turn of events that had resulted in the settlers forgiving a man after he had attempted to kill someone, and he was afraid that he might live to regret his bowing to their wishes.

Malcolm and Pete stopped by to talk before joining Bradley's family for supper. "I didn't know nothin' about this religious business any sooner than you did," Malcolm said. "Not that there's anythin' wrong with havin' religion, hell, I got a little bit myself. I can see how you feel about lettin' Starbeau go after the son of a bitch took a shot at you. I reckon we'd all best keep a close eye on that one, won't we, Pete?" Pete nodded when Malcolm paused, then revealed the real reason for his visit. "These folks are good folks and they need you. I'm just hopin' you ain't thinkin' about washin' your hands of the whole thing."

Joe added a few more limbs to his fire, then replied. "I said I'd lead you through these mountains."

"Yes, sir, you did," Malcolm replied quickly, "and you're a man of your word. I'm obliged." Feeling more secure in the knowledge that the mysterious denizen of the high ridges was not contemplating leaving the mule train stranded, he and Pete walked away, leaving Joe to tend to his fire.

Malcolm and Pete were not the only visitors to Joe's camp that evening. He had just pulled his coffee back from the center of the fire to keep it from boiling too long when he saw someone leave the circle of camp-fires and head toward him. He watched as the figure became clear in the darkness of the tree line. It was a girl—or a woman. It was hard to tell because the figure was a small person, possibly a child. He straightened up and waited, curious as to the purpose of the visit.

"Mr. Fox," she called out as she approached, her voice soft and small, but not at all childlike.

Curious, he rose to his feet. "Yes, miss?" he responded.

As she entered the firelight, he could see that she was indeed a young woman, though tiny in stature. He saw then that she carried something wrapped in a cloth. Holding it out to him, she said, "I brought you some pan bread that I made for supper."

"Why, I'm much obliged to you, miss," he said as he eagerly accepted the gift. "It'll go mighty good with my coffee." He could not help but wonder what motivated the young woman to perform this gracious act. From what he had seen in the faces of the people in the train, he was regarded as something strange and apart from the human race. His unspoken question was answered by her next statement.

"I'm Callie Simmons. I wanted to thank you for saving my father's life." When she saw that he was running the name through his mind, trying to place it, she continued. "I'm Jake Simmons' daughter, and I'm certain that when you stepped in between him and that ogre, Starbeau, you saved his life."

Without knowing how to respond, he simply stammered, "Yes, miss."

She went on. "Pa's a good man, but he's not a big man, so I think he sometimes feels like he has to show people that he's as much a man as anyone." She smiled then. "Anyway, I thank you for what you did, and I hope you enjoy the bread. I'll leave you to your supper." She turned to go, then paused. "The folks on this train aren't as stiff as they might look. You'll see when you get to know us better." She returned to the camp then, leaving him to think about the sweet smile she had given him.

Chapter 4

The days that followed the incident by the river became a constant grind of long hours in the saddle that left the travelers weary and hungry when nightfall finally forced them to camp. There were no complaints from the people, because Bradley and Jake had impressed upon the others the need to pass through the mountains as quickly as humanly possible. The days were already cold and the skies continued to threaten, with heavy snows already blanketing the higher elevations.

Not much was seen of their mysterious guide during the daylight hours. He would start the party out in the mornings, telling Malcolm and Bradley to hold to a particular course. Then he would disappear into the forest and hills, only to appear when it seemed the train had reached a box canyon, or some other apparent dead end. He would then lead them on a detour that sometimes called for them to follow a game trail barely wide enough for one mule to pass, and becoming more and more treacherous with freezing rain. It was not an easy time for man or woman, but everyone, even the children, seemed to understand the desperate circumstances that dictated the demands placed upon them. As before, Starbeau kept to himself, riding sullenly, his arm in a sling fashioned by Nancy Lindstrom to rest his wounded shoulder. He, as much as anyone, wanted to get through the mountains before the passes closed. And although he harbored a deep hatred for the man who led them through one rough valley after another, he was wise enough to know his survival depended upon Joe Fox.

In spite of the rugged terrain, the mule train made acceptable progress for the first few days, even with the foul weather. On the fifth day of travel, Old Man Winter evidently reached the limits of his benevolence when Joe led a saddle-weary group of settlers across a frigid mountain pass where howling winds were already sweeping the snow into six-foot drifts. It served to impress upon the travelers what they would have encountered had they insisted upon continuing their trek to Oregon Territory. Once through the pass, Joe led them down into a wide valley where the surrounding mountains offered some relief from the weather above, and a cluster of crude buildings created a welcome sight that Joe said was Missoula Mills.

"It is a good place for your people to spend the winter months," he told Bradley Lindstrom. "There's a sawmill and a flour mill, and a general store. The Missoula Valley has three rivers running through it, and the mountains all around will protect against the strong winter storms." He didn't mention the fact that in years past his adoptive people, the Blackfeet, had fought a bloody war against the Salish in this valley. It had been before his time, but because of it he had very little use for the Salish, or the Flatheads as some called them.

Bradley stood beside Jake Simmons as the two friends got their first look at the valley. "Well, it ain't the Willamette Valley where we *thought* we'd be spending the winter," he said. "But it looks a sight more invitin' than those deep canyons back yonder." He released a weary sigh and looked at Joe. "What about when the spring comes? We're still gonna be lookin' for the way to Oregon."

"The road you spoke about . . . ," Joe started.

"The Mullan Road," Bradley reminded.

"Yes," Joe continued. "The Mullan Road—it runs through the Missoula Valley—you can follow it in the spring when the passes are open."

"Maybe you'll go with us then."

"Maybe," Joe answered without enthusiasm. "But I'll help you store up meat for the winter, anyway. You're gonna need a lot for this bunch of folks."

"We're obliged," Bradley said. Then, turning to Jake and Raymond, he said, "We'd best get to work buildin' some shelters."

The next two weeks were a busy time for the pilgrims as they hurried to establish a winter camp. They were welcomed by the people of the settlement, who turned out to help the new arrivals, hoping they would elect to make permanent homes here. Joe spent all day every day scouting the breadth and length of the fertile valley in search of game to be dried and stored. Game was in abundance—mule deer, whitetail deer, and elk driven down from the mountains by the weather. Bradley was happy to supply him with all the cartridges he needed, but much of the game was shot with a bow. This was especially true on a day like this one, when he had laid in wait for a group of antelope to come down to the Blackfoot River to drink. Using tree branches for concealment, he managed to crawl close enough to target the rearmost animals, dropping two with his bow before the rest of the herd was aware of the danger. When the swift animals bolted, he laid his bow aside and bagged one more with a single shot from his rifle before they fled out of range.

Max Starbeau sat beside his campfire, alternately clenching and relaxing his left hand, testing the progress of the healing in his shoulder. Nancy Lindstrom had done a first-rate job in removing the bullet and cleaning the wound. It was coming along properly. In fact, it was well enough for Starbeau to help the men build shelters, but he didn't let on to the others. Like a colony of ants, the settlers were digging caves along the river bluffs and shoring them up with lumber from the sawmill. Starbeau was not a man to work for what he needed, a trait that had caused a great deal of speculation regarding the gruff man's presence in the train of settler families. He was well aware of their suspicions, and it served to amuse him as they labored to dig in for the winter. If these Christian folk had any notion of the circumstances that had led him to cross the mule train's path, they would be horrified, and would certainly have sought to cast him out. A wicked smile creased his whiskered face as he recalled the day he happened upon Henry Dodson.

Wanted for a shooting incident in a saloon in Bismarck, Starbeau was traveling the back roads around the town *shank's mare*. He was sufficiently tired and footsore from walking when he came upon a small farmhouse and a man attempting to raise one end of his porch. Seeing an opportunity to possibly gain a free meal, Starbeau turned onto the path to the house and approached the porch. "Looks like you could use a hand, neighbor," he called out, using as cheerful a voice as he could create.

So intent upon his work, Henry Dodson had not noticed the huge man walking up the road. Consequently, he was taken aback briefly when he turned to confront the intimidating bulk of the stranger. Recovering from his initial shock, he slowly let up on the long pole he was using as a lever, and stepped away to greet Starbeau. "Well, I reckon it would be a little bit easier if there was one man to raise the porch and an-other'n to slide a rock under the corner." Taking an additional step back to appraise the imposing stranger, Henry could not help a feeling of precaution. The man had the hard look of a road agent, combined with the size of a grizzly. He certainly had the bulk, however, that met the qualifications called for to force the pole down and lift the porch. *He'll have to be careful he don't turn the house upside down*, he thought. "I reckon the pilaster under this corner musta settled some," he went on to explain. "My wife's been after me to build it up—says the porch is starting to tilt so bad she can't set her rockin' chair straight."

"Well, lemme grab aholda that pole, and you can slide a couple of rocks under it," Starbeau said, and proceeded to take hold of the pole without waiting for Henry's response.

With the leverage provided by the large tree limb, Starbeau easily lifted the corner and held it while Henry placed one, then another flat rock on top of the porch supports. "Let her down now," Henry said and watched while the porch settled on the rock pilaster. Nodding his head in satisfaction, he said, "Mister, I'm much obliged to ya."

Starbeau lifted the heavy timber and tossed it sev-eral feet from the porch. "T'weren't nothin' a'tall," he replied. "What kinda neighbors would we be if we couldn't give a man a hand once in a while?" A crooked smile broke out across the harsh face.

"I reckon you're right, friend. I don't recollect seein' you around here before. Where are you headin'?" He was more than a little curious about why a man wear-ing a handgun and carrying a rifle would be walking this far away from town.

"I'm headin' to town," Starbeau lied. "I've had a little piece of bad luck, had to shoot my horse a few miles back, but I'll buy me another one when I get to town."

Henry shook his head, amazed. "Well, you ain't likely to get to town goin' the way you were headin'. You need to go back to that crossroad about a quarter mile back the way you came. That'll take you to town, but it's a right far piece, especially for a man on foot."

"Well, now don't that make me feel like a fool?" Starbeau said, forcing a chuckle. In fact, his horse had been shot, but not by his hand. The bullets had come from the pistol of a deputy sheriff, and would probably not have killed the horse, but Starbeau had run the animal until it bled to death and collapsed on the road just mentioned by Henry. "I reckon I'll just have to turn around and go back," he said, feigning a sigh.

"It's gettin' pretty late in the day to be settin' out to town on foot," Henry said. "Why don't you stay here for the night? Least I can do is feed you some supper for stoppin' to help with the porch. And you're welcome to sleep in the barn—start out fresh in the mornin'."

"I wouldn't wanna put you out none," Starbeau replied.

"Nonsense," a voice came from inside the front door. "We've got plenty and you're welcome to share it with us." Margaret Dodson stepped out on the porch from the hallway where she had been listening to the conversation between her husband and the strange man.

Both men turned at the sound of her voice. "This here's my wife," Henry said.

Always with an eye for the ladies, plain or proud, Starbeau cast an appraising gaze over the ordinary features of Margaret Dodson. Just short of leering, he managed to say, "Pleased to meet you, ma'am." *It's been a while*, he thought. *You ain't exactly no young beauty, but you've got enough to scratch my itch.* "I thank you kindly for your offer. I'd be obliged."

Thinking about it now, he had to chuckle to himself. She had been a little woman, not much bigger than Jake Simmons' daughter. Of course, she was a good bit older than Callie, but she put up a good fight. Starbeau liked that. He'd had to hit her a half dozen times with his fist before she succumbed. He could still picture her horrified face as he took her—and lying right beside the body of her husband, him with a bullet hole in the middle of his forehead. His only regret was that the woman lacked the fortitude to withstand the beating. He would have liked it if she had not died so soon.

Henry Dodson was evidently a successful farmer, judging by the livestock Starbeau had found in the barn and the corral behind it. Dodson's house had been a lucky find. He packed everything he thought he could sell, trade, or use himself on four mules and Dodson's bay saddle horse. He rode away the next morning a well-supplied traveler.

His reminiscing was interrupted then by the sight of Callie Simmons heading toward the river with a bucket in hand. *You might wiggle that little tail once too often before this winter is over*, he thought. *I've got a little something to settle with your daddy, too.* He slipped the sling back under his arm when he saw Bradley Lindstrom coming his way.

"How's the shoulder coming along?" Bradley inquired.

"It's gettin' there," Starbeau replied, "but slow as hell. I still can't do much with it."

"I was hopin' to hear better than that," Bradley said, trying to keep his suspicions out of his tone. "We're makin' good progress on most of the caves, but it would be good if you could get started on one for yourself. It'd be pretty rough passin' the winter in that tent."

Starbeau reached up and rubbed his shoulder as if testing the injury. "I might not have no choice," he replied. "It's still awful tender. I don't think I'll be much good for diggin' anytime soon."

Bradley hesitated for a moment. He wanted to call the huge man a slacker, but he lacked the necessary grit to do it. "Well, I reckon when some of us get finished, we can help you out."

"I 'preciate it, Lindstrom," Starbeau said, affecting what was meant to be a look of sincere gratitude. The smile on his face grew as Bradley walked away again until it broke into a contemptuous chuckle. "Praise the Lord," he murmured in contempt under his breath. "I wonder where you've got that money hid." He had been thinking about the two hundred and fifty dollars the party had promised to give Skinner at the completion of the journey. It was his guess that Bradley was most likely the one holding the cash. It was something for him to speculate on while he was recovering from his wound. *I'll just bide my time*, he thought, *I can't go anywhere for a while yet*.

A moment later, the malicious grin faded from his face as he caught sight of Joe Fox approaching the banks of the river, leading one of his horses. The horse was pulling a travois carrying what appeared to be three antelope. Starbeau glanced quickly around him to make sure no one was watching him. Then he slowly reached down and picked up his rifle. Pressing the butt against his wounded shoulder, he took deliberate aim at the tall figure astride the paint pony, his finger resting on the trigger. "Bang," he whispered softly, and lowered the weapon to the ground again, knowing that satisfaction would have to wait until spring.

Unaware that he had been framed in the sights of Starbeau's rifle as he guided his horse down through the bluffs, the buckskin-clad rider halted his horses and dismounted. Dropping the paint's reins, he led the packhorse to a large fire before the caves, where most of the preparation of smoked meat was going on. "My stars," Nancy Lindstrom exclaimed upon seeing the carcasses on the travois. "More meat to fix—it's a wonder there's an animal left in this valley."

"They're gettin' scarcer," Joe replied with a smile. "I'm havin' to go farther to find 'em, but you're still gonna need more to carry you folks through the winter."

The owner of the trading post, a man named Horace Templeton, stood next to the fire. He had been pretty much in evidence every day while the pilgrims created their winter quarters. Hoping the party might reconsider moving on in the spring, he had taken it upon himself to daily cite the virtues of the Missoula Valley and Missoula Mills specifically. "We've already got the seed stock for building a proper town," he had appealed to Bradley Lindstrom and Jake Simmons. "All we need to make it grow is folks like you." Though certainly worth considering, they said, there were other things to influence the party's decision. There were friends and relatives awaiting them in the Willamette Valley, and that was where they had set out for when they left North Dakota. Still, Templeton was persistent in his daily visits to the ant hill, as the residents of the town referred to the camp on the Blackfoot River.

Silently witnessing the brief comments between Joe and Nancy, Templeton could only stand and gape for a few seconds before stepping forward and asking, "You're Joe Fox, ain't you?"

Joe did not immediately reply. Turning to face the man, he paused, puzzled that Templeton knew his name. After a few moments, he answered. "I'm Joe Fox," he said, still trying to place the man.

"Well, I'll be . . ." Templeton started, but failed to finish. He favored Joe with a wide smile. "Wait till I tell the boys over at the sawmill about this. I've heard some of the Injuns talk about a man that roamed the high peaks, but I swear, I never thought there really was one. Thought you were somethin' they just made up—a spirit or somethin'.""

Not sure how to take Templeton's comments, Joe's initial reaction was simply to feel uncomfortable. Not knowing how to respond, he said, "I'm Joe Fox, but I ain't no spirit."

Standing next to a big pot of boiling water on the fire, Callie Simmons beamed delightedly upon witnessing the somber mountain man's discomfort. "He's not a spirit," she whispered soft enough that no one should hear. "He's an angel."

"Joe Fox!" Templeton exclaimed again, shaking his head as if he had just witnessed the confirmation of a legend.

Nancy Lindstrom and Cora Simmons, who paused to listen to the comments, both turned a puzzled gaze toward the man who had volunteered to guide them to this valley. Confused by their expressions of wonder, Joe felt an immediate desire to be elsewhere. Turning his attention to the travois, he started dragging a carcass off as several of the other men came up to take charge of the butchering.

"Joe Fox," Horace Templeton repeated softly, then raised his voice to say, "Come on by my store and I'll buy you a drink of whiskey, Joe Fox."

"Thanks just the same," Joe answered, barely glancing in Templeton's direction, "but I reckon I've still got work to do." He felt uneasy with the man's interest in him and distressed to find that his name had become known in the valleys beyond the mountains that were his home. Wasting no time, he led his horses away from the river as soon as the third antelope carcass was removed from the travois.

"Well, now, what do you reckon got into him?" Templeton asked, confounded by what he interpreted as unfriendly behavior.

"I guess he just prefers being left alone," Cora Simmons answered, sensing a disdain for any situation that focused on him as a curiosity.

Smiling to herself, Callie Simmons studied the tall, rangy figure as he walked away toward a grassy knoll where his other horses were grazing with the mules. While Horace Templeton was relating the many stories he had heard about the ghost called Joe Fox to her mother and Nancy Lindstrom, Callie went unnoticed to her tent. Fetching a cup, she returned to the fire and filled it with coffee. Slipping a biscuit in her apron pocket, she then followed Joe to the knoll.

He turned when he heard Callie coming up behind him, and waited for her to speak. "I brought you some coffee," she said, holding the cup out to him. "You looked like you wanted some before Mr. Templeton started talking." She reached into her pocket and produced the biscuit. "You might want something to go with the coffee. I hope it's still hot."

Surprised by the young girl's thoughtfulness, he took the cup. "Thank you, miss. You're right, I did want some coffee—and that biscuit will go mighty good with it."

She smiled sweetly then, pleased by his reaction. "You don't have to call me miss," she said. "My name's Callie. If you don't mind, I'll sit down while you have your coffee. Then I can take the cup back." Not waiting for his reply, she seated herself on a cottonwood log. Since there was no place to sit other than the ground, she said, "You can sit beside me if you want. I won't bite you."

He smiled at that and sat down on the log next to her. He was aware then that he felt no uneasiness when with the girl. He sensed a feeling of honesty about her that made him comfortable. It struck him that he had made a friend, and he realized that he had made no friends since he had left Crying Woman's village.

"I hope that coffee's still hot," she said. "It doesn't take long to cool off in this weather." When he assured her that it was just right, she sat silent for a few moments before speaking again. "You haven't been digging a camp for yourself. Aren't you going to need a cave?"

"No, miss . . . I mean, Callie. I expect I'll make me a camp back up in the hills." He thought he detected a genuine look of disappointment in her face.

"Won't it get too cold to stay up in the mountains?" she asked.

"Well, it'll be cold all right, but not if you're used to it and know how to make your camp. I worry more about my horses than me. I expect I'll leave all but the paint down here with the mules."

"Does that mean we won't see you again until spring?" she asked, encouraged by the fact that he planned to leave his horses here.

He hesitated before answering. "I don't know, maybe. I might drop in to see how you folks are faring."

"Well, you'd be welcome if you decide to come back sooner." She was dying to ask him about his family, where he spent his childhood, how he came to spend his life alone in the wilderness, but she was afraid he might suddenly become reticent to talk to her at all. Taking the opportunity to study him closely while he was seemingly relaxed, she noted the finely chiseled features of his face and the dark eyes that seemed to be looking inside her thoughts. His black hair was long, worn in two braided strands that rested upon broad shoulders, giving him the bearing of a Blackfoot warrior, and yet his English was as refined as any of the men in her party. A white Indian, she thought, with his shirt and leggings of animal skins, and his bow strung on his back. She wondered whether his wants and passions were as feral as his appearance. Her mother would be shocked to know the thoughts prodding her curiosity about this mystery man, she decided with an inward giggle.

Draining the last of his coffee, he stood up and handed her the cup. "I thank you, Miss Callie. That was mighty fine."

"You're welcome," she replied cheerfully. "You know you're always welcome at our fire. After all, you are supplying almost all the meat for us this winter."

"I'm obliged," he said, unable to think of anything better.

"Well, I've got to get back to work," she said when it became obvious he was not going to delay her.

When she had turned and started back to the campfire, he paused and watched her make her way across the bluffs, holding her skirt up just high enough to prevent it from dragging in the shallow patches of snow. Her visit had caused troubling thoughts to play in his mind, thoughts about things he had not considered before. He would find himself lost in thoughts of the young girl tiptoeing through the patches of snow for many nights to come.

Callie's visit to take coffee to Joe Fox did not go unobserved by at least one person. Cora Simmons paused at the racks constructed to smoke the meat for winter to watch her daughter returning from the knoll where the animals were grazing. She sincerely hoped that Callie's visit was no more than a courteous call in an act of Christian kindness, and not something more troublesome. For an interest in that man was akin to an infatuation with a mountain lion. She and Jake might have to have a talk with her.

Chapter 5

The day arrived near the end of September when Joe decided he had done all he could to ensure that the party of settlers would have enough to survive the winter. Now there was little time left to tend to his needs. Taking only a small supply of the dried meat, some salt, a large sack of coffee beans, and, at Callie's insistence, a sack of dried apples; he packed it all on the paint. Malcolm, Bradley, and Jake, along with many others of the community, gathered to see him off as he climbed aboard his horse.

"We'll be lookin' to see you come spring," Bradley declared hopefully.

"Can't say for sure," Joe replied. "You don't need me anymore, anyway, if that road you've been talkin' about really leads to Fort Walla Walla. I don't know much about the country on the other side of Lolo Pass, so I don't see how I'd be much help."

"You'd be a helluva lot of help," Malcolm Lindstrom spoke up, "just like you've been so far. I don't know how these folks would've fared without you leadin' 'em here and supplying all that meat." He had more than a casual interest in hoping to see the recluse

mountain man again. He and Pete had families back in
Dakota, and he wasn't sure he could remember how to
get back through the mountains to the point where they
had first found Joe Fox. If he decided not to take this
party to Oregon, Malcolm and Pete could sure use his
help finding their way home.

Joe nodded soberly to the folks gathered around his
horse. "I'll be back for my horses, anyway," he said as he
glanced around to find Callie Simmons. She was watching him closely, a smile upon her young face. Their
eyes met briefly and he gave her a slight nod. She responded in kind. Then he abruptly turned the paint's
head and was off.

He left with a conflict of emotions raging in his brain.
Never feeling at ease in a large gathering of people, he
was relieved to be free of them. On the other hand, he
was encountering emotions of melancholy that he was
reluctant to attribute to parting from Callie Simmons.
His meeting Callie had introduced a new sensation never
experienced before, and he was not at all sure he was
comfortable with it. She had stopped by his campfire
several times in the weeks that followed her visit with
coffee and a biscuit. Bright and cheerful, she had given
no indication that those occasions were anything more
than being friendly. He was not ready to admit it, even
to himself, but there was little doubt that he would
come back. His horses were just an excuse to see her
again.

"You'd best be careful your eyeballs don't fall out,"
Cora Simmons warned her daughter.

Callie turned then to confront her mother's stern features glaring at her, and she realized that she had been
caught fondly gazing after the tall scout. "Mama . . . ,"
Callie complained indignantly. Her mother had already
warned her against having any interest in a half-savage

wanderer with no roots planted anywhere. She spun on her heel and headed toward the cave, seeking to avoid another lecture from her mother. Much to her annoyance, Cora followed.

"Your papa and me have tried to raise you to take your place in this world as a serious, Christian woman, marry a God-fearing husband, and raise a family in the arms of the church."

"Oh, Mama," Callie responded, "Joe Fox and I are just friends. I'm not thinking about *marrying* him, for goodness' sakes."

"I saw you making sugar eyes at him," Cora insisted. "Who knows what a man like that would do if he had any idea you were sweet on him?" Callie tried to walk faster, but Cora stayed right on her heels. "Malcolm Lindstrom told Bradley and your papa that Joe Fox was raised in a Blackfoot Indian camp. Did you know that? A wild savage—I doubt if he knows right from wrong. I pity the poor woman who takes him for a husband."

"Mama!" Callie scolded, having heard enough of her mother's haranguing. "He's gone, and as you can see, he didn't grab me and carry me off into the woods."

"Well, it wouldn't have surprised me if he had," Cora said. "You just think about what I said, young lady. You don't wanna end up living like an Indian squaw."

Cora stood, hands on hips, watching her daughter until she disappeared into the earthen hovel that served as the family's winter quarters. She had always been in tune with Callie's moods and tendencies, and she was truly concerned about her apparent infatuation with the soft-spoken man of the forest. Even knowing how much Joe Fox had already done for her family and friends, and how grateful they were for his help, she was thankful that he was not remaining in the camp all winter. Callie was only eighteen years old. Maybe she would forget her silly notions about the man over the coming months.

Winter came in with a grudge that year, dumping heavy snowfalls in the mountain passes, accompanied by howling winds that sculpted giant towers in the icy drifts that clogged even the oldest of trails. Although the valley was protected from the raging storms that stalked the mountains around it, still substantial mounds of snow covered the collection of caves along the river bluffs. Malcolm commented that the little community resembled a village of white mole hills. There was little activity in the congregation outside the earthen hovels beyond venturing out for firewood, or answering nature's calls. The caves were warm enough, and more than a few felt obligated to thank Joe Fox for refusing to lead them off into the mountains. Not one soul complained that they should have tried to push on through to Oregon.

Unless the weather was unusually poor, Sunday services were held every week, and thanks were offered for the group's survival. Everyone made an effort to attend, except the sick and, of course, Starbeau. Although apparently unable to venture out on a Sunday, it was noticed by all that the surly malcontent found a way to get to the trading post to trade items from his packs in exchange for whiskey. The rest of the time he stayed in his cave, glaring out at passersby as if blaming each one of them for the cruel conditions. His shoulder fully recovered soon after the men in the party finished his dwelling. All the members of the stranded mule train rapidly came to regard him as they might a great bear in his cave, and were content to leave him to his solitary drinking.

Near the end of February, the weather improved a bit, to the extent that more wood-cutting parties could be organized, as well as occasional trips to Templeton's store to buy what staples he had left on his nearly bare shelves. On a day such as this, when the sky opened briefly to confirm that the sun still resided over the high mountains, Callie Simmons felt the need to venture out to flush her lungs with fresh, cold air. Stepping carefully through a patch of snow, she felt a strong urge to turn and gaze toward the western mountains. Her eyes settled upon a dark object standing out against the whiteness of the snow-covered hills. It attracted her attention because of its gentle swaying motion. At first she thought it to be a fir tree waving in the wind. But then she realized that the tree seemed to be moving toward her. Her curiosity completely captured then, she stared hard in an effort to identify the object, which now began to resemble a great bear, approaching on its hind legs. She shaded her eyes with her hand as she continued to stare through the glare of the lightly swirling snow. Finally coming into focus, the object became a man on horseback, plodding across the snowy meadow, wearing a heavy bearskin coat. She laughed to think that the blinding sunlight upon the white snow had played such a trick on her eyes. In the next instant, her heart skipped a beat when she realized that the rider was astride a paint pony.

Joe Fox. The thought brought a smile to her face, and her hand automatically reached up to tidy her hair. She looked quickly around her to see if anyone else had seen her unconscious motion, pleased to find no one close at hand. Turning her full attention back to the rider approaching, now at a distance of approximately one hundred yards, she could see that the carcass of some animal was riding behind the saddle. *He never comes empty-handed*, she thought, and beamed delightedly as she gazed at a sight that had become so familiar to all the people in the camp. One could not help but admire the partnership between horse and rider, watching the easy motion of the two, moving as if one.

Seeing her standing on the edge of the bluffs, Joe gave the paint a nudge in that direction, and the horse, needing no further guidance, headed straight for her. Pulling up before her, he said, "Well, I see you're still here."

She laughed gaily. "Where did you expect I'd be?"

Her reply caused him to stammer awkwardly, "Why, nowhere else, I reckon." Then realizing the young lady was simply teasing him, he laughed. "Looks like you're makin' it all right." He reached back and patted the whitetail deer carcass behind his saddle. "I ran across this young feller on the other side of that mountain back yonder. He was just beggin' to get shot, so I obliged him. Thought your family might could use a little fresh meat."

"It would be wonderful," she replied enthusiastically. "I'm about to turn into jerky." She stood back then and gave him a good looking over. "I declare, when you rode up I thought you were a bear riding a horse."

Pushing back the hood of his bear coat, he laughed and said, "I reckon a body could make that mistake." He dismounted then. "I'll tote this whitetail over to your fire. I've already gutted him. I can hang him up and skin him for you."

She was thrilled to anticipate the taste of fresh venison, but the little ripple of excitement she felt down the length of her spine was not caused by a craving for fresh meat. She could not explain the feelings she had for Joe, and was not even sure if they were not simply fascination for this wild thing—like the fascination for a lion cub. Maybe she was attracted to him for no reason other than that her mother was so fearful of a union between the savage and her. Whatever the reason, she was just glad to see him after all the cold, lonely weeks since he had gone away. She was about to tell him so when a voice behind her exclaimed, "Joe Fox!"

They both turned to see Jake Simmons coming from the corral that had been built to contain the livestock. He sang out again, so that others might hear him. "Joe Fox is back!" He was successful in causing several more heads to pop out of various caves. One of them, Cora Simmons, frowned as she saw the tall mountain man, wrinkling her brow even more when she spotted Callie talking to him. "Look, Mama," Jake said. "Joe Fox is back!" She did not reply, but followed her husband and several of her neighbors to greet the man striding toward them.

"By golly," Jake exclaimed, grinning from ear to ear. "What are you doin' back here? We didn't expect to see you before spring, and maybe not even then."

"I moved my camp over to that line of ridges to the east of you," Joe replied, pointing toward a low line of hills behind him. "So I thought I'd drop in and see how you folks are farin' the winter. Thought you might want a taste of fresh meat if you ain't been huntin' lately."

They were joined then by Malcolm and his brother. Pete Watson could be seen hurrying up from the stand of cottonwoods that served as the men's toilet, still hitching up his trousers. "By thunder, you're right about that," Jake said in response to Joe. "We could sure use some fresh meat." He looked around at the gathering crowd. "We all could. We can have us a feast! Whaddaya say, ladies? We can build up that fire and roast the whole carcass."

Soon the entire camp was transformed from a sense of cold boredom into a festive air of celebration. One deer was hardly enough to satisfy the needs of thirty-seven people for any length of time, but it was enough to provide one fresh, hot meal for folks in need of something to break the monotony of winter. It was a good bit more than Joe had anticipated. He would have preferred to slip in quietly and leave the deer for Callie's family to use as they saw fit. When he stopped to think about it, however, he had to admit that Jake *was* using it as he thought best, and it appeared it was going a long way toward lifting the spirits of the winter-weary travelers. Several of the men set upon the carcass and hung it from a tree limb. Three men started in skinning the deer at the same time. With knives flashing, it was a wonder to Joe that someone wasn't stabbed.

He was about to step forward to criticize the method in which the hide was rolled back until a beaming Callie Simmons caught him by the elbow and drew him aside. "Let them do it," she said. "You've done your part. Now just sit down over there and watch these folks make fools of themselves, and I'll bring you a cup of coffee."

"They're gonna ruin half of that hide . . ." He started to protest, then paused when he saw her smiling up at him. "Oh, well," he said, "I reckon it don't matter."

"No, it doesn't matter," she said. "What matters is that you got everyone out of their holes, and people look happy again." A moment after she said it, someone started a chant to get Raymond Chadwick to fetch his fiddle. He didn't need much persuasion, and soon, by the time the deer was roasting over the huge fire, he struck up a lively tune. He was handy with a bow, and before long some of the younger ones began tapping their toes to the rhythm. Not to be outdone, the older folks stepped out in the clearing to show off their suppleness. Before long, everyone in the party of settlers was dancing, watching the dancers, or tending the meat. Joe was astonished by the spectacle. He had never seen a demonstration such as this, and he was especially fascinated by the instrument upon which Raymond was able to extract such rhythmic sounds. When he glanced at Callie and found her smiling as she watched his reactions, he nodded and returned the smile. Watching from the other side of the fire, Cora Simmons stared tight-lipped at her daughter, a deep frown upon her face.

One other soul was not enjoying the celebration. Starbeau watched from afar. Near the end of the caves, where Bradley Lindstrom and Jake Simmons had dug their abodes, his mind was occupied with thoughts of the two hundred and fifty dollars that had been saved as final payment to Skinner. With everyone's attention drawn to the dancing, there would never be a better opportunity to slip into the caves and search for the money. Taking one last cautious look to make sure none in the crowd was looking his way, he ducked inside Bradley's cave.

Pausing for a second to adjust his eyes to the gloom inside the tiny cavity, he glanced around until he spotted the saddle packs stacked against the back wall. Moving as fast as he could manage while trying not to leave evidence of his search, he untied pack after pack, rummaging through clothing and cooking utensils, household trinkets and personal pictures of relatives back east. Never one to hold his temper for long, he became more and more irritated as the search revealed nothing of value. His patience expired, he threw the last pack carelessly against the wall of the cave. Suddenly the music from the fiddle stopped and he knew the meat was ready to be served. "Damn!" he exclaimed, ready to admit defeat. Angry then, he stalked toward the mouth of the cave when he caught sight of a small wooden box stacked amid Nancy Lindstrom's pots and pans. He almost passed it by, then decided to take a quick glance since he had looked in everything else. He unconsciously let out a low whistle when he saw the money inside the box. "I knew it," he murmured. "I knew it was here." He took the roll of money out and fondled it covetously for a few minutes before returning it to its hiding place. "I'll be back for you," he said as he replaced the box, being careful to return it to the position he had found it in.

Outside again, he looked around him, satisfied that no one had bothered to look toward the caves. It would not do to take the money now. Even a man as blunt as Starbeau knew that. He was content to wait until the weather improved and he was ready to part company with the unsuspecting pilgrims. He couldn't help chuckling when he thought about it. There were a couple of other chores to be settled as well. He thought about evening the score with Jake Simmons and Joe Fox as he walked toward the party. There was also the issue of fresh-roasted meat that he didn't want to miss out on.

Moving through the gathering of people, now standing in small groups as they ate the freshly roasted venison, Starbeau scowled contemptuously, neither speaking nor being spoken to. Like a grizzly moving through a thicket, he left pools of silence behind him as conversation paused until he had passed. Helping himself to a large slab of meat from the deer's haunch, he sat down on a rock away from the fire and proceeded to eat. As he looked over his neighbors, his glance lit on Joe Fox. The tall hunter was seated on a log beside Callie Simmons, and he was watching the huge bully closely. Starbeau smirked when he caught his eye, and pointed his finger at Joe as if threatening with a pistol.

Seated beside Joe, Callie sensed the sudden tension in his body. She looked up at him to discover the smile had been replaced by a frown. Following his gaze, she discovered the cause of his displeasure. "I wondered if fresh meat was going to rout the ol' bear outta his cave," she said. "Papa thinks he won't stay around when spring comes. Everybody's hoping he'll leave before then." Noticing the tight set of Joe's jaw, she said, "I wouldn't worry about him. He just likes to look mean. I think he's harmless."

"I ain't so sure," Joe replied softly. "That man's got a mean streak. I shoulda killed him when I had the chance." He turned to look directly at Callie then. "You be careful around that man." *He's harmless all right*, Joe was thinking. *Harmless like a rattlesnake.*

"Oh, I will," she replied, pleased by his apparent concern for her safety.

"What is it, Cora?" Jake asked, a touch of irritation in his tone when his wife kept tugging at his coat sleeve. He was in the midst of a conversation with Bradley and his brother, Malcolm, about the possibility of persuading Joe to join them in their journey to Oregon. When Cora insisted that she needed to talk to him right then, he made his excuses and let himself be led over to the side where she could speak privately.

"Look yonder," was all she said at first, nodding toward the other side of the clearing, where Callie and Joe were talking. When Jake failed to respond as she expected, she spelled it out for him. "Our daughter is throwing herself at Joe Fox, and we've got to put a stop to it before something bad comes of it."

Still not quite sure what Cora was getting at, Jake replied, a little bewildered, "What bad are you talkin' about?"

"Dammit, Jake!" Cora exclaimed, causing him to blink hard. Cora used profanity only on occasion when she was genuinely angry or worried. "If we don't do something, Callie is gonna follow that savage off to some tipi in the mountains somewhere and we'll never see her again. Is that what you want for Callie? If you weren't so blind, you'd see that she's been mooning over him ever since he led us into this valley."

Jake took a step backward, suddenly awake to what

his wife was telling him. "I swear . . . ," he muttered, realizing that what Cora said was true—Callie had given Joe a lot of attention. He had just not given it much concern before. "Well, what can we do about it?" he asked, then offered, "I can talk to her, I reckon."

"I've already talked to her till I'm blue in the face," Cora said. "I think you'd best have a talk with Joe Fox, let him know that Callie's not one of his little squaw women that can live in the woods."

Jake shook his head, concerned. "Oh, I don't know, Cora," he started, obviously not pleased with the prospect. "That man's done a helluva lot for us, all of us, and I don't mind admittin' that he probably saved my life when Starbeau tried to trick me into a fight." He shook his head again. "Maybe you're seein' more to it than there really is."

"I reckon I know my daughter well enough to know when she's thinking things she oughtn't. If we don't stop her, she's going to do something she'll spend the rest of her life regretting. And there's no talking sense to her—I know, I've tried. You're gonna have to tell Joe Fox to go sniffing around somebody else's henhouse." She watched Jake's reaction for a moment, then said, "I like the man, too, Jake, but we have to think about what's best for Callie."

Jake took a long, deep breath and let it out in a weary sigh. "I reckon you're right," he said. "We have to think of Callie." He was reluctant to, but he finally agreed. "I'll go talk to Joe."

Although he had been offered the hospitality of Malcolm and Pete's cave in the bluffs, Joe was thinking of staying in the cottonwoods upriver for a couple of days. Now that the festivities were winding down, and people were returning to their caves, it was time to make his camp while there was still light. Cora Simmons had called for Callie to come help with some chore, leaving Joe by himself again. It had been surprising to him that he had enjoyed the dancing and merriment. Normally, he would have sought to avoid any such gathering. The fact that Callie was by his side had a lot to do with it. But even aside from that, he wondered whether he could live in a white man's world after all. His chosen path between the Blackfoot's and the white man's worlds had suited him fine for the past several years. Maybe it was time for him to choose one or the other, and with the feelings he had experienced since finding this mule train, he found himself leaning toward the white man's world. It was something he would have to think about, he decided. Putting the thought away for another time, he picked up the paint's reins and led it toward the grove of trees.

"Heyo!" He heard a call from the edge of the bluffs and turned to see Jake Simmons angling across the clearing to intercept him. "Hold up a minute, Joe," Jake called after him.

Joe stopped and waited for Jake to catch up to him. Watching the little man stepping to avoid the deeper patches of snow reminded him of a coyote pup venturing out for the first time after a snowfall. He had to smile.

Jake was relieved to see the fearsome-looking man smiling. His mission was not one he would have chosen for himself, for he was not sure how Joe would react to what he was about to be told. It would have to be handled delicately. Seeing him heading toward the cottonwoods upriver gave him hope that Joe was heading back into the mountains, sparing Jake the necessity of delivering Cora's message. "You headin' out again?" Jake asked hopefully when he caught up with Joe.

"Nope," Joe replied, "thought I'd stay around for a couple of days. I'm just gonna make my camp in the trees."

"Oh," Jake responded. While Joe stood waiting for Jake to go on, there was a long moment of awkward silence, finally broken by Joe.

"Were you wantin' somethin'?" Joe asked.

"No . . . I mean, yeah, I need to talk to you about somethin'." He took a deep breath and forged on ahead with it. "It's Callie," he said and paused again. Joe gazed at him, puzzled. "Callie's all me and Cora's got," Jake started once more. "We want her to be happy, find a God-fearin' husband when she's old enough, and raise a Christian family out in Oregon with us." When Joe still showed no sign that he understood what Jake was trying to tell him, Jake came out with it. "I ain't throwin' off on you none, but I'm askin' you to stay away from Callie."

Joe made no response right away, but Jake could see the hurt in his eyes when he suddenly realized what Jake was telling him. At that moment he would have taken it back if he could have. "Like I said, we've got nothin' against you. It's what's best for Callie, that's what we have to think about. If you was in my shoes, you'd do the same thing. I mean, you live like an Injun. That ain't no fittin' life for Callie. She ain't used to that."

Having been totally unprepared for it, Joe was stunned momentarily, his head a maelstrom of confusing thoughts. He felt the sting of rebuke by Jake, but also the impression that her parents feared she might actually have feelings for him. Or was he wrong? Was it possible Callie thought him too bold, and complained to her parents? No, he decided. She had given no indication that she was bothered by his company. He realized then that he had never thought beyond the fact that she was on his mind a good portion of the time. *What*, he wondered, *did I think it would lead to? If anything?* When he could not answer that question with any degree of certainty, he thought then of what he could offer her. In view of that, he could not truly blame Jake and Cora for their attitude. Seeing the anxiety in Jake's eyes, he finally spoke. "I have not spoken to Callie of such things," he said softly with no sign of emotion.

"No, I know you ain't," Jake hurried to exclaim. "I ain't sayin' you done anythin' wrong. I just wanted to say somethin' before things got too far. Callie just ain't for you, that's all. I hope there ain't no hard feelin's."

Joe could not react immediately, shocked by the realization that he was deemed unfit company for Callie. Too astonished to be angry, he didn't know what to say. Outwardly, his expression betrayed no hint of the turmoil inside him, causing Jake to think he felt no emotion. Afterward, when relating the incident to Cora, Jake would remark that Joe had not reacted at all. "Just like a stone-faced Injun." He could not know the depth of the hurt in Joe's heart, for it told him that he was not accepted in the white man's world in spite of the color of his skin.

The message delivered, the two men stood silently facing each other for a long moment. Finally Joe responded. "Is there anythin' else you wanted to tell me?"

"No, I reckon that's all I had to say," Jake replied. "Like I said, I hope there ain't no hard feelin's."

Joe continued to look at the little man for a moment more, then without another word, turned and led his horse into the trees. A dozen yards inside the tree line brought him to a suitable place, but he did not set about making his camp right away. Instead, he paused to sort out his emotions and rethink what had happened in the last quarter of an hour. Making a decision then, he tied the paint's reins to a tree limb and returned to the corral to fetch his other horses. He had a strong desire to leave this place and seek the solace of the mountains. The mountains were his strength and the source of his being. When he was a boy, he had gone to the mountains to seek his medicine and had been shown the path he must follow. He thought about the respect he had earned as a Blackfoot warrior. He had counted his first coup when only fourteen years of age and killed for the first time when he was eighteen. He had proven his courage and was respected in his village. His father had been approached by the fathers of several young girls about the possibility of marriage. It was he who had not been ready to marry. Now, with his heart aching, he thought about the possibility of returning to the world of the Blackfoot, but he feared it was too late. It had been too long. He did not belong to that world anymore. He paused then to recall the vision he had received when a boy, and the words that were spoken in his dream: *Neither white nor red are you, but a man alone.* "Enough of this thinking," he resolved. "I must leave this place."

"There! See!" Wounded Elk exclaimed and pointed at the tall figure leading three horses toward the cottonwoods upriver. "He is the one who killed Dead Man and Two Arrows. Look at the ponies he is leading. The spotted one is Dead Man's."

"I see him," Yellow Hand said. He had not been with the war party that had attacked the white men on mules and had cost the lives of all but Wounded Elk and Crooked Lance. Crooked Lance had been the leader of that war party, but he was not with them today. Because of the loss of lives suffered, he was thought to be unlucky, and was not welcome on this scouting party. One of the warriors killed on that day was Yellow Hand's brother, and he had organized a war party to avenge his death and that of the other Gros Ventre warriors. After tracking the mule train for two weeks, they had been forced to abandon the search when the snowstorms in the mountain passes covered the trails.

Yellow Hand had refused to give up the search for

the men who killed his brother, insisting that only fools would try to cross over the mountains in the winter. "They have made a camp somewhere to wait for the spring," he had maintained. And along with three warriors who trusted his leadership, he had scouted a half dozen valleys that offered protection from the winter storms. At last his persistence had come to bear fruit, for here in the Missoula Valley he had found them, burrowed in the ground like prairie dogs.

"We must decide what is the best thing to do," Yellow Hand said. "It would not be wise to attack them since we are only four, and there is still too much snow to ride in quickly and drive off their horses and mules. They are camped close to the white man's village as well."

"What are we going to do?" Long Walker asked. "Why have we traveled all this way if we are going to do nothing?"

"This is what I think," Yellow Hand said. "I think they are not going anywhere until the weather gets better. I think we should go back to our village and mount a full war party. With many warriors, we can kill all the whites. And with many warriors, the people in the white man's settlement will be afraid to come to help them. That is what I think."

The others nodded in agreement with only one questioning comment from Long Walker. "Our village is a long way from this place. What if the white men have gone before we can get back?"

"The mountains are covered with snow," Yellow Hand replied. "It will be another full moon before they are able to travel. There is plenty of time for us to return."

"I agree with Yellow Hand," Wounded Elk said.

"I agree also," Red Sky, the youngest of the four, said. "But we could slip into their camp tonight and steal some of their horses."

"It is better not to warn them to prepare against future attacks," Yellow Hand said. The others nodded their acceptance of his wisdom. He smiled at young Red Sky. "You will have your chance to steal many horses and count coup many times if you have a little patience."

"Not even the one man who led the ponies into the trees?" Red Sky persisted, causing the three older men to laugh.

"It's best not to take a chance that he might shout an alarm to the others," Yellow Hand said, as the four withdrew from the thicket from which they had watched the camp. "If he is the one who killed my brother, as Wounded Elk has said, then it is I who should have the right to kill him. When it is dark, then I'll look for him in the trees. If I can find him alone, I will kill him."

"He's the one who killed Two Arrows," Wounded Elk said. "I saw him. He wasn't with the others when we found them by the river. He came from the mountain ridge behind us and shot Two Arrows and Dead Man. I was lucky to get away before he shot us all."

"He doesn't look like the other white men in that camp," one of the other warriors said. "Maybe he is the ghost the Blackfeet call Joe Fox, who they say walks along the high peaks of the mountains."

"A ghost, eh?" Yellow Hand responded. "He didn't look like a ghost to me. Tonight, when it's dark, I'll find this ghost and kill him."

Chapter 6

With no reason to believe that he was being stalked, Joe Fox led his horses down along the river. At the edge of the trees, where a low, rolling line of hills came down to the river, he climbed on the paint and struck out across the treeless slope. Although darkness was already descending over the valley, he decided to ride on until finding shelter at the base of the mountains beyond another treeless mesa. The covering of snow made traveling at night easy enough to see the breaks and gullies that might otherwise have hampered him. Consequently, he was in no particular hurry to get anywhere. The only urgency he felt was to remove himself from the people he was leaving behind.

After he had ridden for a little over an hour, a light snow began to fall, creating a lacy veil over the dark form of the mountain directly before him now. He pulled the hood of his bearskin coat over his head and pressed on, oblivious to the falling snow. Though heavy on his mind, he decided to put away thoughts of Callie Simmons and her parents, and bring his concentration back to what he knew best—survival. Thinking of his horses then, he determined it time to find adequate shelter for them. A long, deep ravine, carved into the base of the mountain was his choice for a campsite. Sheltered from the icy winds by a thick growth of pines, the defile offered protection for his horses as well as a little grass under a thin blanket of snow. "It won't be much longer, boy," he said as he took the saddle off the paint, "and the winter will start to let up."

Stealing cautiously across the open meadow, Yellow Hand, followed closely by his companions, made his way toward the cottonwoods that framed the river. Once they reached the cover of the trees, they paused to look carefully around them. There was no sign of the man they searched for or the horses he led. There was, however, an easy trail in the snow that told them which way he had gone. Squinting in the darkness of the forest at the tracks left by the horses, Yellow Hand asked Wounded Elk, "Do you still think this man is a ghost? These are tracks a child could follow. I don't believe ghosts leave tracks."

Wounded Elk shrugged, not ready to concede. "All we see here are tracks left by the ponies. The ponies are not ghosts. There are no tracks left by the man, so who can say?"

He was answered by a quiet laugh from Yellow Hand. "We will see if this ghost sheds blood when I kill him," he boasted. "Come now," he said and set out to follow the tracks in the snow.

When the trail left the trees and continued across the treeless hill, they stopped to speculate again. "He leaves the others," Wounded Elk said. "He goes back to his home in the mountains."

"Maybe," Yellow Hand said, disappointed to find that his brother's killer had not camped in the cotton-woods, and unwilling to admit that Joe Fox had managed to slip away while they had sat waiting for darkness. "He cannot hide his trail in the snow. I'll track him down and kill him. My brother must be avenged."

"We will follow him," Wounded Elk said in support of his friend, but deep in his heart he still had uneasy feelings about the man they sought to kill. Dead Man and Two Arrows were both mighty warriors, and they fell before Joe Fox's gun. He would prefer to leave this ghost to go his own way. Yellow Hand's plan to return to their village to organize a large war party was a good one. Rubbing out the party of white mule riders should be revenge enough for Two Arrows' death. He did not share his feelings of reluctance with the others, however.

"I am afraid if we go after this one man in the high mountains," Long Walker said, "it may take too long to catch him. If we are going to attack the white men in the holes by the river, we need to go back to our village and get our warriors ready. The white man is crazy. Who knows when they might decide to leave? They may not wait until the passes are clear."

"There is wisdom in what Long Walker says," Wounded Elk said. "There is much preparation to ready our warriors for battle. This is something we should talk about."

Yellow Hand nodded and considered the comments. Although Wounded Elk sought to hide his reluctance to follow this *ghost*, Yellow Hand sensed his friend's apprehensions. "You may be right, but I know what I must do." Looking at Wounded Elk, he said, "You and Long Walker should ride back to our village to prepare for the attack. Red Sky can go with me to kill Joe Fox."

It was agreed then. Long Walker and Wounded Elk started back on the long trek to the Gros Ventre village while Yellow Hand and the eager young Red Sky set

out after the lone mountain man the Blackfoot called
Joe Fox.

The man they hunted was in the process of making
his camp a little more weatherproof, thinking the ravine a good place to stay for a while before moving
higher up to one of his regular camps by the waterfall.
By the light of a full moon that broke through with the
passing of the recent snow clouds, he selected a spot in
a stand of young pines. Picking four of the young trees,
he bent the tops over and tied them together, forming
a crude shelter. Cutting branches from other trees, he
covered his shelter, making it better able to protect
him from the weather. His hut of pines also allowed
him to make his fire inside, away from any eyes that
might be about. By the look of the sky, there should be
more snow on the way, possibly by morning. That
should help cover the trail he had left in the snow.

When his camp was finished and his horses taken
care of, he roasted some of the dried meat he carried.
He couldn't help but think of the times Callie had brought
him pan bread or some other thing she had cooked to
eat with his jerky. As soon as the thought sprang forth,
he forbade his mind to dwell on Callie Simmons. He
had wasted enough thoughts on foolish fantasies that
could not be. He must walk the path that had been
set before him and leave the white man to his own
world. His self-council was not enough to ease his
mind, however, and he became restless and ill at ease,
with a feeling that all was not well. He decided he
needed to breathe the clean mountain air, free of the
smoke from his fire. Taking his rifle, he left the hut and
stood for a while listening to the sounds of the night.
Looking above him, he saw a knob formed at the rim
of the ravine where more young pines grew in a half
circle. He decided to climb up to the knob to await the
morning sun. It would not be long before it rose. He

had labored all night and he felt the need to rest, but his restless feelings made the thought of sleep impossible. When he reached the knob of pines, he decided it would be a good place to watch the sun come up over the mountains.

The two Gros Ventre warriors paused to study the trail that now led up a draw at the foot of the mountain. Yellow Hand looked up at the sky. "It will be morning soon. I think he has decided to make his camp up this ravine." Red Sky nodded. He was in agreement that if Joe Fox intended to climb the mountain, this draw was not a reasonable path to attempt. It went only a quarter of the way up before ending at the base of a sheer cliff.

With prospects of catching the mountain man while he was sleeping, they hurried along the trail, following it up the snowy draw, eager to reach the camp before sunup. Suddenly, Yellow Hand held his hand up to halt Red Sky. With hand signals only, he directed him to back his pony until reaching a pine thicket they had just passed. As soon as they reached it, Yellow Hand slid off his pony and whispered to Red Sky to do the same. He explained then that they had almost blundered right into the camp. "He has made a lodge with young trees," Yellow Hand said. "His horses are tied in the trees beyond." He looked overhead at the sky again just as the first tiny rays of the morning sun probed the trees at the rim of the ravine. "It will be light soon. We must hurry to be ready."

Leaving their ponies in the thicket, they crept forward until they reached a point some thirty yards from the pine shelter. There they split up on either side of the trail in order to set up a cross fire. Yellow Hand hoped to catch his enemy as he walked out of his shelter, so he waited until the sun had risen over the ridges to the east. Still, Joe Fox did not come out. Too impatient to wait longer, he inched a few yards closer, then gave Red Sky the signal to shoot, and both warriors opened fire with their repeating rifles, pumping round after round into the makeshift shelter, sending pine limbs flying and filling the ravine with thunderous echoes.

After both men emptied the magazines of their rifles, they charged up to the shelter to peer inside. Stunned, they stood gaping into an empty hut. "Up here," Joe Fox said, and they both turned toward the sound, looking up into the glare of the sun as it framed a dark image against a background of young pines. In the blinding light, it appeared to the two assassins that the image stood in a flaming arch, and in the next instant fiery missiles reached out to strike down both of them.

Joe cocked the Winchester, ejecting the last empty shell, and stood watching the two bodies sprawled before his campsite for a few moments to make sure they were dead. When there was no sign of life from either, he made his way back down the side of the ravine, alert to the possibility there may be more than these two. At the bottom of the ravine, he scouted cautiously along the trail until he came to the two ponies tied in a thicket. Satisfied then that they were alone in the attempt to kill him, he was left to ponder the reason. After going back to examine the dead, he was able to identify them as Gros Ventre, and realized that they must have been seeking revenge for the slaying of their brothers. He had been spared because of his feelings of restlessness. He also wondered whether the slight feeling of uneasiness he had experienced while making his camp had been caused by a sense of danger, as if something had been warning him. He did not discount it. It was a trait often manifested in wild animals, and like a wild animal, he had lived many years alone in the mountains.

Both Indians had early models of repeating Henry rifles. Joe checked the action of each and grunted his satisfaction. They would be worth something in trade for supplies. He had survived the attempt on his life, but all was not well, for two of his horses were lying on the ground, having been hit by lead flying from the warriors' rifles. Their screams of pain had gone unheard amid the volley of gunfire. He was relieved to see the paint standing, nervously stomping his hooves and stepping from side to side. On closer inspection he found no wounds. For that he was thankful. He and the paint had been partners for a long time. Then he wondered whether there would be more Gros Ventre coming to find him, but the thought left him quickly, for suddenly he felt very tired and in need of sleep.

He untied the paint and the other, a sorrel he had captured in the first encounter with the Gros Ventre, led them away from the bodies, and tied them again. With the horses quieted down, he went back by the fire and lay down to rest. He would sleep, and afterward he would collect the two ponies in the thicket and leave this ravine to the buzzards.

Callie Simmons slid the cake of pan bread off the huge iron skillet onto a folded cloth, since the bread was larger than any plate she had. She glanced up at her mother and smiled. "I'll bet Joe would appreciate a piece of this to go with his coffee," she said cheerfully.

"I expect he might," Cora replied without enthusiasm. "But he's been living without it for most of his life, so I wouldn't bother taking him any." She glanced over at Jake and met his gaze. "Our supplies are running low as it is, without feeding every wild critter in the woods."

Callie was shocked by her mother's harsh comments, unaccustomed to any show of selfishness from Cora Simmons. "Mama," she replied, "I can't believe you'd begrudge a little piece of bread for someone who's done so much for us."

Her father spoke up then. "Just forget about it, Callie. We think it best if you don't hang around someone like Joe Fox no more. Can't nothin' good come from it."

"And a lot bad," her mother added.

Obviously distressed, Callie almost dropped the cake of bread on the ground, scarcely believing the words coming from her parents' mouths. Her mother had been trying to discourage Callie's friendship with the strange, quiet man from the mountains ever since Joe had first come to rescue them. But her father had never said a negative word in association with the man who saved his life. Dismayed, but not for long, her eyes flashed with anger, and she broke off a generous piece of the fresh bread. "I don't know what's wrong with you two," she scolded. "Joe is the kindest, most thoughtful man I've ever met. He deserves a lot more than a little hunk of pan bread, and I'm taking it to him!" With that, she turned abruptly and left the cave.

"Callie!" her mother cried out and reached for her arm to stop her, but Callie was already out of her reach. "You come back here!" she ordered, but her daughter ignored her. Cora ran out the entrance after the headstrong girl. Jake didn't know what to do, so he followed his wife outside. The girl didn't get far before she ran headlong into Bradley Lindstrom as he was walking past their hovel.

"Whoa, young lady!" Bradley exclaimed as he caught Callie in time to keep her from falling. "Where are you off to in such a hurry?"

"I'm sorry, Mr. Lindstrom," Callie replied, embarrassed by her reckless exit from her family's cave. "I should have been looking where I was going." Recovering her composure then, she answered his question. "I was going to take Joe some fresh pan bread, if he's still in his camp."

"Joe's gone," Bradley said, and glanced up to see Jake and Cora as they stepped outside after their daughter.

"Gone?" Jake asked. "Did you say he was gone?"

"Yep," Bradley replied. "Musta lit out last night sometime—didn't say nothin' to nobody about leavin'."

Jake cast a quick look in Cora's direction and she returned his gaze with a slight nod, silently recognizing his apparent success in serving notice to the wild young man. Jake acknowledged her approval with a nod of his own.

Bradley went on to convey his concern. "He said he was gonna stay around for a few days, but he's already gone. Luke Preston's boy was over in those cottonwoods early this mornin'. There wasn't no sign of Joe, and he found tracks leadin' out toward the mountains to the south." Bradley paused to scratch his head thoughtfully. "What I'm afraid of, though, is if he's ever plannin' to come back, 'cause we were sure hopin' we could talk him into leadin' us to Oregon come spring."

"Could be he's just gone huntin'," Jake said, experiencing a slight feeling of guilt for the possibility that he had cost his friends the services of Joe Fox.

"Don't look that way," Bradley said. "He took his horses with him, all of 'em."

"Well, I reckon there ain't nothin' we can do about it," Cora said. "It's hard to depend on a man like that." She glanced at Callie. "Wild ones, you can never tell what they'll do."

"I don't know," Bradley replied, not necessarily in agreement with Cora's assessment of the man who had proven to be pretty damned dependable in his eyes. "I hope he'll change his mind about goin' with us come spring." He called to mind a conversation he'd had with Joe the day before. Raymond Chadwick was there as well. Joe had said then that he had a camp in the mountains two days' ride from this valley, where he sometimes stayed part of the year. It was one of his favorite hunting spots, he had said, at the base of a waterfall that fed Otter Creek. If Joe really was gone for good, maybe it would be worthwhile to try to find that camp and hope they found him there as well. "Well," he finally said, "I expect I'd best go see if my mules are doin' all right." He strode off toward the corral, leaving the three of them to consider this unexpected development.

Seeing the look of disappointment in Callie's face, Cora sought to smooth her daughter's ruffled emotions. "Callie, honey, your pa and me were just trying to keep you from making a mistake that would ruin your whole life. And now you see we were right about Joe Fox. He's gone without so much as a *kiss my foot* to anybody."

Callie cocked her head to one side, and frowned at her mother as a suspicion struck her that her parents had something to do with Joe's sudden departure. All at once she was overcome with mixed feelings of anger and humiliation. She stared at her parents accusingly and charged, "You said something to him, didn't you?"

"Callie, baby," Cora tried to explain, "it's best to forget that man. You're not ready to be making decisions that might affect the rest of your life." She turned to her husband for support, but he could only shrug and nod.

"Oh, my God," Callie said despairingly, mortified, thinking of what Joe must have thought. "Oh, my God," she repeated.

"We're only thinking of you," Cora said.

"Oh, Mama, why couldn't you just leave it alone?" Callie lashed out, furious now with her parents' interfering. She threw the piece of bread she had been holding on the ground, spun on her heel, and stalked off toward the cottonwoods to be alone in her sorrow.

"Maybe I oughta go after her," Jake said.

"Leave her alone," Cora advised. "She's just hurting a little now, but she'll get over it. Then she'll realize that she wasn't really in love after all."

One individual seemed to find the confrontation between mother and daughter amusing. Starbeau chuckled when he saw Callie walk away in an apparent huff. *You can really swing that little behind of yours when you've got your dander up*, he thought. Seated on his saddle blanket in the mouth of his cave, taking in the morning sun, he could not hear the conversation between Bradley and the Simmons family except to catch a word or a phrase here and there when a voice was raised. It was enough to tell him that there was a thread of discord between daughter and parents, and it had something to do with Joe Fox. He drew satisfaction from anything that caused trouble for Jake Simmons or Joe Fox, and it was doubly pleasing if that something meant trouble for both of them. He was almost certain that he had heard Bradley Lindstrom tell Jake that Joe Fox was gone. He hoped that was true. He hated Joe Fox as much as he had ever hated any man. More than that, although reluctant to admit it, he feared him, feared the man's pragmatic reaction to threat. Starbeau was dead certain that Joe Fox was about to finish him off that night he shot him in the shoulder and would have completed the job if the others had not persuaded him to stop. The thing that caused Starbeau to fear the rangy mountain man was the cold, emotionless way he had prepared to kill him, with no show of excitement or anger, as if it were no more than the dispatching of a wounded animal. A man like that was dangerous, and given the chance, more specifically Joe Fox's back, Starbeau wouldn't hesitate to kill him.

"Lucky for him he's gone," he growled to himself,

said mostly to boost his pride. Then he smiled when it occurred to his sluggish brain that with Joe Fox gone there was no one to challenge him. His size and bluster would once again cause fear and demand respect. His smile widened until it broke into a mischievous chuckle. Before that morning, he had just about decided to leave this camp of God-fearing Bible thumpers and forget about going to Oregon. The two hundred and fifty dollars hidden in the little wooden box in Bradley Lindstrom's cave would give him a right comfortable grub stake for a while. *Maybe I'll go down to Butte,* he thought. *Don't nobody know me there.* He looked up at the sky then. *I'll just wait a little while longer for the weather to get better.* He felt smug when he thought that Joe Fox wouldn't be around to track him when he left with the money.

Chapter 7

Spring arrived early that year. Everyone in the camp was eager to vacate their dank, dark earthen hovels and continue on to what they hoped would be their promised land. There was still some trepidation, for no one could know for sure when all the passes would become clear of snow and ice. So they waited, and the men talked about it, and everyone prayed together for guidance at the Sunday service. The one thing that dismayed Bradley was there was no sign of Joe Fox. He, Jake, and Raymond talked about the possibility of sending someone to find the reclusive mountain man. After much discussion, it was decided that the likelihood of finding Joe's camp was remote at best. So they prayed some more for some sign that it was safe to start out over the mountains, hoping God would send a message in some form, biblical or physical. A message was, in fact, on the way, but not the one the people were praying for.

A war party, numbering twenty-three Gros Ventre warriors, plus five young boys eager to prove themselves in battle, went into camp less than two days from Missoula Mills. Wounded Elk sat down before the fire to confer with Long Walker and Little Buffalo. "I fear they are both dead, killed by Joe Fox," Long Walker said. It had been a full moon with no sign of Yellow Hand and Red Sky, when they should have returned to the village many days ago—unless they were not successful in killing the Blackfoot ghost. "I fear that their deaths might bring bad luck to our attack of the white camp."

"What say you, Wounded Elk?" Little Buffalo asked.

"I think that we have two more of our brothers to avenge," Wounded Elk replied. "I don't think their deaths could bring bad luck to our mission, because we do not go to attack Joe Fox. Our fight is to avenge the warriors killed by the white men with no wagons."

Little Buffalo and Long Walker considered what Wounded Elk had said, then agreed that his counsel was probably wise. With the exception of the two missing warriors, all the other signs had been favorable. The weather had been kind to them on the journey from their village, and they had made good time in reaching the Missoula Valley. "What should we do about the white man's settlement upriver from the people that live in the ground?" Little Buffalo asked. "We don't know how many there are, or if they will come to help the mole people." His concern was shared by Wounded Elk and Long Walker, for all three were well aware that they were far from their home range.

"I think if we follow my plan, we will kill the mole people and be gone before the whites at the trading post can come to help them." When the others agreed, Wounded Elk said, "Good, we should get to their camp before the sun comes up two more times."

As Wounded Elk had said, the Gros Ventre war party reached the creek from which Yellow Hand had watched the white camp before. Wounded Elk halted his warriors there to wait out the night before the dawn attack. They would proceed from this point on foot, leaving four of the young boys to hold the horses. While they waited, the warriors applied new war paint and asked Man Above to favor them in battle. When it was time, half of the war party followed the creek down to the river, then worked their way back up the river to be in position between the water and the bluffs, facing the cave openings. Two of Wounded Elk's bravest warriors stole across the open meadow in the gray light before dawn to pull rails from the corral to create a hole to drive the livestock out. When the first rays of the sun inched across the isolated patches of old snow, the rest of the war party advanced toward the village of caves—slowly at first, then gradually gaining momentum as the sun showed its face, until a cry of alarm from the camp signaled a full charge and the raiders opened fire on the few early risers walking between the caves and the corral.

At almost the same time, war cries were heard from the corral, and the horses and mules were stampeded through the gap. Flushed from their beds by the hellish sound of war cries and gunfire, the settlers grabbed their weapons and raced out to defend their camp, only to be cut down by the warriors below the bluffs as they emerged from the caves. Those lucky enough to have been missed by the volley of shots scrambled back inside to construct hasty ramparts, using their packs, bedding, and anything else to protect themselves.

The attack was well planned, with the warriors by the river keeping the settlers pinned in their earthen barricades while the rest of their war party charged up behind the caves. If all went as Wounded Elk planned, all the whites would be trapped in their holes in the ground. He had underestimated the tenacity of the white settlers to defend their families and possessions, however. Malcolm Lindstrom and Pete Watson were quick to recognize the danger of holing up inside the catacombs of caves. Scrambling outside their hole, they took positions on the ground between their cave and Jake Simmons', and began firing at the Indians led by Wounded Elk. Down the line of dwellings, several of the other men did the same, and soon the warriors' attack was blunted and they were forced to halt and seek cover.

Meanwhile, the warriors below the bluffs found themselves with no real protective cover from the rifle fire coming from the caves. After the initial barrage, the besieged settled down to snipe at the Indians on the edge of the water. Soon, due to an absence of effective cover, one by one the Gros Ventre casualties began to pile up until they were forced to withdraw down the river. Encouraged by the arrival of reinforcements from the sawmill and general store, the embattled settlers were able to vacate the caves and join in the fight behind them. The battle became a single-front skirmish as the warriors from the riverbanks joined Wounded Elk and his warriors in the open field before the line of caves.

Amid the heat of the conflict, Max Starbeau at first cursed himself for not having left the mule train when he first had the notion. He had dallied too long on his decision to head for Butte. With no thoughts of helping defend his fellow travelers, he sought to escape the battle altogether, his priority being the preservation of his hide, and the others be damned. But his greed would not permit him to go without the money in Nancy Lindstrom's little wooden box. It occurred to him then that the attack by Indians might have given him the perfect opportunity to liberate that money. The thought forced a smile to appear on his craggy face.

Easing his bulk out of his cave, he made sure there

were no Indians remaining below the bluffs before moving cautiously down the line of caves. "Come on, Starbeau!" Luke Preston shouted as he ran by him. "We've got 'em on the run!"

"Right behind you," Starbeau replied, then paused to let Preston disappear over the top of the mound. He watched for a moment and saw that Luke was right. The Indians were withdrawing and the men from the settlement were giving chase. Starbeau grinned. *Go get 'em, boys.* Then he turned his attention back to the row of caves. There was no one in sight. He wasted no time in getting down to Bradley Lindstrom's cave, and without hesitating, ducked inside. In a hurry, he went directly to the stack of pots and pans where he had first seen the wooden box. There it was, just as he had left it. He snatched it from the stack, opened it, and exhaled a great sigh of satisfaction to find the money still there.

"Now you can put that right back where you found it."

Startled, he turned to find Nancy Lindstrom huddled against the back corner of the cave with a shotgun aimed straight at him. In his haste to get his hands on the money, he had failed to see her hiding behind a pile of bedclothes. With no possible explanation available to him, he took the only option still open. "Well, now, just hold your horses, ma'am," he said while his hand dropped casually to rest on the handle of his .44. "This ain't what it looks like."

"I think I know what it is," Nancy retorted. Those were her last words. Starbeau suddenly drew the pistol from his belt and fired, hitting the surprised woman squarely in the chest, and knocking her back against the wall. To be certain, he took a step toward her and placed another shot in her forehead.

He went to the mouth of the cave and stopped to listen before stepping outside. The sound of gunfire

told him that the counterattack was still going on, and
evidently successful for the settlers. He then stuck his
head outside and looked left and right. Seeing no witnesses to his evil deed, he stepped out and walked
briskly away, the money a comforting lump in his
pocket.

His mind on other things now, he trotted along toward the fighting in hopes he might find his horse. The
counterattack had been spirited enough so that the
raiding Indians had had no time to herd the horses and
mules, consequently they were scattered along the river
and over the open meadow. He would have struck out
for Butte right then if he had his horse. He didn't care
about the mules, or most of the things he had packed
on them. With the money, he didn't need the household items in those packs. He would have preferred to
be gone when Nancy Lindstrom's body was found,
but no one saw him, so he wasn't overly worried.

There was no rejoicing over the successful defense
of their mule train, for there had been lives lost. Immediately after the final retreat of the Gros Ventre war
party, the weary settlers went about the business of
recovering their livestock and mending the corral, with
the unhappy task awaiting to bury their dead and
comfort the survivors. Most of the victims were men,
cut down as they ran out of the caves in the initial
assault. Some, like Nancy Lindstrom, were harder to
explain. Nancy had been shot at close range, yet no
one had reported seeing any Indians on top of the
bluffs. It was just one of life's mysteries to a grieving
husband until he happened to find that the money
was missing from the little wooden box.

It was highly unlikely that an Indian had taken the
money. Nothing else had been disturbed, so all suspicions went directly toward Starbeau, but there was no
proof one way or the other. Bradley insisted upon fac-

ing the huge bully with the accusation, anyway, and along with his brother, Malcolm, and several others, he called Starbeau out shortly after burying Nancy.

"You're barkin' up the wrong tree, Lindstrom," Starbeau slurred when confronted by the delegation. "I was fightin' them damn Injuns alongside everybody else. You got a helluva lotta nerve askin' me about how your wife got kilt. How the hell would I know? I might oughta break your back for you, throwin' somethin' like that up in my face." He looked around at the others with Bradley and smirked. "She probably got shot 'cause you were someplace hidin' from the Injuns."

"I've asked around, Starbeau," Bradley replied, showing no fear of the big bully. "Nobody remembers seein' you at all when we were driving those Injuns across the meadow."

"That ain't all of it, Starbeau," Malcolm interjected. "There's a little matter of two hundred and fifty dollars that's missin' from Bradley's cave, and I'm thinkin' you're the one who most likely took it."

"Why, you son of a bitch!" Starbeau exploded. "I oughta kill you right now." He dropped his hand to rest on his pistol, and stopped only when he saw several rifles immediately bob up to a firing position. Changing his tone then, the familiar sneer returned to his face. "I reckon I ought'n to hold it agin you. I mean, losin' your wife and all, but I ain't the only sinner in this outfit. Coulda been anybody, includin' the damn Injuns, that stole that money. I'm lettin' you get away with it this time, Lindstrom, but I'd better not hear no more talk outta you about no stolen money." He glared at them for a moment before ordering, "Now go on and get the hell outta my face before I lose my temper."

Not ready to concede, Bradley started toward the big man, but Malcolm and Raymond Chadwick caught him by his arms and pulled him away. "That's all we can do right now, Brad," his brother said, knowing that Starbeau would most likely tear Bradley apart if they fought.

"We got no way to prove it," Chadwick said. "What if we're accusing the wrong man?"

Starbeau snickered contemptuously. "That's right, Lindstrom. You'd best listen to him. You can't prove a damn thing, and if you keep runnin' your mouth, you're liable to have to back it up." He shifted his gaze then to focus on Jake Simmons and grinned. "And there ain't no half-breed to save your ass this time." The comment caused Jake to flush slightly before glaring defiantly at the belligerent troublemaker.

Bradley started toward Starbeau a second time, but this time Malcolm and two of his friends dragged him back and started walking him toward a large campfire in the center of the clearing behind the caves. "We ain't done with this yet!" Bradley called back over his shoulder.

Still standing before Starbeau, Raymond Chadwick took it upon himself to speak for the whole community. In a voice calm and quiet, he gave the huge troublemaker notice. "I'm speakin' for the congregation now, Starbeau. We've done our best to give you every opportunity to salvage your Christian soul, but I reckon there's just some things that prayer won't change. So we think it best if you go your own way now, and let us go ours."

Starbeau chuckled delightedly. "You're throwin' me out?" he asked, laughing. "Well, much as that sorrows me, I guess I'll just go then. Hell, I'll leave first thing in the mornin'." He was still chuckling as he turned and left Raymond standing there astonished that the quarrelsome bully found it so humorous.

The burials and cleanup continued throughout the rest of the morning and into the afternoon before some sense of normalcy returned to the now-depleted group of pilgrims. Doing what she could to help, Callie visited several caves where women had been widowed to offer her comfort and assistance. There was little she could do to ease their grief, but she felt the need to at least make coffee, fix the children something to eat, and provide a shoulder to cry on.

Left to himself, shunned by the congregation, Starbeau readied his horse and pack mule for an early-morning departure. From a natural sense of survival, he was careful which way he turned his back while tying up his packs. Ordinarily he would not have given a thought to the need for such caution among the gentle Christians he had traveled with from Bismarck. But Bradley Lindstrom was lying around the camp somewhere, sulking over his dead wife. He might get himself worked up to the point where he thought about taking a long-range shot at the man who murdered his wife. The irony of it caused Starbeau to grin, thinking about how frustrated Lindstrom must be, knowing that Starbeau probably killed his wife, and not being able to prove it. *And got away with the money, too,* Starbeau added, extending his smile even wider.

Starbeau was right about the grieving widower. Bradley Lindstrom could not be consoled. Nancy had been his life, and he could not bear the thought of living without her. The marriage had produced no children, but they felt blessed as long as they had each other. Now it was as if the light of life had been blown out, and nothing remained but the darkness in which his lonely soul must dwell.

His brother, Malcolm, and Pete Watson remained with him to try to give him support until Bradley begged to be left alone with his memories of Nancy. Reluctant though they were to leave him in such an obvious state of grief, they gave in to his insistence that he would be all right. It was growing dark and he expressed the need for sleep, so they filed out of his dwelling and left him to grieve alone.

The despondent new widower sat there with his back against the wall where Nancy's body had been found until he heard no more noises outside, telling him that the camp had settled in to cook their suppers. Confident that no one would notice, he crawled to the front of the cave and strapped on his pistol belt, knowing that what he was determined to do was not sanctioned in the eyes of the Lord.

Outside, in the fading twilight, he slipped between the caves and walked along behind them to the end of the row and Starbeau's dwelling. He paused a moment to consider the saddled horse and loaded pack mule tied to a pine sapling a few feet from the cave's entrance. With dogged determination and fear of facing the world without Nancy greater than that of facing Starbeau, he called out for the brute.

"Who is it?" Starbeau demanded when he heard his name called. Pulling his pistol from the holster and belt lying beside the entrance to his cave, he edged up to the opening and peered out in the growing gloom. Recognizing Bradley Lindstrom then, he guessed the reason for the visit. Remaining at the edge of the opening with his huge body all but concealed, he said, "What the hell do you want?"

"You know what I want," Bradley replied. "I want you to face me. I aim to kill you for murderin' my wife."

"I told you I never done it," Starbeau said, still using the edge of the opening for cover. He cocked the pistol and held it beside his leg.

"We both know that's a lie. Come on outta there and face me."

Starbeau edged his head out far enough to look

around to make sure there were no witnesses before answering. Then, unable to resist the opportunity to taunt his victim, he said, "Yeah, you're right. I shot the bitch. I even thought about doin' a little more, but a man would have to be damn hard up to want any of that." A wide grin spread across his face while he waited for Bradley's response to that.

His mind consumed by the rage within him, Bradley still fought to retain his sense of purpose. "Come on outta that cave and face me," he demanded again. "The Lord will decide who shall survive."

Without further hesitation, Starbeau stepped outside and in one quick motion shot Bradley down before the unfortunate victim knew what was happening. "The Lord decided," Starbeau taunted calmly, and put the fatal shot in Bradley's defenseless body. He reached down then and took Bradley's revolver from the holster and placed it in the dead man's hand. Standing erect again he turned to walk away, only to be startled by the sight of Callie Simmons standing paralyzed by the shock of what she had just witnessed. "Where the hell did you come from?" he asked. Seeing then that she was too shocked to answer, he said, "You saw it. He tried to kill me, but I got him instead. It was self-defense."

Finally finding her voice, she blurted, "You murdered him! He was just standing there, and you murdered him! Just like you murdered his wife."

"Now, that ain't so," he insisted. "Look at him. He's got his gun in his hand." As he talked, he moved closer to her.

"You put it in his hand after you shot him," she cried. "I saw you." Recovering from the shock that had immobilized her, she realized the danger she was now in, and spun on her heel to run for help. But he had slowly moved too close, and with a couple of quick steps, he caught her by the arm. She started to scream but was immediately silenced by the barrel of his pistol across the back of her skull, knocking her unconscious.

Quickly looking around him again, in a hurry to finish this business before others came to investigate the two gunshots, he saw people emerging from the caves, but no one at the far end where he was. Knowing he must permanently silence the girl, he pulled his knife from his belt and grabbed a handful of her hair. Pulling her head back, he exposed her white throat, but hesitated before slicing her windpipe. *I've got a better use for you, missy*, he decided, picking up the limp body and hurrying to his horse.

With a quick look toward the other end of the caves, he tried to calculate the amount of time he had. A crowd of people had gathered, and were working their way cave by cave up the line. It was enough time, he figured, to bind and gag the girl. When that was done, he pulled a couple of the packs off the mule and threw Callie across in their place. Working fast for a big man, he vacated his cave with all he thought he would need, and while the crowd of searchers was still fifty yards away, he dragged Bradley's body behind the cave, then led his horse into the cottonwoods on the other side of the clearing. With one more look back to confirm that he had not been spotted, he stepped up in the saddle and loped off along the creek, leaving the ill-fated mule train behind him.

A quarter of an hour passed before someone shouted, "Over here!" The crowd of pilgrims rushed to the spot behind Starbeau's cave. "It's Bradley Lindstrom," Frank Bowen blurted excitedly. "He's been shot dead."

Lighting the way with a torch, Jake Simmons held it close while he and the others bent down to confirm Bowen's identification. "My Lord in Heaven,"

Jake gasped upon seeing Bradley's startled expression frozen forever on his lifeless face. He stood back away from the body when Malcolm pushed his way through the crowd.

Upon seeing his brother lying cold and still in the muddy clearing, he fell to his knees beside him and roared out his grief. First Nancy, then Bradley, it was almost too much to bear. He and Pete had come all the way from the Dakota Territory to find Bradley. After finding him, to have it end this way, was more than he was prepared to deal with. He rocked back on his heels, oblivious to the mud, and sobbed. The first suspect that popped into everyone's mind was Starbeau. "Come on," Pete Watson said, "let's get him out here!" He led the way around to the front of Starbeau's cave. Malcolm staggered to his feet to follow. There would be no notice to part company. This time, it was almost a unanimous decision that it was time for a hanging.

"He's lit out!" Luke Preston yelled from the entrance to Starbeau's cave. He turned to face the crowd that had grown to include everyone in the camp. Holding up a discarded pack, he said, "His horse is gone, too, and it looks like he left in a hurry."

"The low-down murderin' dog," someone in the group uttered. "Some of us oughta go after him." His comment was met with grunts and nods of agreement, but no one moved to form a posse right away.

"Where's Callie?" Cora Simmons asked her husband.

Jake looked around at the gathering of faces, unable to find that of his daughter. "Callie!" he called out. When there was no answer, he yelled her name again. There was still no answer, so he asked, "Has anybody seen Callie?" No one had.

"The last I saw her," Jenny Preston offered, "she was going in to comfort Ida Parsons. Her remark caused a rumble of murmuring in the congregation, for Parsons' cave was the last one in the line before Star-beau's.

"No, no, no . . . ," Cora Simmons uttered in anguish, as she pushed her way through the people gathered at the mouth of the cave, and looked inside. Her face pale with dread, she exhaled a small sigh of relief. She had feared she might find the body of her daughter there. Her relief was only for a moment, however, before she began to call out Callie's name again. There was no answer. The crowd, having caught the fever of Cora's alarm, began to disperse, all looking for the missing girl while Cora and Jake hurried back to their cave in hopes she was there.

Every inch of the riverbank was searched, and the cottonwoods, the meadow, the corral. The girl was gone. The moon was high in the sky before the last of the searchers gave up and returned to the fire to report their failure. "He's got her," Cora gasped, almost collapsing before Jake caught her and lowered her gently to the ground. "That monster took her," she sobbed loudly. "He took our baby."

"We'll find him," Jake promised, trying to comfort his wife while fighting to keep his emotions under control. "We'll get her back."

Malcolm Lindstrom was already a step ahead, calling for volunteers to go with him and Pete. Every man there volunteered to join the posse, some wounded and not really fit to ride. Malcolm picked eight of the volunteers. "Get saddled up," he shouted. "We've already lost too much time."

Still shaken, but determined to go after his daughter, Jake left Cora in the hands of Raymond Chadwick's wife, Pearl, and hurried to join the posse. There was no clear trail to follow, especially in the dark, but the one they decided the most likely was the one through the cottonwoods to the south. It was the trail cut by Joe Fox when he had left the camp the first time. Since there had been a bit more traffic over the same tracks from Indians and Joe's horses when he left for good, it would have been difficult for a real tracker to determine if any of the tracks were recent. Urgency ruled the night, however, and with the need to take some positive action, the riders stormed out through the cottonwoods, churning up any fresh trail had there been one.

Out of the trees and onto the broad treeless plain that rolled toward the distant mountains they rode, determined men, resolute in their intent to find Starbeau and Callie. Unprotected by trees, however, the snow on the open plain had melted during the recent weeks of warmer weather. The riders were slowed by the need to inspect the ground more closely for tracks in the darkness of the night. Soon the posse was broken into smaller groups as men circled about, checking the little isolated patches of old snow in gullies and ravines. Finally, when the moon was sinking behind the mountains, even Jake was forced to admit that they were going in circles and might as well give up. It was a difficult decision for Jake, his mind already half-crazy with thoughts of Callie in the hands of that evil brute, but there were promises by all to take up the search in the morning when they could see.

"It ain't that long till daylight," Jake protested when several of the men prepared to return to camp. "We might as well stay right here till sunup." Feeling helpless and frustrated, and eaten up inside with worry, he did not want to return to tell Cora they had failed.

Malcolm spoke for the rest of the men when he said, "We left in a kinda hurry, Jake. And we ain't that far from camp as it is. So we might as well go on back and pack in some supplies. We don't know how long this is gonna take. We'll get back on it in the mornin', ready to ride to Texas if we have to. I got as much reason to catch that son of a bitch as you do."

"I expect you're right," Jake conceded. Feeling weary and defeated, he climbed back up in the saddle and followed along behind the posse.

Chapter 8

At first she fought him any way she could—fingernails, teeth, fists. Her efforts were a pitiful attempt to ward off his assault, and in fact, served only to add to his fiendish pleasure. Though not frail, she was a small girl and no match at all against the imposing bulk of Starbeau. When he was no longer amused by her desperate efforts to deny him the satisfaction of violating her virginity, he struck her with his fists, one hammer-like blow after another until she lay unconscious, a helpless sacrifice on the altar of evil.

When she awoke, it was to a world of pain and sickness, and disappointment to find that she was, in fact, still alive. Moments before she lost consciousness, she had prayed that God would take her soul, but He had not seen fit to end her torment. As she lay there on the ground, she did not open her eyes, afraid that he would see that she was awake and attack her again. Her body ached with deep bruises all over as if she had been trampled under a horse's hooves. Her thighs and knees burned with the pain of muscles stretched beyond their human limits. And she felt sick, dizzy and nauseated, realizing at that moment that she was going to vomit. The wave started in her stomach and rolled upward, and she knew she could not prevent it from gushing forth. Suddenly it crested, forcing her to roll over on her side, unable to stop it. She didn't know until then that her jaw was broken, and she almost screamed out when the spasms of her stomach forced her mouth to open wide.

"Gawdamn," Starbeau mocked. "Ain't you a pretty sight?" He got up from beside the fire and walked over to stand looking down at her. "I reckon you learned your first lesson. It don't pay to make me mad, and you're gonna get a whuppin' every time you don't give me what I want." Disgusted by the vomit dripping from the side of her mouth, he stuck his foot out and rolled her over with the toe of his boot. "Get yourself up from there and clean that mess offa your face." When she did not move, he drew his foot back as if to kick her, and she struggled to do as he had ordered.

He watched her closely as she stumbled to a small stream nearby and dropped to her knees at the water's edge, oblivious to the soaking of her torn skirt. Though flinching with a stabbing pain each time she touched her swollen jaw, she managed to douse her face with water, washing away the remains of vomit and blood. Somewhat revived then, she faced the panic starting again inside her, and she felt she could not endure more of the hell she had just gone through. Raising her head slowly, she turned to gaze across the creek and the trees beyond. How far could she get, she wondered, before he would run her down?

"I wish you *would* try it," Starbeau remarked, the familiar malicious grin upon his face. He picked his rifle up and cocked it. When she failed to accept his challenge, he laughed and said, "Get your lazy ass over here. You ain't gonna have no picnic, just enjoyin' my company. You're gonna have to work for the pleasure of takin' care of my needs." He waved her over toward his pack mule with his rifle. "There's coffee, bacon, and flour and such in them packs. You can cook me up some breakfast." He paused to fix her with his accusing gaze. "You know, like them cakes of pan bread you was always fixin' for that damn half-breed. And let me tell you right now, it better be good or I'll whup you till you can't stand up."

Afraid to do otherwise, she did as she was told, accompanied by a constant rambling of coarse threats and promises from the belligerent brute. As she went through the motions of preparing a meal for him, she tried to think of some way to escape this hell she had been cast into. Her life's dreams were all shattered, ruined beyond repair, but thoughts of suicide were replaced with thoughts of escape and retaliation. At the present, however, escape seemed unlikely, so she endeavored to endure whatever abuse awaited her until an opportunity presented itself.

Feeling smug and very satisfied with himself, Starbeau watched his captive closely, admiring the slim hips and tidy bottom he had ogled all the way from Dakota Territory. He smiled when he thought about the taking of that body, violent though it may have been. The fact that she had been utterly reviled by him failed to bother him. He had never had a woman who was not reviled by him, even when they received money for the repulsive contract. Rather than depress him, it amused him. His foul, oversized body was such a source of intimidation to both men and women that he had always used it to his advantage. He smiled when he recalled the look of fear in Jake Simmons' eye when he faced him down. *I'd like to see that runty little bastard's face right now*, he thought.

Thinking of the girl again, he thought, *It's gonna be a real shame to have to kill her, but I'll have to before I get to Butte.* He would have to cut back to the south in the morning if that was to be his destination. A faint grin appeared at the corners of his mouth when he thought about what must have gone on back in the caves when they discovered him gone. They no doubt formed a posse to come after him, but he sat now by his campfire, taking his time, unworried about the possibility of a posse catching up to him. *This ain't the first time I've been chased*, he thought. Figuring that Jake and his friends would probably follow the trail through the grove of cottonwoods, he had instead backtracked the trail the Indians had taken, planning to make a wide swing back to the south trail after he was sure they were not on his tail. It had evidently worked because there had been no sign of anyone, even after camping in this spot overnight. "Hurry up with that grub," he scolded. "I'm hungry." He leaned back against a tree trunk then to enjoy watching the frightened young girl. *Yes, sir, I'd like to see that little runt's face if he could see his precious little gal right now.*

Haggard and weary, Jake Simmons' face showed the strain of a day of searching that yielded no results. The search party had been unsuccessful in picking up any recent tracks that might give them some place to start looking. It was as if the big man and his two horses had simply disappeared in the thin mountain air. Raymond Chadwick was the first to express the feeling of the whole posse. "It's a waste of time, Jake," he said when they stopped at a small stream to water the mules. "I mean, I'll go out again tomorrow if you want, but we ain't got a notion where to look. He's got away clean. That's just all there is to it."

"Raymond's right," Malcolm said. "We ain't doin' no good out here. I think the only chance we got to find Callie is Joe Fox, and I don't know if he can track 'em. But he's the best chance you've got."

Jake thought about it for a long moment before

speaking, thinking about the last time he had talked to Joe. "I don't know if he would agree to do it," he said.

"Why wouldn't he?" Malcolm replied. "He's been willin' to help with everythin' we asked him to do."

Jake slowly shook his head. Only he and Cora knew that he had told Joe to stay away from Callie, which was more than likely the reason the tall mountain man had left their camp so abruptly. "I don't know," he said. "Besides, who knows where he is?"

"I might," Malcolm said. "He told Raymond and me that he's got a camp about two days' ride from here near a waterfall. If you'll give me a minute, I'll think of the name of that creek."

"Otter Creek," Raymond said. "It was Otter Creek."

"That's right, it was," Malcolm said. "I figure all we got to do is find that creek and follow it up the mountain till we find the waterfall. I bet ol' Templeton at the tradin' post knows where Otter Creek is." The other members of the posse all agreed to the plan. Tired of riding all day with no hope of results, they were in favor of any plan to get them out of the saddle, knowing there was no need for them all to look for Joe.

"I reckon we ain't got no choice but to try," Jake said, while wondering whether Joe would be carrying a grudge and refuse to help.

"I'll go with you," Malcolm said, "me and Pete." He looked at his brother-in-law for confirmation and Pete nodded. "We'll find him if he's still there."

It was agreed that they should start out at sunup the next morning. Malcolm volunteered to go to the trading post that night to talk to Templeton. As he had guessed, Templeton knew exactly where Otter Creek flowed into the river, and drew a rough map for Malcolm to follow. "It'll take a day, maybe a little more, to get to this spot," he said, pointing to the confluence of the creek and the river. "I ain't ever been up it far enough to get to the waterfall—didn't even know there was one. So I don't know how long that will take you."

Cora Simmons, always a strong-willed woman, was now almost incapacitated by the abduction of her daughter. She had not slept or eaten since that fateful night when they discovered Callie gone. Pearl Chadwick and Jenny Preston had tried to comfort her, one of them with her almost all the time. When Jake told Cora about the plan to try to find Joe, Cora burst into loud sobs, mystifying Jenny Preston, who was with them at the time. "What if he won't do it?" Cora sobbed. "He's got good reason to tell us to go to hell."

"He's the best chance we've got," Jake replied patiently. Then, noticing the look of astonishment upon Jenny's face, he reluctantly explained the reason for Cora's outburst. "Maybe he's got a good reason not to help us," he said, "but he's the only hope we've got right now."

Malcolm Lindstrom sat on his horse at the mouth of a wide creek, studying the rough map, then comparing it with the features of the terrain. "This has gotta be it," he said to the two men accompanying him. "There's that knob of firs at the foot of the hill and the big rock that looks like a turtle on the other side of the creek."

Pete Watson nudged his horse up beside Malcolm's to take a look at the map himself. "Looks right to me," he said. Then he took a long look up at the towering mountain beyond the hill, its peak still covered with snow. "That sure 'pears like the kinda country he favors, don't it? I hope to hell his camp ain't all the way up that mountain."

Malcolm and Jake, though making no reply, were thinking along the same lines. It was rough-looking country all right, but as Pete commented, where else would one expect to find Joe Fox? "Well," Malcolm remarked, "let's get started. Maybe we'll find him before dark—if he's still there."

The passage along the creek was easy enough until they followed it beyond the small foothills and up through a forest so thick with firs that it was dark as night. Winding their way through the trees, around boulders and smaller rocks, they found it difficult to follow the creek bank, making it necessary to swing wide around rock formations to search for the creek again. The higher they climbed, the more difficult it became, and soon they were forced to dismount and lead their horses. About halfway up the mountain, the creek narrowed as it rushed through a narrow flume formed by solid rock. They paused at a deep pool at the bottom of the flume to let the horses drink.

Pete laid on his belly at the edge of the pool to drink with the horses. After he had his fill, he rose to his knees and wiped his face with his sleeve. "Whooeee!" he exclaimed. "That water's so cold it makes your teeth ache. Damn, it's good, though."

"I expect a man would be hard put to find any better," Malcolm replied. He held his canteen at the end of the flume where the water gushed out to form the pool. He took a long drink from the canteen, then filled it again. Standing then to gaze up toward the top of the chute, rushing with the icy runoff from the snowy peak, he began to have doubts, wondering whether they had followed the wrong creek. Scanning the steep slope above him, he could see no sign of a waterfall. He turned to Pete and Jake to express his concern. "I don't know if we've wasted half a day or not," he said, "but standin' here, lookin' up this mountain, I don't see how there could be a waterfall up above us."

Jake walked over beside him and peered up the mountain. "I don't know," he wavered, hating to think they were on the wrong trail. "Maybe if we get up to the top of this chute, we can see better."

They decided to leave the horses there at the bottom of the flume, thinking it too difficult to make the steep climb while trying to lead them. After a half hour climb up the rocky face of the mountain, they finally reached the top of the flume. "Damn!" Malcolm exclaimed, for he could now see that the stream had disappeared. A few dozen yards farther up, they discovered the reason—a knee-high cavern in the rocks from which the water flowed. The stream was underground above them.

"Well, there ain't no damn waterfall on this mountain," Pete fumed, "at least not on this stream."

They stood and scratched their heads for a few minutes while they discussed it, but it was the opinion of all three that there was no sense in continuing to climb higher and higher up the wrong mountain. It was especially difficult for Jake to give up and turn around, with the image of Callie in his mind, and wondering whether she was alive or dead. Thoughts of what horror she might be enduring were constantly crossing his mind to the point where it was all he could do to keep from crying out his anguish. But there was nothing he could do about the dead end they had come to, so he turned around and followed Malcolm and Pete back down the slope.

When they reached the pool at the bottom of the flume they were startled to find a buckskin-clad figure squatting on his heels on top of the largest of the rocks that formed one side of the natural basin. His rifle resting across his thighs, he had watched their progress down the mountain with curious interest. Malcolm, who was leading, stopped so abruptly that Pete stumbled into him, almost causing both to fall. "Joe Fox," Malcolm pronounced.

"This is the second time I've found your horses with nobody watchin' 'em," Joe responded, equally surprised to find the three men on the mountain. With the grace of a mountain lion, he rose to his feet, and stepping from one rock to another, made his way quickly to the ground. "Are you lookin' for me?" he asked.

"We're hopin' you'll help us find Callie," Jake blurted. "She's been took by that devil Starbeau! I know there's probably some hard feelin's between me and you, but I'm hopin' you'll do the Christian thing and set 'em aside and help us track Starbeau." Desperate to plead his case, he tried to talk as fast as he could before Joe had a chance to say no. "We've done tried to track him, but we lost him. It takes somebody like an Injun or somethin' to track him, 'cause he ain't left one track, and you're the only one we know of. And if you need me to say I'm sorry for what I said to you before, hell, I'll say it. . . ."

He was about to spout on, but Malcolm finally interrupted him. "Take it easy, Jake. He ain't said no yet." Taken aback by the little man's frantic plea, he looked at Joe, who seemed as puzzled by the outburst as he. He then went on to calmly relate all that had happened since Joe left the camp, and how Callie had come to be abducted.

There was only a flicker in the mountain man's eye to register the distress he felt inside when told of the abduction of Callie Simmons. Malcolm feared at first that Joe would deny their plea for help, for he saw no expression of concern on the man's face. It was not until Joe spoke that the three settlers could know for certain. "I must take care of my horses. Then we can go," he said.

"God bless you," Jake uttered. "Cora and I both thank you."

Joe paused to study the worried man for a moment, his face revealing no emotion. "I do it for Callie," he said and led them into the trees. Although he revealed no evidence of it in his facial expression, the news that Callie had been taken, and by a perverted scoundrel such as Starbeau, caused his insides to churn with anguish. He cursed himself for leaving the settlers' camp, thinking that if he had remained, he might have protected Callie. At least, had he been unable to prevent her abduction, he would have had a fresh trail to follow. The thought of her fate at the hands of Starbeau was enough to bring his blood to a boil.

After a walk of about ten minutes, they came to a clearing in the forest with grass and several springs bubbling from the earth. The horses were grazing in the mountain meadow, and off to one corner of the clearing they saw his camp and the ashes of a campfire.

"We'll help you carry your possibles and drive your horses," Pete said.

Joe shook his head. "No need. I'll take all I need on the paint. I'll leave the horses. They'll take care of themselves till I come back for 'em. I'll be travelin' light." At this moment, finding Callie was more important than the horses, or anything else, but he knew the worst that could happen in regard to the horses was that they would wander off and he would lose them.

A thought entered Malcolm's mind as they were watching Joe pack up to leave. "I thought you told me your camp was near a waterfall," he commented.

Joe cast a sideways glance in his direction as he continued stuffing some dried meat into a parfleche. "It is," he said. "We just came from it."

Puzzled by the answer before it struck him, Malcolm understood then. He had pictured a typical waterfall, pouring over a cliff, while Joe considered the water rushing down the flume a waterfall. He smiled then. "Oh, yeah, I reckon we did at that."

Malcolm thought he, Pete, and Jake had pushed their horses pretty hard on their search upriver for Joe. Their trek was a casual stroll compared to the pace set by the solemn mountain man on the return trip. Joe knew there was no time to waste. Starbeau could not take Callie with him to any place where she might have a chance to cry for help. It was painful for Joe to speculate upon, but he figured Starbeau would be eager to reach someplace where he could spend that two hundred and fifty dollars Malcolm said he had stolen. Consequently, Callie's days were numbered. Starbeau would use her until tiring of the novelty, then kill her before going on to a town or trading post where he could spend his ill-gained wealth.

Seeming never to tire, the paint Indian pony set a demanding pace for the horses ridden by the three men following. Before the first night's camp, first one and then another dropped behind until they were strung out for over a quarter of a mile. With dusk approaching, Joe rode back to tell Malcolm that he would wait for them ahead where a stream emptied into the river. When the three weary riders and horses reached the stream, there was a fire burning and coffee boiling. Figuring each man could fix his own food, he chewed on elk jerky as he watched the three pull the saddles off their horses and leave them to graze with the Indian pony. "I'll be leavin' before sunup in the morning," he told them before rolling up in his blanket to sleep. It was a simple statement, but they understood that he was telling them that he would not wait for them if they weren't ready to leave.

It was early afternoon when Joe and three weary companions arrived at the caves by the river, and the entire camp turned out to greet them. Among them, Cora Simmons stood anxiously waiting, her eyes red from crying and lack of sleep. Tears of hope welled up anew when she saw Joe, and she ran to meet the riders. Jake stepped down and caught her in his arms, and together they turned to thank Joe for coming. "God bless you," Cora said, almost choking on the words, for fear God might strike her down for her hypocrisy. Joe said nothing in reply, but simply nodded.

"There's a bunch of us ready to ride with you, Joe," Raymond Chadwick announced. His statement was followed by a solemn chorus of confirmation from the men in the congregation.

Joe took a moment to look over the crowd before responding. "I'll be goin' alone," he told them. He didn't bother to explain his reasons, leaving them to gaze at one another in surprise. He knew it was going to be difficult enough to track Starbeau without having the nuisance of a mob of farmers getting in his way and possibly tramping all over a trail that was already too old for most men to follow. "If you want to help, I'd be obliged if you could spare me some coffee beans. I'm about out."

"Why, sure," Raymond replied. "We'd be more'n happy to give you some coffee, but ain't you gonna need some help? I mean, what if you catch up with that devil?" Then, noticing the look in Cora's eye, he added, "I mean *when* you catch up with him."

"I'll be goin' alone," Joe repeated.

Malcolm shrugged. "Right," he said, seeing no point in pushing the issue. "I expect you'll be leavin' first thing in the mornin'. We followed some tracks out of those trees to the south, figured he'd be headin' in that direction, but they petered out after we reached the high ground beyond that mesa."

He was about to expound on their search, but Joe interrupted. "I'll be goin' now, as soon as I rest my horse."

"It'll be dark in two hours," Jake said.

Joe fixed the little man with a cold stare. "Two hours might make a lot of difference to your daughter," he said.

When he was ready to go, he turned to Malcolm and Pete. Nodding toward the mountains to the east of the valley, he asked, "Did your posse ride down the valley over that way?"

"No," Malcolm replied. "It didn't make much sense to go that way. There ain't nothin' to the east but mountains and Injuns. That's where them Gros Ventre came from. We figure Starbeau would hightail it down the valley, back the way we first came."

Joe nodded again, and without a word of good-bye, stepped up on the paint and rode out of the little clearing and the line of caves carved out of the bluffs. They watched him as he crossed the narrow creek on the far side of the clearing, but instead of turning to the right through the stand of cottonwoods, he guided the paint to the east. "Well, where's he goin'?" Malcolm complained. "I just told him Starbeau had to have gone the other way."

"I expect he knows what he's doin'," Pete said. "He always does."

The tracks were old but still there, between the creek and a shallow draw to the east. They were the tracks left behind by the war party that hit the settlers' camp. Joe dismounted and knelt to examine them. They verified the recount of the raid he had been given by Malcolm and Pete. Unshod horses, their hoofprints going in both directions, told him that the Gros Ventre had come and gone down the same draw. He was looking for prints from a shod horse, figuring that Starbeau would have been smart enough to try to mix his tracks with the plethora of hoofprints. It was a gamble on his part to hope to find tracks this long after the abduction, but he had to bet that Starbeau took this route. There wasn't a chance in hell that he would be able to pick out any tracks after the posse had obliterated those through the cottonwoods, so he had no choice.

The paint munched casually on the short grass beside the trail, following slowly along behind Joe as he moved down toward the draw, his eyes searching, his fingertips feeling the hardened ridges of the prints. The tracks were too old. He moved forward, searching and feeling. Suddenly he stopped. There it was, the print he was looking for. The faint outline and sharp marks of a horseshoe that had been invisible up until then, now stood out in his vision like a shining sign. With some feeling of confidence that Starbeau had fled in this direction, he continued to search the path before him. A second print, then another and another appeared as he trained his eyes to focus on the shod images and ignore those of the Indian ponies.

The puzzle to be solved now was how far Starbeau remained on this trail before he changed directions. Joe knew that the brutal bully had to turn off somewhere before reaching the mountains, less he find himself a guest of the Gros Ventre. He continued the painfully slow process until all at once there were no more prints, only those of the unshod horses. He had missed the turnoff. He rose to his feet and looked back the way he had come, searching for a likely spot to leave the trail. He decided on a shallow stream a few yards back, and returned to examine the area more closely.

There was no sign that Starbeau had left the trail, but Joe could find no shod prints on the east side of the creek, so he felt confident that his man turned up the stream. In the saddle again, he guided the paint into the water and slow-walked him up the middle of the fast-flowing water while he scanned the banks carefully. He could find no tracks that would indicate a point at which Starbeau left the water, but he felt certain that he would have headed upstream. After almost a quarter of a mile, the stream became narrow as it cut a trench through a thick stand of willows and berry bushes. Even though he flattened himself against his horse's neck, he was still swatted by the low hanging branches. "Damn!" he swore when a sizable branch snagged his sleeve, and he halted the paint to free himself. *Maybe I missed some sign back a ways*, he thought. Then something caught his eye. Close to the limb that had him ensnared, he saw another branch that had recently been broken off. Confident again that he had not missed a sign, he disentangled himself and pushed on. A little way past the willows, he found what he was looking for.

Coming to a small clearing where the stream forked around a sandy spit, a clear set of hoofprints led up the soft dirt of the bank. He didn't have to dismount to read them. Two horses, both shod, the prints were deep, indicating the horses were carrying heavy loads. *Starbeau didn't think he had to be careful anymore*, Joe thought as he followed the tracks out of the water and pulled the paint to a halt in the middle of the clearing and stepped down to the ground. The cold ashes of a fire marked where they had camped. Nearby, he found traces of dried blood in the grass, enough to feel a stab of pain in his gut, but not enough to indicate a slaughter. *She's still alive*, he told himself while trying to discipline his mind to detach itself from his personal feelings.

There was no need to scout the clearing more thoroughly. He had the answer to the question he had most sought an answer for. The question to be answered now was where did they go from here? To find his answer, he began to scout the perimeter of the clearing until he found prints in a uniform pattern leading away to the south. Crossing the stream again, they led him into a dense pine forest where he lost the trail and proceeded on only instinct and guesswork. With no sign to lead him, he had to rely upon the lay of the land and which seemed to be the most obvious path down through the pines. The worrisome question kept repeating itself in his mind, even though he tried to suppress it.

How much time does Callie have? Tracking this way was too slow. He was afraid he would never catch up to them before it was too late. Still, there was little choice. Picking up the trail again at the edge of a line of grass-covered, almost treeless hills, he pushed on until darkness forced him to camp. Looking toward the mountains that lay ahead to the south, he could only pray that Callie was still alive.

Chapter 9

Starbeau grinned as he thought to himself, *She ain't swishing that little tail back and forth like she used to before she got rode good and hard.* Sitting in the shade of a tall pine that had somehow managed to grow up through a crack in the huge boulder he was using as a backrest, he made himself comfortable while he watched the battered young girl carry wood for his fire. She had made an attempt to escape when they had stopped at midday to rest the horses, mistakenly thinking he was not watching her closely when she went to fill the coffeepot. It was a desperate attempt and she paid a painful price in the form of a beating that left her bleeding and bruised. Though small in stature, she had never been a frail girl. But the abuse at the hands of the evil monster had taken its toll, and the small portion of food allotted to her was not sufficient to sustain her. She was not sure how much longer she could survive.

"That's enough wood for now," he yelled at her. "Get over here and cook my supper." He watched as she dutifully did his bidding. He was going to miss the pleasure of ravaging her body, he was thinking. But he was about to reach the point where he deemed it time to put her out of her misery. He didn't know the country well enough to be sure, but he figured that he should be reaching some of the mining camps before riding very much farther. Her defensive practice of pretending she was dead when he had his way with her was infuriating to him, anyway. *Like mating with a possum*, he thought. He made up his mind then. *One more go-round and I'll cut her throat.* Having made the decision that this was to be her last night, he smiled to himself in anticipation of the night's entertainment. The killing promised to be the more enjoyable part to Starbeau. *I might even let her have a little bit more to eat tonight*, he thought.

Lost in the moment of anticipating his evening's entertainment, he was suddenly distracted by the girl's movements by the fire. In the process of adding more wood, she had abruptly frozen, bent over with a sizable limb poised over the flame, but suspended motionless. Something had caught her eye, causing her to stare at the forest beyond the stream. Following the direction of her gaze, he was startled to discover three Indians at the edge of the trees, mounted, silently watching the activities of the girl by the fire.

He immediately grabbed his rifle and prepared to fire, but the Indians made no move to attack. Instead, they calmly watched both the white man and woman for what seemed a long time to Starbeau as he remained seated by the pine tree trying to decide whether to shoot or not. Maybe they were friendly. He didn't know one Indian from another, so he couldn't say what tribe they were. He had heard that the Flatheads and the Kutenai used to live in this part of the Bitterroots, and they were supposedly friendly with the white men. Then, remembering the raid by the Gros Ventre, he decided he'd better shoot while he had a sitting target.

"Friend," one of the Indians declared as Starbeau raised his rifle, causing him to pause.

"Is that a fact?" Starbeau murmured sarcastically to himself and paused a second longer to look his visitors over more carefully. He noticed then that two of the Indians were carrying parts of a sizable deer behind them. *I could sure use some fresh meat*, he thought, and got to his feet. "Friend," he called back. "Come on in, friend."

The Indian who had spoken before held up his hand in a gesture of peace. Then the three split up before slowly riding into the camp, having no doubt learned that some white men were friendly, some were not. Starbeau had to smile when he realized they knew his repeating rifle gave him superior firepower, so they had spread out in case he started shooting. *They're thinking I'll get one, maybe two of them*, he thought, *but the other one would have time to get me.* He decided not to take the chance. Dropping his rifle by his side, he waved them in.

Callie backed slowly away from the fire while keeping it between her and the three Indians, frightened by the curious stares of the visitors. The older one, who had spoken before, looked from the girl to the huge man striding toward them with his rifle held with one hand at his side. He then quickly scanned the camp, making a mental note of the packs before he spoke again. "You have coffee?" he asked. "We will trade you some fresh meat for some coffee." While Starbeau was mulling that over, he informed them that he was called Gray Wolf and they were Salish and friends with the white man, and their village was north of there.

"I guess I could let you have a little," Starbeau said, "for a good portion of that meat."

Gray Wolf nodded, then pointing to Callie, he asked, "Bear?"

"What?" Starbeau grunted, confused. Then it struck him that Gray Wolf wondered whether Callie had been attacked by a bear to be so battered and scarred. He had to chuckle. "No, she's just a little slow in learnin' how to behave."

Gray Wolf did not understand. "Woman slave?" he asked.

"Never mind the woman," Starbeau said. "How about that meat? I need most of what you got there."

"Coffee," Gray Wolf said while his two companions continued to stare at Callie.

"All right," Starbeau said, "coffee." While keeping his eye on the three Salish men, he ordered Callie to get a double handful of coffee beans from his packs. "That one sack's about empty, put 'em in that."

When Callie came back with the beans, she gave them to Gray Wolf and immediately stepped away. Gray Wolf looked inside the sack at the small amount of beans, glanced at one of the men standing beside him, then spoke to him in the Salish tongue. The man nodded and went to his horse. Taking his knife, he sliced off a small portion from the haunch and offered it to Starbeau.

"Hell, I've got to have a helluva lot more than that!"

"More coffee," Gray Wolf said.

"I can't spare no more coffee," Starbeau insisted. "It'll be a spell before I get to where I can get some more. I need more of that meat you're carryin'." He started to raise his rifle again, but thought better of it when he realized that the Indians had slowly positioned themselves on three sides of him. He immediately changed his tone. "Listen," he said, "I can't spare any more coffee, but I need all the meat you've got there." He nodded toward his packs. "Maybe we can trade somethin' else for the meat."

Gray Wolf consulted briefly with his two friends before speaking to Starbeau again. "We trade you all the meat for the woman."

Callie gasped in horror, repulsed by the very notion. She had heard horrible tales about white women who were captured by savages. Realizing she was a pawn between two different, but equal, terrors, she found herself hoping Starbeau refused the offer, thinking that she at least knew his version of hell. She was disappointed to see the look of amusement on his face as the thought struck him. She was bound to die, anyway, he was thinking, and this way she would just die a slower death at the hands of the Indians. He considered the enjoyment he had been looking forward to when it came time to kill her, but he told himself that he could sure use all that fresh meat. Finally, he threw his head back and laughed. "Done, that's a proper trade." Hearing his response, Callie immediately turned and ran. Her reaction caused Starbeau to roar with laughter. "There she goes! Looks like you're gonna have to run her down."

One of the Salish hunters jumped on his pony and bounded after her. No longer fearing the rifle slug between her shoulders that she had been threatened with before, Callie ran as hard as she could with nothing in her terrified mind but escape. Within seconds, she heard the pounding of horse's hooves behind her, and she tried to veer off her path into a juniper thicket. Running with wild abandon, she ignored the stinging thrashing of the branches as they raised welts on her face and arms. Breaking free of the junipers, she almost stumbled as she staggered up a grassy rise toward a pine forest. A dozen steps from the edge of the forest she was suddenly lifted off the ground by a strong arm wrapped around her waist.

Though she kicked and flailed her fists in her panic, it served only to amuse the three men watching the show. Lame Horse, the young hunter who had caught her, did not find her antics amusing, however, since he was the recipient of her frantic flailing. Galloping back to the fire, he dropped her at Gray Wolf's feet. When she tried to scramble to her feet and run again, he placed his foot on her behind and shoved her flat on her face. Driven almost out of her mind with fear, she lay there, panting for breath, knowing it was useless to try to run again.

Lame Horse stood over her while his companions transferred most of their meat to Starbeau's horse. When they were finished, he said, "Good trade," and stepped back with his rifle ready while the Salish hunters prepared to leave. Tying Callie's hands together, Lame Horse looped a length of rope around her wrists. Holding the free end of the rope, he climbed on his horse and the three visitors departed. Starbeau called after the stricken woman as she was forced to follow on foot. "You mighta thought I was a little hard on ya," he said. "Wait till them Injuns get through with ya." She could still hear his laughter as she was led off through the pines.

Two Bears moved cautiously up to join Gray Wolf at the rim of a long ravine. "Where?" he asked, and Gray Wolf pointed to a stand of a half dozen pines at the lower end of the ravine. Two Bears nodded when he saw them, four mule deer lolling in the shade of the trees. "We should get two of them, maybe three if we're quick enough," he whispered, then complained, "We would be on our way back to our village now if Lame Horse had not given all our meat away."

Gray Wolf smiled. "It was his kill. He had a right to do with it as he wished."

Two Bears was not as forgiving as his older friend. "The meat was for all to share," he said. "What does he want the white woman for, anyway? She's already beaten half to death."

"He says he will give her to his wife to do her

chores," Gray Wolf replied softly while still watching the deer. "Little Moon is lucky to have such a thoughtful husband."

"Ugh," Two Bears snorted, well aware that Gray Wolf spoke facetiously. "He is back at the campfire playing with his little white woman while we do the hunting. I think Little Moon would break a stick across his back for his thoughtfulness."

"Maybe he will offer to share the woman," Gray Wolf said, joking.

"Humph," Two Bears snorted again. "Who would want her after she has been mating with that great grizzly that traded her?"

"Lame Horse," Gray Wolf replied, and both men laughed then. "Come, let's slip down the side and get our meat."

Callie tried to brace herself mentally for what she knew was going to happen. With all emotions inside her reduced to shame and sorrow, she had come to perceive her body, even her soul, as nothing more than clay—a lifeless form without past or future, something to be casually used, then thrown away. Even so, she found she was unable to completely will her mind away from the soulful stare of the fearsome warrior. Looking down, avoiding the intense gaze of her savage master, she waited, wanting only to have it over with.

Lame Horse did not thrust himself upon her violently, however, as the savage Starbeau had. Instead, he seemed more curious about her person. Intrigued by her sandy hair, he reached out to feel it, causing her to recoil in fear. He paused and gave her a puzzled look, then took a large strand of her hair in his hand, feeling it as if judging the texture of a bolt of cloth. Releasing her hair then, he reached down and caught the hem of her tattered skirt. She tried to jerk it away from him. His reaction was calm and deliberate as he struck her face sharply with the back of his hand. There was no indication of anger in his expression. It was as if he were simply administering a lesson of discipline to a child—or a horse. When she lifted her eyes to meet his gaze, it conveyed a message that he would not tolerate disobedience. When he continued his inspection, she no longer resisted, knowing it would not save her.

He slowly lifted her skirt, and was at once appalled by her torn and blood-encrusted undergarments. Anger sprang from his face then, with no thought of sympathy for the obvious torment the woman had suffered. Instead, he was disgusted, thinking she was dirty. Furious with thoughts that he had been cheated, he grabbed a handful of her underwear and ripped it from her body. Casting it upon the ground in revulsion, he took her by the hair and pulled her stumbling to the creek they had camped beside. There, she was unceremoniously dumped into the cold, knee-deep water with the command to clean herself.

She was still in the water when Gray Wolf and Two Bears returned with the carcass of a mule deer draped across each horse. Upon seeing the woman in the creek, trying to clean herself without exposing too much of her body, Gray Wolf assumed that Lame Horse had sampled the fruits of his slave. "So," he said, "are you satisfied with your trade?"

"I have heard that white women are different between their legs than our women," Two Bears said.

Gray Wolf laughed at his young friend's comment. "All females are the same," he said. "Ask Lame Horse. He will tell you."

Still somewhat disillusioned by his disappointing inspection of the girl, and seeing the two freshly killed deer, Lame Horse answered in a surly voice, "How should I know? I would not lower myself to lie with her. She is dirty, not worth the meat I traded for her."

Amused by the entire turn of events, Gray Wolf could not help but laugh at his sullen friend. "Is that why she is cleaning herself in the creek?"

Lame Horse ignored the question, instead commenting, "I am thinking that maybe we should trail this white man and kill him and take the meat back." He glanced toward Callie, still in the water. "I will decide about the woman. Maybe I will kill her and then go after the big ugly white man."

Gray Wolf stroked his chin as if giving Lame Horse's words serious consideration. When he spoke, it was with the tone of an elder offering the wisdom of experience. "That is one thing we could do, but the white man has the gun that shoots many times. If we can surprise him before he has a chance to use it, then we can kill him. That would be good. But we are armed with nothing but our bows. We would have to get close to get a shot, and if we did not kill him, it would be like wounding the grizzly bear. With his gun, he might kill one or more of us." He paused to let Lame Horse think that over; then he continued when the sulking brave made no reply. "We did not ride the war path when we left our village. We meant only to hunt." He gestured toward the deer carcasses. "We have plenty of meat to share." He paused again, looking at Callie. "And you have a present for Little Moon."

Lame Horse did not reply, but shrugged in an apparent dismissal of his plan to go after Starbeau. The matter settled, they decided to butcher the deer and prepare to return to their village on the western side of the mountains that formed the valley. Callie, having no knowledge of the language being spoken, had no idea what the discussion between the three had been about. So she was unaware that she had again escaped a sentence of death. But while they seemed engrossed in talk, she had remained in the water, slowly inching her way downstream, hoping they did not notice. Her thoughts of escape were quickly extinguished, however, when Gray Wolf pulled the carcass from his pony, jumped on its back, and quickly circled around to head her off. Guiding his pony into the water, he herded her toward the bank, where he spoke to her in English. "Lame Horse is not a patient man. If you try to run again, I think he will kill you."

Dripping wet, her breath laboring from her efforts to keep from being trampled by Gray Wolf's horse behind her in the water, Callie climbed up the bank and stood awaiting her fate. She was relieved to find that her immediate lot was no more than an order from Lame Horse to help with the butchering.

After they had skinned the first carcass, Lame Horse tossed a long knife at Callie's feet, and stood watching her reaction closely, wary of her thoughts with a weapon in hand. He said nothing but motioned toward the skinned deer and waited for her response. She picked up the knife and immediately went to the carcass, where she began to carve chunks of meat from the haunch. She had never butchered any animal before, but she had sometimes watched her father when he had, and she was eager to show her usefulness in case they were deciding whether or not to kill her.

Lame Horse and Two Bears exchanged glances of astonishment before Lame Horse lapsed into a fit of anger again. "No!" he roared and pulled her away from the carcass when it was apparent that she did not know how to butcher properly. "You ruin the meat! You waste too much!" He picked up the pieces she had cut away from the haunch and thrust them in her lap. "Go roast this to eat tonight," he said. "We will do this."

Pausing to witness the incident, Gray Wolf and Two

Bears grinned at each other, amused by their friend's continued troubles with his captive. Seeing their impish smiles, he snarled, "Stupid white woman, she knows nothing."

Unfortunately for Callie, her treatment at the hands of the Salish hunters was little better than that she had experienced while a captive of Starbeau, with one exception—for which she was grateful. Although she was occasionally beaten with Lame Horse's bow whenever she displeased him, she was not sexually assaulted. It was ironic that she had Starbeau to thank for that. Lame Horse had been so repulsed by the injuries she had suffered that left her so scarred and bloody, he lost his lust for her.

There were no thoughts of hope for her survival, however, as she trudged along ancient game trails behind the Indians' horses, her wrists rubbed bloody by the rawhide rope that bound her. There were times during the long walk when she felt she could go no farther. And only the promise from Lame Horse that he would kill her if she could not continue caused her to stagger along behind him. The end of each day found her reeling from exhaustion, her feet swollen and bleeding, but still she was ordered to find wood, make the fire, and cook their meat.

Finally, after the third full day, she reached the point where she no longer cared if she lived or died. When the three men had eaten their fill, she dropped wearily to the ground beside the fire to try to make a meal for herself out of what was left. Watching her, as he always did, Lame Horse waited until she had picked some morsels of meat from the bones and prepared to eat them, then commanded her, "Get up from there, you lazy bitch, and bring the parfleche from my horse."

It was the final straw. Callie gritted her teeth, feeling the anger boiling up inside her. "Get it yourself, you goddamned dirty savage!"

All three men blinked in surprise, astonished to hear her make even the smallest sound. After the shock of her insolence faded, Lame Horse jumped to his feet in a fit of rage and stormed over to the fire, his bow in hand. Accustomed to his beatings now, Callie hugged her knees and rolled up in as small a ball as she could. Lame Horse set upon her with a will, raining blows upon her back with the flat of his bow. Callie took the beating, just as she had suffered those before, until her own long-suffering anger finally exploded and surged through her veins like fire. When Lame Horse paused to take a breath, she reached into the campfire and grasped a burning limb. Striking back with a vengeance fueled by the beatings and abuse of the past few days, she struck him across his knee, causing him to howl with the pain. Abandoning all hope of survival, she scrambled to her feet, swinging the flaming limb from right to left before her, her fatigue forgotten, pushed from her mind by a flood of energy throughout her body.

Taken completely off guard, and hobbled by the sharp pain in his kneecap, Lame Horse staggered backward to escape the fiery onslaught by the crazed woman, each swipe of the burning limb barely missing his face. He tried to catch the limb, but yelped again with pain when he felt the sting of the hot flame sizzle in the palm of his hand. Forced to release the timber, he backed away again, and this time he tripped over his bow, which had fallen behind him when he tried to catch the limb. Landing on his back, he was immediately set upon by the infuriated girl, who proceeded to administer a series of blows that eventually extinguished the flames, each blow leaving a smutty print on the unfortunate Salish warrior's deerskin shirt. Lame Horse had no choice but to roll over and over to escape the enraged woman.

With no thought toward coming to the aid of their comrade, Two Bears and Gray Wolf found the episode highly entertaining, in fact, so much so that both were stricken with fits of laughter. Lame Horse, however, could find no humor in the humiliating incident. At a safe distance from the crouching demon now, she with her smoking club ready to defend herself, his eyes fairly sparked with indignation. "You are a dead woman," he spat. "I will carve your liver from your body and feed it to the dogs."

"You can go to hell," she spat back at him, sustained by the anger within her soul, and knowing at last that there were worse things than death.

Her defiant reply to her tormentor caused only more laughter from the two witnesses, much to Lame Horse's embarrassment, which, in turn, served to add fuel to his anger. He drew his long skinning knife from his belt, and limping slightly from the pain in his knee, he started toward her again. She backed away, but only a couple of yards to the fire, where she quickly exchanged her smoking timber for another in full flame, clearly prepared to fight to the death.

No longer laughing, Gray Wolf watched until it appeared that Lame Horse was truly intent upon killing the woman. "Wait," he said, "the woman has shown great courage. It would be wrong to kill her for fighting for her life."

The comment caused Lame Horse to hesitate. Gray Wolf was older than he and Two Bears, and his word was respected in their village. Lame Horse was still not ready to forgive what had amounted to an insult to his pride as a warrior, however. "What you say may be true," he replied, "but she clearly is too dumb to train, so why waste food and water on her?" His temper cooling down a little, he said, "She is my property, and I no longer want her, so I will kill her."

Gray Wolf shrugged. He was truly impressed by Callie's will to stand and fight against a warrior such as Lame Horse. "Let me say this," he began. "My wife could make use of this worthless woman. I will give you my white pony for her."

This caused Lame Horse to pause again. The white mare was a favorite of Gray Wolf's, and it would certainly compensate him for his loss of the woman. He replaced his knife in the sheath. "It is agreed," he said, "but I think you have been cheated."

"Perhaps so," Gray Wolf replied, smiling.

Unable to understand the words between the two men, Callie stood, poised to expend her last breath in defense of her life. Though the language was unfamiliar, she sensed that they were discussing her future. She was glad when it appeared that the older one, called Gray Wolf, had been persuasive in his argument. Still wary, however, she took another step backward and held her weapon before her when he started to approach her.

"Put the limb back in the fire," he said, his tone almost fatherly. "No one is going to hurt you. You may rest now."

Whether she chose to believe him or not, she wasn't certain. But suddenly the passionate rage that had sustained her left her body, and with it, the strength to resist. Exhausted, she dropped to her knees, her strength spent, and her mind a dizzy eddy in her brain. She was afraid she was finished. If they chose to kill her, she could no longer resist.

Gray Wolf took the burning limb from her hand and threw it in the fire. "We will reach our village tomorrow before the sun is straight over our heads. Tonight you can rest." He led her over beside a small tree and she obediently lay down. They continued to keep an eye on her until she was asleep.

"I think there will be no more trouble from her this

night," Two Bears said, with a slight smile for Lame Horse.

"Maybe so," Gray Wolf replied, "but I'm going to bind her hands and feet tightly in case she wakes up like a mountain lion again."

Chapter 10

Joe Fox jogged along a well-defined game trail, leading his horse behind him. On foot, he could study the ground more closely while still holding to a pace sufficient to rapidly close the distance between him and Starbeau. It was a pace that he could maintain for hours and served to rest his horse at the same time. It was also necessary on this morning because the trail he followed crossed and recrossed a stream several times, as if Starbeau was undecided in which direction he should travel. Joe speculated that it could also mean that it had been late in the day when Starbeau and his captive made these tracks, and he was searching for a good place to make camp. This hunch proved to be accurate.

After the last change in direction, the trail led back to the stream again as it ran through a small clearing dotted with rocks of all sizes. Near a large boulder with a pine tree growing out of its center, he found the remains of a campfire. Joe dropped the paint's reins and let the horse graze in the grass between the rocks while he scouted the campsite. Suddenly he stopped, took a step backward, and knelt to examine a track he had almost missed. It was an unshod print and it was as fresh as the tracks he had followed into the clearing. Moving more slowly now, he scouted farther, finding more of the unshod tracks. Starbeau had had visitors— *Indians!* Scouting the clearing in a wider circle, he could find no indication of a fight, which caused him to seriously ponder the meeting. It appeared they had peacefully parted company, for he found the same two sets of tracks he had followed from Missoula Mills on the far side of the stream. And they continued to lead southeast toward the mining camps.

Taking time to satisfy his curiosity, he scouted back along the stream in an effort to find the trail left by the Indians. In a few minutes' time, he found what he was looking for, a clear trail left by two horses, maybe three. They led off toward the northwest. Satisfied, he turned to continue trailing Starbeau when he was stopped cold by the sight of a clear footprint in the soft dead leaves by the water's edge. Too small to be that of a man, it had a clear shape of a heel, unlike a print a moccasin would leave. His thoughts now spinning in his head like a whirlpool, he followed the trail left by the horses, picking up the tiny print of the girl's shoe wherever the ground was soft enough. *The Indians now have Callie!* The thought caused anew his sense of urgency. The deeper indentation of the toe of her print told him that she was being pulled by a rope.

He got to his feet again and looked long and hard in the direction indicated by the tracks. They led to the northwest, toward the mountains beyond the Missoula Valley. Who were her captors now? Flathead, Kutenai, Pend d'Oreille? It was hard to say. In theory, many of these tribes were friendly with the white man, but theory perished when out of sight of the treaty tents. From the footprints he had found, it was obvious to him that Callie was being led like a prisoner.

He took a moment then to turn and look in the direction Starbeau had gone. He knew in his heart that he could not rest until the score was settled with the cruel murderer and rapist. The knowledge that Callie would still be safely with her family had he simply pulled the trigger when he had Starbeau under his rifle still haunted his conscience. There was no decision to be made at this point, however. Starbeau would have to wait. He turned his thoughts and his concentration on the trail before him, praying that she could survive until he found her.

One day's travel from the rocky glen, he came upon a smaller clearing beside a creek and the remains of another campsite. Almost reluctant to go farther, afraid of what he might find, he walked his horse slowly into the clearing, glancing sharply from side to side. Pulling the paint up beside the burnt-out campfire, he dismounted and began to examine the ground around the coals.

There was not a great deal of sign to tell him what had happened to Callie that night. A few discarded bones told him that the Indians, a party of three he now decided, had eaten deer meat for their supper. And while there were signs that a scuffle had taken place near the fire, there was no fresh blood anywhere on the grass or sand, giving him hope that Callie was not involved. A few yards away from the ashes, he found a large piece of cloth that caused him immediate concern. It appeared to be part of a woman's undergarment, and it was covered with blood, but the blood was old and crusted, again giving him hope that it was evidence of an earlier wound and she had not been harmed by her Indian captors. Not permitting himself to dwell upon what might be happening to Callie, he immediately set out to follow the trail again, planning to push on until darkness forced him to stop.

If Callie thought her lot had improved when she was traded to Gray Wolf for a horse, she was to be disappointed once more. Gray Wolf himself was not the source of her continued hardship. Credit for that belonged to Bright Basket. As Gray Wolf's first wife, she was his *sits-beside-him* wife, sitting at his right side in the tipi. His other two wives were Bright Basket's younger sisters and their positions in the tipi were closer to the door.

Bright Basket was not pleased to see the young white girl led into the village by the hunters, and she was quick to express her displeasure to her husband when she found that the girl was his property. "Why have you brought this coyote pup into my lodge?" she demanded. "Are you still so young that you think you need another wife?"

"Maybe I am so old that I don't need to hear your sharp tongue," he retorted, glaring his annoyance with her insubordination. "I have no need for another wife. I bought her for you—to help with your chores."

"Humph," she snorted, somewhat relieved to hear Callie was not to be a wife, but still opposed to her presence in her lodge. "Are you complaining that the three women in your tipi do not take care of you properly?"

Gray Wolf sighed patiently and shook his head. "Your rattling makes my head hurt. Lame Horse traded some deer meat to a white man for the woman. Then he decided he didn't want her, so he was going to kill her. She is small, but she can fight like a mountain lion. It would have been a shame to kill her. So now she is yours to work for you."

Bright Basket snorted confidently, but was wise enough not to badger her husband further on the matter. She marched over to Callie, who had been left to be gaped at by the crowd that had gathered around Gray Wolf's horse. With hands on hips, Bright Basket walked around the frightened girl, looking her over intently. Noticing the many bruises and scars on the girl's arms and legs, she commented, mostly for the crowd's benefit, "You must be a lazy slave, or you wouldn't have so many scars. Now that you are mine, you will not be lazy, or I will beat you to death." With no idea what the Indian woman was saying, Callie could only stare back at her, which seemed to aggravate Bright Basket. She turned to speak to her sisters, who had come to stare at the white slave. "She can gather the wood for the fire. Watch her carefully." Then, turning back to Callie, she ordered her to go and collect some wood for the fire. Callie did not move, having been subject to the obviously angry woman's tirade for several minutes with no notion what she was being told. Her failure to respond to Bright Basket's commands caused the Salish woman to scream at her for her insolence. She grabbed the quirt from Gray Wolf's saddle and set upon the unsuspecting girl.

Caught by surprise, Callie could not move fast enough to avoid the stinging rawhide whip, and she cried out as the angry Indian woman delivered blow after blow, raising painful welts on her arms and face. She tried to run, but the crowd of laughing women caught her and shoved her back for more punishment. Desperate to save herself from the angry woman, Callie braced herself to fight back, even if it meant her death. She took the sting of the whip on her arms and managed to grab it before Bright Basket could pull it away. With a good firm grip on the rawhide quirt, she held on with all the strength she could muster. It soon became a tug-of-war between the battered girl and the larger woman, much to the delight of the spectators.

The circle of women expanded to give the two combatants room to maneuver as they tugged back and forth. No matter how hard Bright Basket jerked and fumed, Callie could not be shaken. Finally, when it became apparent that the white hostage was not going to give in, the women converged upon her, knocking her to the ground. Unable to defend herself against the angry mob, Callie was forced to submit to an onslaught of kicking and hitting.

"Enough!" Gray Wolf commanded, his voice heavy with anger. The women halted their attack at once and backed away, leaving the beaten girl lying still. "What good will the girl be if you beat her to death?" Bright Basket took a step backward when Gray Wolf walked over to stand over Callie. Disgusted with his wife's jealous reaction to the hostage, he noted the welts and fresh cuts, as well as bleeding from some of her old wounds. *I should not have interfered when Lame Horse wanted to kill her*, he thought. *She will probably die, anyway, and I have wasted a good horse.* "Take her to the river's edge and let her clean herself," he ordered. "Then give her something to eat. If she is better tomorrow, we'll decide what to do with her."

"What if she is no better tomorrow?" Bright Basket asked.

Gray Wolf shrugged. "Then we will kill her. She may die before then, anyway."

Satisfied with that answer, Bright Basket's smirk returned to her face. "I'll let her clean herself if she can, but I'll not have the coyote bitch in my tipi. She can sleep outside with the dogs." With help from one of her sisters, she dragged Callie to the river's edge and unceremoniously dumped her into the water.

The cold water struck her senses with a shock as she sank in the shallow pool close to the bank. Moments away from unconsciousness when she was thrown into the rapidly moving current, she was revived enough to struggle to the surface and gasp for air. The thought of escape flashed through her confused brain, but only for a second. Her arms and legs were too weak to make a sudden attempt to swim to the other side. Letting her feet settle to the bottom, she found that she was in water up to her shoulders. Looking then to the other side, she recognized the sullen features of Lame Horse. He was sitting on a white pony, watching her, and she realized that an attempt to escape by swimming across the river would have accomplished nothing more than putting herself back in his clutches. There was nothing for her but to accept her captivity.

Bright Basket's patience lasted only long enough for Callie to make a few feeble efforts to clean herself before she was ordered out of the water. By employing sign language, the Salish woman made her instructions understood, and Callie meekly emerged from the river. Dripping wet, she was led to Bright Basket's lodge, where she was bound hand and foot, then tied to a small tree with a short length of rope. There she lay, shivering in the afternoon sunshine, a curiosity for the children of the village and an object of open scorn by the women.

As the afternoon waned and the shadows lengthened, gradually the visits of the curious became less frequent. Cramped and cold though she was, she mercifully fell asleep, her mind and body being too tired to remain awake. She was awakened by Bright Basket's sister as she rudely poked her with her toe. Seeing that the captive was not dead, Bright Basket's sister placed some meat on the ground near Callie's face. Then, without bothering to untie her hands, the sister left her to grovel for her supper.

As she struggled to inch her way close enough to take some of the food in her mouth, she realized that evening was descending upon the village. It was nothing more than an unconscious thought, for she was past the point of caring whether it was day or night. Her fate was certain and she was sure that her future extended no farther than the dawn of another day, for she made up her mind that she would not cling desperately to life any longer. She would take her own life if there was no other opportunity to escape. Such morbid thoughts were forgotten for the moment when one of the many dogs in the village picked up the scent of the meat on the ground and trotted over to share in her meal. Realizing then just how hungry she was, she struggled as best she could, with her hands and feet bound, to crowd the mongrel away from her food. He was not easily discouraged, however, and it soon became a contest between the two to see who could capture the biggest portion of the meager supper. Hampered by the pain in her jaw, she was forced to eat slowly and carefully, so it was no real competition for the hungry dog. Cursing the cur as he ran off with the last piece of meat, she heard the sound of laughter, and rolled over on her side to discover Bright Basket watching her.

"You eat with your brother, coyote bitch," Bright Basket scorned and laughed again.

"You can go to hell," Callie returned.

Although neither woman understood the other's words, the tone was unmistakable. Bright Basket drew near and aimed a kick in Callie's stomach before leaving her slave to sleep as best she could. Finally the cooking fires died down and the camp settled in for the night, and Callie was at last alone with her thoughts of the fate that had been cast upon her. The night seemed to make her many pains more intense as she tried to accomplish some position that would be more comfortable. Finally convinced that sleep was impossible, she willed her mind to think of other things and people. She regretted the fact that she had quarreled with her father and mother over her visits with Joe. She wished that she could somehow tell them she was sorry. Then her thoughts centered on the mysterious man of the forest who had appeared out of the wilderness to guide her family and friends out of the mountains. She let her mind drift lazily for a few minutes as she pictured the sharply chiseled features, the dark, soft eyes that seemed to speak to her without a word being spoken. For a moment, her heart cried out to him, but only for a moment before her bruised body reminded her that she would never see him again. It made no difference, anyway, she told herself, for she was ruined as a woman. Her innocence torn from her body by a cruel demon of a man, she could no longer be desired by any man. Even the brute, Lame Horse, was sickened by the sight of her. The thought almost made her cry out in despair. She shook her head violently as if to shake meaningless thinking from her brain. She was certain now that she would never be able to sleep, but exhaustion finally came to claim her troubled mind. She drifted off to sleep, only to be awakened once again in the wee hours of the night.

At first she thought she was dreaming, but the chill on her skin told her that she was awake. In the next instant, she felt a gentle tightening on the rope and realized that someone was behind her. Immediately alarmed, she tried to cry out, but a powerful hand clamped tightly over her mouth before she could make a sound. Terrified, her first thought was that Lame Horse had returned to extract from her that which he had first sought. She struggled against him, but he was too strong, and rolled her over to face him. Helpless to stop him, she stared up at him, but her eyes played tricks on her, for the face she thought she saw was not Lame Horse's.

"Callie," the soft voice whispered, "don't be afraid. It's me. I've come to take you away from here." Certain that she was dreaming now, she started to cry, devastated by the cruelty of such a dream. "Callie," he said again, "do you understand what I'm sayin'? It's me, Joe."

Swept under by a wave of emotion, she realized that it was real. With eyes wide open now, she nodded rapidly, and he slowly removed his hand from her mouth. "Be real quiet," he whispered. "I'm gonna cut you loose. Then we gotta get outta here. Can you walk?" She nodded. "Good." He finished sawing the rawhide ropes that held her, then looked around him at the sleeping Salish village. When he was satisfied that all was still quiet, he lifted her to her feet. "Come," he said, "the horses are in that stand of trees near the riverbank."

Too frightened to do anything but obey his instructions, she started to follow him, but collapsed to the ground after taking a couple of steps. Her legs, numb from being trussed up for so long, refused to support her. Pausing less than a second, he reached down and picked her up as gently as he could manage. Holding her in his arms, he moved silently between the tipis, placing his feet carefully to avoid making a sound. Once past the outermost lodge in the circle of tipis, he quickened his pace to a trot, unhampered by the girl in his arms.

When he gained the cover of the trees, he slowed to a walk, and continued until he came to a tangle of young willows. On the other side of the willows, two horses stood tied to some branches—one, his paint pony, the other a white mare. He started to put her down, but before he could, she tightened her arms around his neck and hugged him, holding him for a long moment. She said nothing, but he felt her tears on his neck and knew what she wanted to tell him. She released him then and he set her feet gently on the ground. "Can you stand now?" he asked while still supporting her.

"I think so," she said. "I don't know what was wrong before."

"Most likely had the blood cut off from your legs too long," he said. "Don't matter anyway. Can you ride?" She said that she could. "I think this horse will do fine for you. I stole her from their horses on the other side of the river. I'd rather not have a white one, but this one came over to meet me and acted like she was just waitin' for me to come get her." He held out his hand to help her. "Come on, up you go. We'd best get movin'." He had fashioned a bridle and reins from one piece of rope with a couple of half hitches, Indian style. "Sorry I didn't have time to find a saddle for you."

"I don't need a saddle," she said, looking back over her shoulder, afraid she might see someone coming after them. "Let's just get away from here."

"Yes, ma'am," he said, and climbed on the paint. "We're gonna go for a little swim. Hang on real tight." He guided his horse down through the willows to the river. Once they reached the other side, he led them straight up the valley, making the best time possible in the dark of night. There were not many hours left before daybreak, so he wanted to put a lot of ground between them and the Salish village.

With the coming of the morning sun, it was apparent to him that Callie needed rest and food. It would have been his preference to continue riding until it was necessary to rest the horses, but upon looking back at Callie, he could see that she might not make it that far.

Looking around for the best place to stop for a while to let her rest, he slowed the horses to a walk until they came to a small stream winding its way down from a mountain pass high above them. "This'll do," he said and turned the horses upstream. "We'll climb up this stream a ways till we get outta sight and high enough to see anybody that might be thinkin' about followin' us." She nodded gamely, but he could see that she was fighting to stay on the mare's back. So he decided not to climb as high as he was originally thinking, and picked the first suitable spot, a small glen where the stream widened to flow over a rocky ledge. It wasn't high enough to give him a view of the valley floor, but it likewise could not be easily seen from below.

Dismounting, he moved quickly to her side and caught her as she leaned toward him, almost falling from the mare's back. "Easy does it, Callie," he said as he helped her walk to a flat rock by the stream.

"Thank you," she said, grateful far beyond those two simple words. "I must look a sight."

He smiled. Although she attempted to smile back at him, he could tell it was painful due to a serious-looking split on her lower lip. He tried to hide his initial reaction to her frightful condition he could now plainly see in the morning sunlight. But he was not wholly successful, for she lowered her gaze to fall upon her hands, which were folded in her lap. His heart ached for her and the torment she had obviously suffered. Her arms and legs bore the scars, and bloodstains on her tattered clothes were testimony to the many beatings she had survived. But the more serious injuries he had read in her eyes before she had averted them. These were injuries burned deep into her soul, and might never be healed. It required no imagination to speculate on the hell she had endured while a captive of the murdering monster Starbeau. He knew of nothing he could say or do to alleviate that pain. The best he could do was to attempt to get her mind on other mundane things.

Noticing that she was shivering in the morning chill, he said, "I'm gonna get a fire started to warm you up a little. Then I'll find you somethin' to eat. I've got coffee in my saddlebag. You'll feel a sight better once you get a decent meal in you."

She started to protest that she could help him, but he quickly rejected her offer, telling her that she could tend the fire once he got it started. She gratefully conceded, leaning back against the rock to rest. Her battle with Bright Basket had drained her energy, and the small portion of meat she fought the dog for had not been enough to rebuild any strength. Deer jerky was all he could offer her at the moment. She accepted it even though she still found it painful to chew. "I oughta be able to find you a little somethin' more than jerky to eat," he said, taking his bow from his saddle. "The woods are full of food." Noticing an immediate look of alarm in her face, he said, "I won't be gone long," and placed his rifle beside her. "Besides, I need me a cup of that coffee when it gets through boilin'." He walked off into the woods then.

True to his word, he was not gone long. The coffee had finished boiling only ten or fifteen minutes before she heard him call out to her that he was back. She guessed that he spoke to prevent her being startled by his sudden appearance, knowing his habit of materializing where there was nothing before. "It ain't much," he said, holding up a squirrel, "but it's fresh meat." He immediately started skinning the squirrel while she poured coffee in the cup he had placed before her. She watched as he skinned and gutted the squirrel in a matter of minutes, and placed it over the fire to roast.

"I thought you said you wanted some of this coffee," she said when he settled himself on the other side of the fire.

"I'll have some a little later on," he replied, and busied himself with tending the squirrel.

She sipped from the cup, wincing when the hot liquid touched the partially healed split on her lip. Then it occurred to her. "You don't have but one cup, do you?"

"Never needed more'n one," he said. "It don't matter. I'll wait till you're done."

"We'll share," she insisted, filled the cup to the top, and passed it over to him.

"Much obliged," he said and drank down over half

of the cup. Then he took his sleeve and carefully wiped the rim before refilling the cup and passing it back to her. "That'll hold me for a while." He turned his attention to the squirrel on his makeshift spit. "This little feller is about done."

"That's not a lot of breakfast for a man your size, is it?"

"This is all for you," he said. "I ain't really hungry. I just wanted some coffee. Guess I ate too much of that jerky."

She knew he was lying, but also knew he would never admit it. In a few minutes he took the squirrel off the fire and handed it to her, still on the spit. As she took it from him, a thought entered her mind. *I wonder if angels sometimes wear buckskins.* Then a more ominous question occurred and she asked, "Will they come after us?"

"Can't say for sure," he answered. "Sometimes it's hard to say what an Indian will do, especially a Flathead. But I don't reckon they'll be any too happy when they figure out that somebody walked right into their camp and took you." Seeing the smile fade from her face, he tried to reassure her. "We'll be movin' on from this spot as soon as you're feelin' up to it, just to be safe. I've got to get you back to your folks."

"Maybe they've already started for Oregon," she said.

"They're not gonna start without you," he insisted. "Besides, there's still some snow in the high passes."

She said nothing, but she could not rid her mind of the thought that she was forever damaged. No man would ever want her now, and maybe even her parents wouldn't. She somehow felt that they would blame her for the black stain upon the family.

Chapter II

Although Joe had told Callie that Indians were unpredictable, he had chosen not to tell her that on this particular point they were almost certain to be predictable. He knew that the escape of the white captive may not have been that important to them, but the loss of the horse would surely call for retaliation. In fact, the war party was already tracking them while he and Callie were discussing it.

The early-morning quiet had been split by Bright Basket's piercing scream of anger when she found the ropes severed and her captive gone. She was still running through the camp alerting everyone about the missing girl when Lame Horse forded the river to report his newly acquired mare gone. Seething with anger, he stomped back and forth in the fire circle venting his rage. Feeling doubly cheated, first for trading the girl to Gray Wolf, and now having the white mare stolen before he even got to know the horse.

The men gathered in the center of the camp to confer on the matter. There was little doubt that the girl had not managed this thing alone, which further inflamed Lame Horse as well as most of the other men.

It was insulting to think that someone had walked right through the middle of their camp and freed the woman, then added the insult of stealing a horse to carry her.

"I will find this person and kill him," Lame Horse declared. "Who will ride with me?" All but the old men volunteered and Lame Horse selected a dozen of the younger warriors to ride with him. They went immediately to prepare themselves and their horses. Two Bears was one of those selected, but Gray Wolf was not, for Lame Horse felt that he had been too soft with the girl. While the rest of the war party were making ready to ride, Lame Horse and Two Bears scouted the opposite side of the river, looking for the raider's trail. After about twenty minutes, a howl went up from Two Bears, signaling that he had found their tracks. Lame Horse rushed to join him.

"Here!" Two Bears exclaimed as Lame Horse slid from his pony's back. "Two horses, they go up the middle of the valley."

Lame Horse took but a second to confirm his friend's opinion. He leaped upon his pony's back and rode around and around in a circle, signaling for the war party while Two Bears went ahead to scout the trail. By the time the rest of the warriors caught up to Two Bears, he had a clear picture of the escape route, and they were soon in hot pursuit.

Eager to put more distance between them and the Salish warriors he knew would be coming, Joe studied the young woman intensely as she cleaned the bones of the squirrel. *She doesn't look too strong*, he thought. *She must be a whole lot worse off than she lets on.* He decided that she needed more nourishment than one puny squirrel could give her, but he was afraid to take the time to hunt when still this close to the Salish village. He was sure she also needed time to rest and recover from the horrible ordeal she had undergone. The problem at the present time, however, was that they could ill afford to take the time.

In spite of his concern, she insisted that she was ready to ride again after she had eaten. He still had doubts, but he also knew that it was too dangerous to stay where they were. In an effort to make it easier for her, he took his saddle off the paint and placed it on the mare. Although it was no more than an Indian saddle, one he had made, it still gave her more to hold on to. He pulled his rifle from the sling, jumped on the paint, and with a gentle nudge of his heels, started up toward the ridge above them.

Intent upon at least gaining the far side of a line of ridges to the west before stopping again, Joe led Callie along the side of the closest ridge, weaving his way through thick growths of firs, gradually climbing toward the crest. Looking back frequently to see how she was doing, he was met with a determined smile. *So far, so good*, he thought. The forest abounded with deer sign, and at one point he spotted a buck and three does below them on a ledge. It would have been an easy shot, but he was reluctant to use his rifle. He was going to have to kill a deer for Callie's sake, but it would have to be shot with his bow.

With the afternoon sun gradually descending, they crossed over the top of the ridge, and with the sun looking directly in his eyes, he started a slow descent, following a stream that appeared to have popped out of a rocky defile. From above, he could see what appeared to be a clearing about halfway down the slope with the stream wending its way through the center. *Looks like the place to camp*, he thought, and turned to take another look at Callie. There were no longer traces of the determined smile. Instead, she appeared grim and haggard, and he hoped he had not pushed her too far. "Halfway down this slope," he told her, "and we'll make our camp and I'll hunt somethin' to eat." She managed a grateful nod.

On this evening, Callie did not volunteer to help set up the camp. After settling her comfortably by a fire, he filled his coffeepot in the cold mountain stream, and set it to boil at the edge of the flames. With nothing to offer again but jerky, he said, "This'll give you some strength till I can get us somethin' better." The gnawing in his stomach told him that he couldn't go much longer without something substantial himself. When she was settled, he left her to take care of the horses; then, assuring her that he would not be far away, he took his bow and disappeared into the forest.

Deer frequented the slope he had camped on; he was sure of that. There was plenty of sign: droppings, tree bark rubbed off, even hoofprints, but there were no deer close around. He figured they had been frightened away by the approach of the two horses and riders. Finally, when it became dark, he had to abandon the hunt for the night, knowing Callie might be fearful that something had happened to him. *It'll have to wait till morning,* he reluctantly decided. It mattered little to Callie because she was sound asleep when he returned to camp. He carefully removed the coffee cup from her fingers, and covered her with his blanket. *I'll go out again before sunup and see if I can't sneak up on game of some kind,* he thought and sat down to finish the coffee.

Lame Horse and Two Bears walked along the trail leading down the broad valley, one on each side, searching for the hoofprints they had followed from their village. Behind them, some two hundred yards or so, the others waited so as not to obliterate the fresh tracks. So sure were they that the two they chased were running as hard as they could down the length of the valley, they had evidently failed to consider that their prey might have left the main trail and turned up into the hills. Finally Two Bears stopped and said, "They did not come this far unless their horses grew wings." There was not one track between the two warriors and the place where the rest of the riders waited.

"We must go back and find the place where they left the trail," Lame Horse responded impatiently. "I want the woman and the one who freed her." They turned around then and started back toward the others. "Do you think it is the big grizzly bear who traded her to me for the meat?" Not waiting for an answer, he said, "I hope it is. I want his scalp for my lance."

Back with the other warriors, they reported that they had been too hasty in their assumptions, and it was now necessary to backtrack to search for the place where the two had eluded them. The warriors were quick to take on the challenge, and everyone began searching the back trail, eager to be the one to find the missing tracks. As the afternoon grew shorter, the enthusiasm for the chase began to drain. With no luck in finding the clue they sought, some of the warriors began to grumble that maybe Two Bears was right. Maybe the horses did grow wings and fly. They searched all the way back to the point where tracks were found in the trail. It was at the crossing of a small stream and obvious then that the woman and her rescuer had ridden up the stream.

Lame Horse's passion was refreshed. He immediately started up the stream, but he sensed a loss of enthusiasm by his followers. Halting his pony briefly, he paused to consider the situation. "I will go on alone," he said. "There are too many of us to surprise them. I can get close without alerting them."

"I will go with you," Two Bears said. "There are two of them, so there should be two of us."

"This is true," Lame Horse replied, "but one of them is a woman. I will kill the big man who stole her." He was convinced that the man he chased had to be Starbeau.

"If this is your wish," Two Bears conceded, knowing Lame Horse felt the need to redeem himself for the times he thought he had been cheated.

There were no objections from the other warriors, they having tired of the chase. They wished him good hunting and turned back toward the village, leaving him to track the escapee and her accomplice alone. He hurried up the stream, in an effort to make use of what daylight remained.

Just before the forest became shrouded in the early darkness, Lame Horse came upon a place where the stream became wider, and the remains of a small fire. He smiled to see they had not ridden far before stopping to rest. Already he was gaining ground. The charred bones of a squirrel told him that they had lingered long enough to eat. With increasing confidence, he pushed on through the thick forest of firs, intent upon following the tracks for as long as there remained enough light to see them. When darkness set in, he paused to look at the crown of the ridge above him. Judging by the path he had followed so far, he considered the intended direction and at approximately where they may have gained the top of the ridge. With that point in mind, he pushed on into the night, fueled by his anticipated pleasure upon running them to ground.

Upon reaching the top of the ridge, he was forced to rest his tired pony before continuing his search. He took the time to ponder his next move. At best, he had gained more time on his prey, but he had to accept the fact that, though he may be somewhere close to their trail, he could not find their tracks in the dark. It was cause for despair, for his passion for Starbeau's and Callie's blood had progressed to a state of lust. The thought that they might yet escape him agitated him to the point where he felt the necessity to pace back and forth. In an effort to walk it off, he walked out to the edge of a rocky shelf and stood gazing out over the dark forest below him. Suddenly there was a quickening in the beat of his heart, for he thought he had caught something out of the corner of his eye. Nothing more than the brief flicker of an insect possibly, but it was enough to compel him to fix his gaze upon the western side of the ridge. *There it is again*—a faint reddish flickering about halfway down the slope, and he smiled as he realized it was a campfire. He had caught them!

His initial reaction was to charge down through the black forest, but a second thought cautioned him to take time to plan his attack. The bearlike brute that had taken her had the rifle that shoots many times, and he had no weapon to match that. So he must work in close to the camp and strike before Starbeau knew he was under attack. It was already past the middle of the night, but there was time to cautiously make his way down through the trees and be in position to strike before the sun came up. He complimented himself for his show of restraint, and smiled again when he thought about the respect he would gain with the big white man's scalp—and the power he would gain with the acquisition of the repeating rifle. As for the woman, he would use her, as he had originally intended. Then he would kill her.

Joe Fox awoke early, before daylight. Pausing only to look in the girl's direction to make sure she was sleeping, he gently laid his rifle beside her. With only his bow and quiver, he disappeared into the forest that surrounded the tiny clearing. He thought his best chance to get a shot at a deer would be a few hundred yards below his camp, so he followed the stream down until he came upon a game trail. He figured that this might be a spot where the deer came to drink, so he sat down beside a sizable tree and waited.

Above him, a menacing figure knelt, also beside a large tree, and watched the camp intensely. Lame Horse hesitated, scanning the clearing, searching for the man whose empty blanket he could see on the opposite side of the fire from the sleeping woman. Cautious of the possibility of walking into an ambush, he crept closer to the very edge of the clearing and waited. When minutes passed with no sign of the huge white man, Lame Horse became impatient. The sun was coming up, its fingers already stealing through the trees. Still the white man was nowhere to be seen. As a precaution, Lame Horse turned to look behind him. There was nothing. Behind the sleeping woman, he could see his little white mare standing beside a paint pony, and he began to wonder, remembering the large bay that Starbeau had ridden before. Shifting his gaze back to the woman, he noticed the object lying beside her bed. As the sun began to break through the predawn gloom, he could better make the object out and realized it was a rifle—*the repeating rifle!*

He was astonished to think that the white man had left the deadly rifle with the woman and gone to relieve his bowels or look for food, or whatever. It didn't matter where he was if Lame Horse could get his hands on the rifle. He would have the power! Taking a last look around the clearing, with no one else in sight, he got up with an arrow notched in his bowstring, and moved quickly and silently across the clearing.

He paused for a moment to gaze at the sleeping woman, casting a churlish grin upon her scarred face. Then he carefully reached down and removed the rifle from her blanket. Unable to contain the feeling of power now within him, he thrust the weapon over his head in one hand and threw his head back to issue a triumphant war cry. Callie was instantly snatched from a deep sleep, horrified to find the evil demon standing before her, a scornful grin upon his cruel face. She screamed and tried to scramble away from him, but he was quick to place his foot on her chest and pin her to the ground. "Where is the white man?" Lame Horse demanded, pointing the rifle at her face.

With the shocking realization that the nightmare she once again found herself in was real, Callie could not answer. "Where is he?" Lame Horse demanded again.

"Right behind you, you Flathead son of a bitch," Joe Fox answered.

Lame Horse spun around ready to shoot, but hesitated, startled to discover the tall, lean man in buckskins, a warrior like himself, instead of the bulky brute, Starbeau. His astonishment caused him to pause only for a moment, replaced by contemptuous amusement at the sight of the drawn bow aimed at him. "Hah," he grunted, "I have your gun," and he raised it to aim at the imperturbable man slowly walking toward him, closing the distance between them. With a sneering grin on his face, he calmly pulled the trigger. The grin turned into a look of disbelief when the rifle failed to fire. He glanced quickly down at the recalcitrant weapon. When he looked back up, the arrow was already on its way. It struck him in the throat. He dropped the rifle and clutched at the arrow with both hands. The second arrow struck his chest and he staggered backward, and would have fallen on Callie had she not rolled out of his way.

Landing heavily on his back, the impact with the hard ground causing the arrows to rip away at his neck and chest, he was helpless to defend against the inevitable. His eyes stared wildly at Joe as the knife was about to be drawn across his windpipe. "It is Joe Fox of the Piegan Blackfeet who sends you to the dark place," he growled. The fatal stroke was swift, and Lame Horse was no more.

Callie sat on the ground, still shivering from the frightening awakening and the execution of Lame Horse. Only moments before, she was certain that Joe was going to be killed, and she found it hard to believe even now that he was not. The fierce countenance that was Lame Horse's last sight on earth, relaxed to return to the calm and gentle face that she knew to be Joe. "You're safe now," he said, then watched her carefully before asking, "Are you all right?"

"I think so," she answered, though not convincingly.

He reached down and helped her to her feet. "He was alone," he said. "There are no others, so you'll be all right now." He freshened the fire before turning to leave again. "I'll be right back. I killed a nice young doe that I left in the woods back there. There's also a black horse tied to a tree up the slope a ways." He smiled. "We've both got saddles now."

"How did you know the rifle wouldn't fire?" she asked as he walked away.

"He didn't cock it. There was no cartridge in the chamber. I left it that way in case you grabbed it while you were still asleep. I figured if you wanted to shoot at somethin', you'd have sense enough to cock it."

Since there was no longer a sense of danger from the Salish warriors, they remained in their camp for the rest of that day while Joe skinned and butchered the deer. They both ate roasted venison until they could hold no more, and Joe showed Callie how to smoke most of the rest of the meat to use later on. It was a healing time for Callie. More than the physical rest, she was able to recover some of the confidence that had been a characteristic when first he met her. The mental scars were far from healing, and in all likelihood would never be forgotten completely. But she felt comfortable in Joe's company, and she was glad that it was he who was there to help her, and not her parents. Maybe, she thought, she would be able to face them by the time they returned to Missoula Mills. Thinking back now on her horrible captivity, she realized that her prayers for rescue had all been for Joe. And in answer to those prayers, he had come for her. She also knew that it was to be her secret, and that unless bridled, thoughts like that could cause her a great deal of heartbreak.

Just to be sure, Joe left again for a short time that afternoon to scout the upper slope and the trail they had come down. There was no sign of anyone and he felt reassured that Lame Horse had been the lone warrior with the incentive to follow them once they had left the valley. Callie could take as much time as she thought she needed before starting out again because there should be plenty of time before the mule train was ready to leave for Oregon. He was relieved to see signs of her recovery. He could well imagine the agony she had endured at the hands of her captors. The physical scars were evidence enough of that. The thought of her torture was enough to renew his promise to himself to see that Starbeau paid for his crimes, not only those inflicted upon Callie, but also for the murders of Bradley and Nancy Lindstrom. There should be no place on earth for vermin like Starbeau, and he vowed that there would be no place on earth where the ugly brute would be safe from him.

Upon awakening the next morning, Callie decided that she should not wait any longer to return to her family. She wished that she could delay until her wounds healed, but it was obvious by the touch of her finger-tips on her cheek that there would remain thick scars even after healing. She tried to resign herself to the fate that her face would be marked for life.

Joe packed up the camp, along with their supply of smoked meat, and tied the bundles on Lame Horse's pony. Continuing in the direction they had traveled the day before, he looked for a way around the mountains to the west, planning to strike the Bitterroot Valley and follow the Bitterroot River north to its junction with Clark's Fork River and the pilgrim's village of caves at Missoula Mills.

Chapter 12

They came out of the mountains and descended into the valley of the Bitterroot, striking the river at a point where tall Ponderosa pines stood guarding a sandy bank. Looking north up the broad valley, Joe figured they were two days from her parents' camp at Missoula Mills. Upon Callie's insistence that she was tired, they made camp by the river early in the day although there were still a good two hours of daylight left. She didn't want to confess that she was really not ready for their journey to end. She secretly wished it would take a week to get to Missoula Mills. To him, she would only confess that she was reluctant to meet her mother and father and the rest of the people she had traveled with from Dakota until she had regained her strength. Although she had no mirror to verify it, she was pretty certain that she looked as if she had been mauled by a grizzly, which was not too far from what had actually happened to her. There were bound to be many questions asked. Knowing that they would be next to impossible to ignore, she did the only thing she could at the moment, and that was to stall, playing upon Joe's patience and hoping the extra time would give her a chance to take better control of the mental anguish of a reunion after her abduction. She longed to see her mother and father, but she dreaded to have them see her.

When the two-day journey stretched into the third day, Joe decided that it was time for Callie to face her family and friends. After plenty of rest and solid food, she had apparently recovered her physical strength, so she might as well get it over with. He told her as much on the morning of the third day, when they had camped the night before just twelve miles from Missoula Mills.

"You're right," she confessed. "I know I've been dragging my feet. I just dread for everyone to see me like this." She felt the stigma of having been violated, and could not help the feeling that she would be forever looked upon as damaged and unclean. She wanted to say how she wished she could stay with him, but she didn't dare for fear of his rejection.

He could read the anguish in her eyes and guessed what was really distressing her. "Callie, you're not to blame for what happened to you. You're not guilty of a damn thing." He smiled at her then. "As far as how you look, I think you're looking fit and fine now," he insisted. "Most of the bad places have healed over pretty good—just a few little pink scars on your face. Those bruises on your arms and legs are already turnin' yellow. They'll be gone in a few days."

She couldn't help but smile at his attempt to appear earnest. "I swear, Joe Fox, you're about the poorest liar I've ever seen." No one had to tell her that her cheek was disfigured permanently from a slash that should have had stitches before it started to heal, and from the feel of the lump left by her broken jaw, the bones would never knit successfully again.

He blushed, having been caught in his attempt to lift her spirits. "Well, you look fine to me," he said, "but you might as well go on back and let 'em all take a good look at you, and then you can get on with your life."

His words sent a sharp pain through her heart, but she knew he was right. She couldn't hide in the bushes all the rest of her life. "All right," she said with a show of determination, "let's quit lollygagging here by the fire and go home." Her decision made, she got up and went to fetch the white mare. Not waiting for his help, she threw the saddle on the horse and led it back to the fire. Responding to her actions, he loaded the packs on the black horse, and then saddled the paint. In a short time, they were in the saddle again and headed for the reunion.

Luke Preston sat on a table-sized rock at the river's edge, holding a fishing pole fashioned from a willow limb. There were plenty of fish, trout from their appearance, but none showed any interest in the piece of raw bacon on his hook. The weather was getting to where it was almost pleasant on some days, this day being one such. Most of the folks were starting to get antsy about vacating the holes they had spent the winter in, and there had already been several meetings to discuss the possible date to leave for Oregon. Horace Templeton had attended one of the meetings, and while he admitted that some trappers had told him that Lolo Pass was clear, he tried to sell the group on the merits of staying and settling there in the valley. "Now that you folks have spent the winter here, you saw firsthand that this is a sheltered valley, and it wasn't near as bad as you'd expect," he had said. "There's good prime land for farmin' or whatever you want—plenty of water. You've got the Clark Fork, the Bitterroot, the Blackfoot, all comin' through the valley. Why, folks, this beats Oregon six ways from Sunday."

He gave a good argument, and the men had given it

a lot of thought, with one family, Luke Preston, his wife, and son, thinking seriously about remaining in the fertile valley. But Oregon was where their friends and families were, so it was pretty much settled for the rest of the group. The only question left to answer was when. That question was hardest on Jake and Cora Simmons, reluctant as they were to leave without Callie. It had been more than two weeks since Joe Fox left to find Callie, and each additional day that passed seemed to confirm that the girl was lost for good.

Luke shook his head sadly when he thought about the torment that Jake and Cora must be suffering. He pulled his line from the water and got up to try to throw it farther out toward a large rock in the middle. Something caught his eye, and he turned to look toward the south. *Two riders and a packhorse*, he thought, *probably going to Templeton's.* He started to turn his attention back to his fishing when something about the lead rider made him look again, this time staring harder. After a minute it struck him. "Jesus, Mary, and Joseph!" he exclaimed. "Joe Fox!" And the smaller figure on the white horse behind him had to be Callie!

He dropped his pole and ran up the bank toward the village of caves, shouting as loud as he could. "It's Callie!" he yelled over and over, running down the length of the entire line of caves. "Callie's back! Callie and Joe Fox!" Within a matter of minutes, the entire party of pilgrims was out of the caves and running to meet the two riders approaching the camp. Holding her skirt above her ankles as she ran down the muddy track, Cora Simmons elbowed her way past her neighbors in an effort to get to her daughter. Running to catch up with her, Jake was right on her heels.

Seeing the sudden appearance of the entire population of the cave village coming to meet her, Callie forgot the fears she had dwelt upon for the past three days. And the reluctance she had felt for seeing everyone again disappeared, replaced by an overpowering feeling of joy at the sight of her parents running to receive her. Unnoticed in the excitement of the reunion, and the cries of welcome from the congregation, Joe reined the paint back to let Callie go on in front.

Beaming with the joy of the homecoming, Callie slid down from her horse and ran to embrace her parents. As they closed the distance between them, Cora caught a sob in her throat when she was close enough to look into her daughter's face. Callie, seeing the shock in her mother's eyes, immediately stopped, her fears of rejection returning. It was only for a moment, however, as Cora's anguish was overcome by the sheer joy and thankfulness for Callie's return and she rushed to receive her in her arms. Embraced by her mother and father, Callie could no longer hold her emotions in check, and soon all three were crying.

Joe had not dismounted, preferring to keep out of the way. He reached down to take the mare's reins, and led the horses aside before stopping to witness the homecoming. It went as he had hoped at first, with mother and father happily embracing their daughter, and the crowd of well-wishers closing in around them, laughing and welcoming Callie back. Then suddenly the noisy crowd grew silent as Jake took a step back to look closely at his daughter. The crowd saw then what struck Jake, the scarred and battered countenance that once was the face of an angel. Jake's face blanched and he was helpless to prevent the cry of anguish that escaped his lips. He turned away, his fists clenched, his face twisted by anger, and uttered a low moan through his gritted teeth that rose to a painful howl of frustrated rage.

It was the worst thing that could have happened from Joe's point of view, and he saw the unfortunate results immediately. He looked at Callie and saw the light of joy disappear from her face, to be replaced by the haunting look of panic and despair. Cora, realizing the damage her husband's damning reaction had been, sought to minimize the hurt to her daughter. With her arm around the girl's shoulder, she said, "Come on, honey, let's go home," and led her toward their cave. The congregation parted to let them pass with several softly spoken words of welcome and comfort with timid pats on her arms and back as if afraid they might hurt her. Joe imagined that Callie could hear the low murmur of voices behind her as she walked away. *That coulda gone a whole lot better*, he thought as Malcolm Lindstrom and Pete Watson walked over to join him.

"I knew if anybody could bring her back, it'd be you," Malcolm said as he shook Joe's hand. "She looks like she took a helluva beatin', poor thing. It's a damn shame."

"What about Starbeau?" Pete asked.

"He got away," Joe replied, then explained that Callie had been taken by a Flathead hunting party.

"I was hopin' you'd catch that son of a bitch and settle up with him for murderin' Brad and Nancy," Malcolm said, obviously disappointed. "Me and Pete gotta go back and give our families the bad news. I ain't lookin' forward to that. It'd be easier if I could say the man who killed 'em is dead."

"I ain't done lookin' for Starbeau yet," Joe said, his tone soft and deadly.

"You ain't figurin' on goin' on to Oregon with these folks, then?" Malcolm asked.

"Reckon not," Joe answered.

"I think Chadwick and some of the others are hopin' to persuade you to go along to lead 'em across the mountains," Malcolm said.

"It ain't likely," Joe replied. "I've got things I've gotta do." He shrugged and added, "They don't need me to take 'em. If what folks say about that new wagon road to Walla Walla is true, then they oughta be able to follow it." Thoughts of Starbeau had never been out of his mind, but now that Callie was safely home, going after the murderer was his one priority.

"Which way do you figure Starbeau went?" Malcolm asked, knowing full well what *things* Joe had to do. When Joe replied that he guessed Starbeau had most likely headed for the mining towns like Butte or Helena, Malcolm said, "Me and Pete are gonna head back home. I ain't too sure we can find our way back the way we came. If you're headin' that way, maybe we could go with you."

Joe paused before answering. He knew that Malcolm still hoped to settle with Starbeau for murdering his brother, but he was thinking that he'd had enough of being a guide for somebody. And now that Callie was safe, he was in a lonesome frame of mind. Looking into the earnest faces of the two men he had first led to this part of the territory, he found it hard to refuse them. "I'll tell you what," he said. "I'll take you to Butte. You know how to find your way back to Bismarck from there."

"Good enough," Malcolm replied. "I appreciate it, especially since we don't know friendly Injuns from hostiles. When are you plannin' to start out?"

"In the mornin'," Joe answered, "at sunup. If you ain't ready to ride by then, I'll figure you changed your mind."

As he had done before he'd left the little congregation by the river the first time, Joe made his camp in the cottonwoods away from the caves. He was to receive two visitors before he turned in for the night.

"Hello the camp," a voice called out. Joe looked up to see Jake Simmons approaching his fire. He didn't respond, just laid aside the bridle he was repairing and watched as the little man drew near. "I heard Pete Watson say you was leavin' in the mornin', and it wouldn't be right if I didn't come thank you for bringin' Callie back. Me and Cora want you to know we appreciate what you've done for Callie and us." When Joe responded with only a nod, Jake foundered for lack of what to say to the silent response. "I reckon we could pay you a little somethin' for your trouble. It wouldn't be much. We ain't got much."

The irony of it almost made Joe laugh. "You know, Jake," he said, "that's the second time you've insulted me. The first time was when you let me know I wasn't good enough to keep company with your daughter. And now you're askin' me if I want money for bringin' her home."

Flustered, Jake could only sputter, "Uh, well, I'm sorry. I reckon I didn't have any business . . ."

"It doesn't matter one way or the other," Joe interrupted. "You've said your piece. Was there anythin' else you wanted?"

"No," Jake replied, "I reckon not." He stood there shifting his weight nervously from one foot to the other for a long silent moment. He had hoped that there would be no hard feelings lingering from his rather rude request before. When it was apparent that Joe had no notion of putting him at ease, he shook his head and said, "Well, I reckon that's it."

"I'm leavin' that little white mare for Callie," Joe said. "The two of them seemed to hit it off real good."

"I'll tell 'er," Jake said. Then, totally bewildered, he spun around and returned to his camp, not really sure what he had expected.

It was later in the evening when his second visitor arrived. He was just about ready to roll up in his blanket when Callie made her way through the dark cottonwoods to find his camp. When he recognized her as she slipped into the firelight, he got to his feet to meet her. "How did you get out this late?" he asked.

"I told them I was going to the toilet," she said.

"Your pa was here just before dark," he said.

"I know. He came back muttering something about a hard-headed Injun," she said. In the light of the fire, he could see the slightest hint of a smile on her face. "They say you are leaving in the morning." He nodded. "Were you going without telling me good-bye?" When he could only shrug in answer, she said, "Well, Mr. Joe Fox, you don't get to do that with me. I haven't thanked you enough for what you did. I can never thank you enough, as long as I live."

"You don't have to thank me, Callie. Nothing could have kept me from goin' after you."

"I know that, and I want to thank you for it," she said.

"All right," he said, at a loss for words. "You're welcome." They stood looking at each other for a few empty seconds, both suddenly finding themselves a little embarrassed and unsure of what to say. Finally, he asked, "Are you doin' okay?"

"Yes," she replied. "If they ever quit staring at me when they don't think I can see them." When another awkward silence fell between them, she changed the subject. "Where are you going from here? Mama heard Malcolm Lindstrom say you were going after Starbeau. I hope that's not true."

He looked surprised. "Well, I reckon it's true enough," he said.

"That man's a monster," she said. "I'm afraid for you. If you're doing this for me, I don't want you to. He's over and done with and it's best if you just forget him."

He was fairly astonished that she would plead for him to forget Starbeau after what the man had done to her. As for her concern for his safety, he had never considered that he would come out on the short end of a fight with the huge man. It was no more in his mind than hunting for a grizzly or an elk. He would stalk it and kill it, and the world would be a better place because of it, and the score would be settled. And then maybe he could forgive himself for not pulling the trigger when he had his rifle in Starbeau's face.

"He owes for what he did to you, Callie," he said after a long pause. "But there's the other thing, too. He murdered Bradley and Nancy Lindstrom—and stole the money that belonged to all of you. A man like that ain't got no right to live on this earth, and I reckon I'm the one who the cards were dealt to."

She was about to argue the point when they heard her name called from behind the caves. "I guess they're lookin' for you," he said. "You'd better go on back. They're worried about you."

"You take care of yourself, Joe Fox," she said. "You'll be in my prayers."

"I'm obliged," he said simply.

She turned to leave, hesitated, then turned back toward him to gaze upon his face for a moment before she rushed to him and threw her arms around him, holding him close to her breast. He held her gently, like a precious thing, afraid that if he allowed his feelings for her to escape, he might crush her in his embrace. She longed to kiss him, but was afraid to offer her lips up to him, afraid that the firelight would display her disfigured face. They clung together for a few moments more, each wishing it could last forever while the sound of her mother's calling became more frantic. "You'd better go," he said and released her. She stepped back quickly then for one last look at him. Suddenly a heavy shroud of melancholy settled about him, and he realized that it was painful to say good-bye forever. "Callie, if you ever need me, if you can get the word to me that you need me, I'll come." She was not sure how to respond to him. Were his words a confession of genuine affection, as she so desperately wished, or words of pity for her plight? Fearful that she might force him into an awkward position if she interpreted his declaration to be more than simple courtesy, she merely thanked him for his kindness, then turned and disappeared into the darkness.

In a few minutes, he could hear her answering her mother's call. Although too far away to make out the words, he could imagine the worry Cora must have expressed to a daughter who had only recently returned from the dead. Suddenly the circle of light around his campfire seemed smaller, and he threw more wood on the flames. He stood transfixed for a long time, remembering the embrace, memorizing the feel of her slender body as it pressed tightly against his. His mind labored to make sense of it—affection or gratitude? "I guess I'll never know," he whispered.

Chapter 13

Malcolm and Pete were waiting for him while he laced up his packs on the black horse. The two men had made sure they were at his camp well before sunup for fear he might have started without them as he had threatened. As the morning light began to eat away at the heavy darkness, the three travelers mounted their horses and Joe Fox led them away from the caves that had seen them through the winter. He set a comfortable pace that the horses could maintain for a long while, knowing that he could cover ground quickly until reaching the place where he would start tracking Starbeau. As best he remembered, it had been a two-day ride to the little grassy clearing with the pine tree growing out of a boulder. It would be a shorter trip this time. As it turned out, the time was shortened to a little over a full day, allowing them to arrive at the clearing the morning of the second day.

He knew the trail was probably too old by this time and the best he could hope for was to learn enough to speculate on Starbeau's general direction, and maybe then guess his destination. Thoughts of his anguish the first time he found this campsite returned to his mind as he searched to find the two sets of shod tracks that led to the south. And he thought of Callie, and the impact the discovery of the one small footprint had upon his mind.

"This the place where that bastard traded Callie to the Injuns?" Pete asked, interrupting Joe's reverie.

"That's right," Joe replied, and brought his mind back to the business at hand. A few minutes later, he found the tracks he was looking for. He paused and let his eyes follow the direction indicated by the faint hoof-prints. Picking a point that looked like the easiest way to head up over the next ridge, he got on his horse and started toward it. Pete and Malcolm followed.

When he reached the spot he had picked out, he dismounted again to search the ground to confirm his hunch. His two companions dismounted and helped scout the short grass hillside. After a quarter of an hour, Joe stood up and looked to the top of the ridge to the east. Pete and Malcolm also stood up and walked over to stand beside him. "Couldn't find a sign," Pete said. "Reckon maybe he didn't come this way?"

"He came this way," Joe replied and knelt to point at the grass where a small stone had been dislodged and a slight indentation left beside it. It was no more than an inch long, but it told Joe that a horseshoe had left it. "It's been too long," he said. "Tracks will be hard to find from here. There's a long valley beyond this line of hills. I expect that's where he headed." He could only guess where the belligerent Starbeau had in mind, and according to what Malcolm and Pete told him, it was unlikely he knew the country he was traveling in. So it made sense to him that a man like Starbeau, with a pocketful of money, would likely look for any place where he could spend that money. Based on that line of reasoning, it was a good bet that when Starbeau struck the valley, he followed it south, figuring there had to be some settlements somewhere along the river.

"If he follows the valley far enough, he'll come to Deer Lodge."

"What's that?" Malcolm asked.

"A town," Joe replied. "I've never been there, but I've heard that there's a prison there." He didn't explain that there were very few towns he had ever visited. He didn't like towns.

"A prison?" Pete exclaimed. "Well, damned if Starbeau ain't goin' to the right place."

"I don't reckon he'll turn himself in," Malcolm joked before remembering that Starbeau had murdered his brother and sister-in-law. No one laughed.

Close to nightfall, they came to a small trading post sitting on the bank of the river. There was a crude sign painted on a wide board that proclaimed the establishment *Lowry's Store*. From the look of the freshly milled lumber, it hadn't been there very long. "I don't know about you fellers," Pete said, "but I could use a drink of likker. It's been a while."

"A little snort would go good right now," Malcolm said. Whiskey had been in short supply while camping with the religious party in the mule train. If anyone in the entire camp had anything stronger than cider, they had kept it a secret. "How 'bout it, Joe?"

"Maybe," he said. It had been a lot longer since Joe had imbibed strong spirits, not since a French trapper had shared a jug with him when he was learning English with Father Paul. He had been a little cautious about drinking ever since. The fiery liquid had sneaked up on him after several drinks and robbed him of his reflexes, and he decided he didn't like being drunk. As a result, on the occasion when a drink was offered, which was very seldom, he limited himself to one drink. It was soon after that when his Blackfoot father and mother were killed by Crow Indians, and Joe decided his life path was to live alone in the mountains where there were no thoughts of drink.

*   *   *

Frank Lowry stepped out on the porch of his little store when his dog alerted him that he had visitors. "Evenin', gents," he said in greeting as he looked the three strangers over. His first impression was, *Two white men and an Indian.* "What can I do for you fellers?"

"We could sure use a drink of likker," Pete declared. "We've been ridin' for a couple of days, and need something to cut the dust in our throats."

"Sorry, fellers," Lowry said. "Looks like you're outta luck here. I don't sell whiskey—nothin' but dry goods and staples to the few families that live in the valley." When he saw the obvious disappointment in Pete's face, he said, "I wish I had some myself. I'd offer you a drink. But you're gonna have to go on into Butte to find a saloon. I've got flour and salt, sugar and tobacco, everything else you might need." He took a sideways look at their tall friend dressed in animal skins with his hair in two long braids. "I've even got some bright beads and calico cloth." He covered half his mouth with his hand and whispered in Malcolm's ear, "A little word of advice, friend—ain't no saloon in Butte gonna sell that Injun no whiskey."

Although Joe heard the comment, he pretended not to. He was proud of the Blackfoot blood in his veins. Malcolm, however, took the word of advice as an insult to a man he had acquired a great deal of respect for. "Listen here, mister, this ain't no Injun. This is Joe Fox, and if it wasn't for him, there's a lotta white folks that wouldn't be alive right now."

Lowry was taken aback. "Hold on, there, friend. I didn't mean no harm. I thought I was doin' you a good turn."

"No harm done," Joe said, stepping in. "Maybe you can do us a good turn at that. We're tryin' to catch up with a feller. Might be he came by here—big feller, ridin' a big dun horse—maybe two weeks ago."

"If it's the one I think it is, I wish he'd stop back by," Lowry said. "He bought a lot of goods—tobacco, sugar, bacon, coffee. He wanted whiskey, too. I wish I'd had some to sell him. He had plenty of money."

"That sounds like our friend," Joe said. "Was his name Starbeau?"

"Mighta been at that," Lowry said, trying to recall.

"Much obliged," Joe said. "How far is it to Butte?"

"Fifteen miles," Lowry replied, then tried to apologize again. "Listen, mister, I didn't mean no harm. Stop in if you're back this way again. I can give you a good price on any supplies you need." He was still talking as they mounted and pulled away from the store. "Hope you catch up with your friend," he called after them.

"Who were you hollerin' at, Frank?" Lowry's wife asked when she came from the living quarters behind the store.

"Two fellers and an Injun that talked like a white man," he said, "lookin' for a friend of theirs."

The three travelers were amazed to find Butte a regular city, something none of them had expected, with several crossing streets and a main street with stores and shops for most anything a person could want to buy. Having never been in a city of any size, Joe was more astonished than his two companions, and could not help but gape openly at the many people scurrying along the busy street like so many ants in a hill. It might have been hard to determine who did the most gaping, however, Joe or the citizens on the busy street. For it was a rare sight these days for the good folk of Butte to see what appeared to be a genuine savage, a throwback to the days before the mining town was civilized. Had it not been for the fact that this Indian riding up the middle of Main Street on a paint Indian pony was accompanied by two white men, there might have been a call for some of the folks to alert the sheriff.

Aware of the stares he was getting in return for his own, Joe's distrust of the white man's town was confirmed. He had no choice but to go on, however. Starbeau's trail led to this place. For the first time since knowing the man, Malcolm sensed a bit of uncertainty in the half-white warrior. He understood at once that Joe was completely out of his element, and it occurred to him that it was an opportunity to repay some of the debt he owed the man. "I'm thinkin' if I was Starbeau, ridin' into town like we are now," he said, "I'd most likely head for the first saloon I came to." He glanced at Pete to see if his brother-in-law had picked up on Joe's sudden confusion.

Pete took a quick glance at Joe, whose gaze had been captured by a mannequin dressed in a woman's lacy frock, complete with parasol. He nodded to Malcolm and said, "I expect that's what he'd do, all right. What do you think, Joe?"

Brought back to the purpose of his visit to the town, Joe immediately agreed. "You're right," he said. Then, seeing the Copper King, he said, "There's one there."

"I could use that drink we were tryin' to get last night," Pete said.

They tied their horses up in front of the saloon and stepped up on the boardwalk. Still staring at everyone who walked by, Joe pulled his rifle out of the sling as he stepped up on the walk. "I doubt you'll need that rifle in here," Malcolm said.

Joe looked at him quizzically. "Well, I ain't gonna leave it out here," he said, looking up and down the street as if expecting to be attacked.

"Joe," Malcolm inquired earnestly, "have you ever been in a town before?"

Joe shook his head. "No, not like this one, not with so many white people." He could not escape his Blackfoot upbringing and the distrust they held for white men.

Malcolm nodded compassionately. "Well, me and Pete have, so we'll help you get the information you're lookin' for. Right, Pete?"

"Right," Pete replied, then asked, "Whaddaya intend to do if we find Starbeau here in town?"

Again, Joe Fox looked puzzled by the question. "Kill him," he replied.

"Well, now," Malcolm hastened to say, "that might be a problem." Whereas the solution the quiet warrior proposed seemed quite biblical—an eye for an eye—the town's law enforcement might see it differently. And Malcolm knew he would hate to see Joe go to jail for something that God and everybody else could see needed doing. "You see," Malcolm tried to explain, "they have lawmen here whose job it is to bring murderers like Starbeau to justice. They don't just let everybody take the law into their own hands."

Joe thought that over for only a second before commenting, "I don't see how they can stop me."

"Dammit, Joe," Malcolm responded, losing his patience, "you gun a man down in the streets and they'll throw you in jail for the rest of your life. It don't matter if the man deserved killin' or not. And if there's one thing I know about you, it's that you won't do so good locked up."

Joe thought about it for a few moments before responding. "Starbeau killed your brother and his wife, and you know what he did to Callie. He deserves to be killed. It ain't no business of the people in this town."

"They'll make it their business," Pete finally interjected. "White folks live by laws, and Butte's a law-abidin' city now."

"It's a dumb way to live," Joe said.

"Me and Pete are just tryin' to keep you from spendin' the rest of your life locked up in a little cell, away from your mountains," Malcolm pleaded. "Listen, why don't we just try to find out if he's in town? If he is, we can maybe get the sheriff to arrest him, and they'll take care of his punishment."

"What if we see him, and he shoots me?" Joe asked.

"Well, then you can shoot him," Pete answered.

"That don't make no sense to me," Joe said. "If I shoot him, the sheriff will lock me up. But if he shoots me, I can shoot him? Why can't I just shoot him and be done with it?"

Malcolm and Pete exchanged frustrated glances; then Pete answered, "I don't know. You just can't."

Joe could see the frustration he had caused in his two companions, so he said, "I'll do what you say. When we find him, we'll go get the sheriff. Okay?" They both nodded, relieved. *If we find him, I'll kill him,* Joe thought to himself.

"What the hell . . . ?" the bartender exclaimed when he saw the three strangers walk into the saloon. Amazed, he stood gawking at them as they approached the bar.

"Howdy," Malcolm said. "We'd like a shot of your good whiskey and maybe a little information."

Looking Joe up and down for a long moment, the bartender finally responded, "In the first place, we don't serve no Injuns in here, and in the second place, I'm gonna have to tell you to take that rifle outside."

By that time, all of the saloon's patrons had discovered the wild-looking customer at the bar. "Better give him some firewater, Tom, before he scalps you," someone called out from a table near the back. The comment brought a laugh from the others, especially since Tom was bald as a bedpost.

Joe turned to gaze out across the barroom, his rifle held casually in one hand. His eyes, cold as black ice, seemed to challenge each man individually. The noisy room suddenly grew as silent as a tomb as each man there seemed to sense the potential for chain lightning to strike if the wrong word was said. After a few moments, Joe turned back to the bartender. "I don't want any of your *firewater*," he said calmly. "Give my friends the whiskey they asked for."

The bartender said nothing, but hastened to set two shot glasses on the bar and fill them. Pete and Malcolm both tossed their drinks down and asked for another. The bartender complied, again without comment. "These are on me, Pete," Malcolm said, and tossed the money on the bar. Feeling the respect gained thanks to the mere appearance of Joe Fox, he said, "Now, we're lookin' for a friend of ours name of Starbeau—big feller—you seen him?"

"Can't say as I have," Tom answered, his eye never leaving Joe Fox's face. "Any of you fellers know somebody named Starbeau?" he asked. No one answered.

"Much obliged then," Malcolm said. "That's all we wanted to know." With every eye upon them, they walked out to the street again.

Behind them, the noisy saloon came to life again. "Man, I didn't think there were any wild ones like that within fifty miles of here," one of the patrons said to Tom. "Reckon we oughta go tell the sheriff there's a wild Indian roaming the streets?"

"Nah," Tom replied. "I reckon they didn't do no harm, but I'm just glad as hell that Injun didn't want a drink."

As far as Joe was concerned, the visit to the saloon accomplished nothing. There was no way of knowing how many strangers had been in the Copper King during the past few weeks, big and small, and it was unlikely anybody would have remembered Starbeau's name if he had given it. He relayed these thoughts to Malcolm and Pete when they returned to their horses. They couldn't deny the possibility, but persuaded Joe to try a couple more saloons. There were plenty in town to choose from, and if Starbeau spent any time at all in Butte, surely someone would remember him. After all, they argued, he was one to leave an impression. It then occurred to Joe that the first place he should have checked was the stables. If Starbeau had spent any time at all in Butte, he would have to stable his horse. A young boy who stopped to gawk at the *wild man* gave them directions to the nearest stable.

"Big feller," Nate Lewis responded, "ridin' a big ol' broad-chested dun. I remember him." He paused to prop his pitchfork against a stall. "Left his horse with me for three nights—paid good money, too. He rode outta here day before yesterday." Like the patrons in the Copper King, Nate took a good long look at the tall Indian standing behind Malcolm.

"You recall his name?" Malcolm asked.

"Not right off. Started with an *S*, Starman or somethin'. Shorty Wesson over at the Miner's Chance might know. The big feller spent a lot of time over there."

"Starbeau?"

"Yeah, that sounds about right," Nate said. "Whaddaya lookin' for him for?"

"We're just some friends of his," Malcolm answered, "and we heard he was in town."

"Did he say where he was headin'?" Joe asked.

Nate eyeballed the menacing figure dressed in animal skins, a look of astonishment on his face, as if surprised Joe spoke to him in English. "Why, no, he didn't say which way he was goin'."

Joe nodded and Malcolm said, "Much obliged." They turned to leave.

When they had almost reached the front door of the stable, Nate called out behind them, "He said he'd be back in a day or two."

"Much obliged," Malcolm repeated, and exchanged glances with Joe. When they reached their horses, Malcolm suggested that it might be a good idea if they sought out the sheriff now.

"Not yet," Joe replied softly but emphatically. "Maybe we'll talk to Shorty at the Miner's Chance."

"All right," Malcolm said, "but why don't you let just me and Pete go in this time?" He paused a moment. "Have you got any white man's clothes?" The look on Joe's face was answer enough.

"You know," Pete said, "I've been thinkin' about this thing—about talkin' to the sheriff. What makes you think he's gonna take our word for it that Starbeau done all them things? He don't know us from Adam's housecat. And he might not give a shit about somethin' that happened up at Missoula Mills."

"Well, I don't know," Malcolm sputtered. "We're just tryin' to keep the law offa Joe's back." In fact, he had no answer to Pete's question. A faint smile crossed Joe's lips. Those were his thoughts on the issue all along, and the reason he had never changed his mind to settle with Starbeau himself.

The visit with Shorty Wesson produced positive information. Shorty was quick to say he certainly remembered Starbeau, a big man with a big thirst, and apparently plenty of money to satisfy that thirst. He had rented a room upstairs over the bar for two nights and paid in advance. According to Shorty, Starbeau said he'd be back, to hold his room for him. The question now was what to do while awaiting Starbeau's return. There was no decision to be made by Joe regarding where he would wait. He had no money for stables, so he would make his camp outside of town in the hills, and during the day, he would select a spot where he could watch the goings and comings at Nate's stable.

The decision for Pete and Malcolm was more complicated than Joe's. Now that they had arrived in Butte, they knew their way home, and no longer needed Joe to guide them. They camped with him on that first night and Pete spent a portion of the evening arguing with Malcolm about the wisdom of getting involved in what might develop into a serious gunfight. He understood his brother-in-law's desire for vengeance. Even if they found Starbeau and came out on top, there was still a good possibility of getting locked up by the law. It had been a long winter for them, away from their families back east. They had fought both the weather and the Indians, and lost family members and friends, but there was an obligation to return home to the folks who had passed the winter without them. They longed to see the monster Starbeau receive his just deserts, but they wondered whether they were pushing their luck a bit too far to stay and be a part of Joe's plan for justice. It was Pete's insistence that Joe would likely run Starbeau to ground and settle up for all of them that finally swayed Malcolm to his line of thinking. They announced their decision to Joe over the evening campfire.

Feeling as though they were deserting a friend, Malcolm broached the subject. "Joe, me and Pete have been talkin' it over and we think it's way past time that we got ourselves back home to take care of our families. We're still lookin' at a month and a half or two months before we get home, if we start tomorrow."

"I think that's a good idea. I 'preciate you helpin' me," Joe said, referring to the two saloons and the stable where they did most of the talking. "Those fellers in the Copper King looked like they'd like to take a shot at me."

"There ain't no hard feelin's about us takin' off before you get settled with Starbeau, is there?" Pete asked. "Because if there is—"

"There ain't," Joe interrupted before he could finish. "Starbeau is for me to take care of, and I don't reckon I need any help with that." He didn't tell them that he was glad they had decided to leave. He worked better alone, and he was already concerned about having to look out for the two of them. So it was a light air that hung over the camp on that evening.

The next morning Malcolm and Pete were up early, packing their saddlebags, getting ready to start out to the southeast on a course that would eventually take them to the Yellowstone. At Pete's insistence, Joe accepted a gift of an extra bag of coffee beans and a box of .44 cartridges. "Put one of these in Starbeau's ass," he said.

Joe smiled and nodded. "I'll ride with you to the edge of town." They were good men, he thought, so he decided to make sure they started out in the right direction. At the edge of town, he pulled the paint over at the bank of the river. "I hope your trip back to your families is a good one."

They both pulled their horses up beside his and shook hands. "Take care," Malcolm said. "That Starbeau is a dangerous son of a bitch." Joe nodded in acknowledgment.

"You watch your back," Pete offered as he shook Joe's hand.

"I will," Joe replied. "You watch your'n. There's still some stray bands of Sioux and Crow hangin' around the Yellowstone." He reined back on the paint when the horse started to follow along behind them, and watched them until they were out of his view. Then he turned around and went back to keep an eye on the stable.

Chapter 14

Joe Fox was not the only person keeping an eye on one of Butte's businesses. For the past morning and night, Starbeau had kept vigilance on a small bank on the northeast side of Butte. He still had a large portion of the two hundred and fifty dollars he had stolen from Bradley Lindstrom, but judging by the rate he was spending, he was going to need a lot more. And the little Miner's Bank of Butte was the perfect solution to his problem. Most of the time while he had watched it, there were only two people there, and one of them was a woman. The building was sitting in a grove of trees by itself, offering cover for anyone with a notion to rob it.

After a night on a creek bank from which he had set up his lookout, he satisfied himself that no one ever came by to check on the bank. It was almost too easy. He decided he would go back to the Miner's Chance for one more night of drinking and maybe a turn with a whore, and hit the bank as soon as they opened the following morning. Just after sunrise, he rode up to the stable and dismounted.

Surprised to see someone so early, Nate Lewis came

from the tack room when he heard the dun snort. Seeing who it was, he said, "Good mornin'. You're gettin' in mighty early this mornin'. You musta been ridin' all night." He took hold of the dun's bridle while Starbeau stepped down. "There was some fellers lookin' for you just yesterday."

This caught Starbeau's attention at once. He paused, his hands still on the saddle horn. "Who was it?" he asked.

"Said they was friends of yours," Nate said, "three fellers, two white and one that looked like an Injun."

Starbeau froze for a long second while a sensation akin to a bolt of lightning shot up his spine. He looked quickly over his shoulder toward the open door he had just entered. Then, without a word, and barely a glance at Nate, he stepped back up in the saddle, hauled the reins around, and left the astonished stable owner standing there scratching his head. At the door, he hesitated before riding out into the open street. He might guess the identity of the two men with him, but he was dead sure the Indian was Joe Fox.

There were very few men Starbeau had encountered in his entire life that he was wary of, and none at all that he actually feared—with the exception of Joe Fox. Starbeau's oversized hulk and fearsome features were usually enough to make most men hesitate to cross him. Consequently, he was not obliged to participate in many face-to-face, man-to-man encounters. Over the past few years he had killed one less than an even dozen, counting women and children, most of them while their backs were turned. If he ever got the chance, he would kill Joe Fox the same way. But he was not eager to face the tall, lean man of the mountains. Joe Fox was different from anyone Starbeau had ever come across before—a cold, emotionless killer who seemed unfamiliar with fear. He swallowed hard when he remembered the merciless eyes that gazed down at

him while he lay wounded and helpless under Joe Fox's
rifle, the muzzle looking as large as a cannon when it
hovered barely inches over his face. He thought he
was a goner, and would have been—no doubt about
it—had not Lindstrom stepped in to prevent it. He
survived that day, and it taught him a lesson where the
dangerous half-breed was concerned—as you would
with a rattlesnake, it was best to avoid him. And that
was just what he had in mind to do on this occasion.

He changed his plans for a night of drinking and
whoring now that the menacing shadow of the half-
breed hunter was on his trail. It would be too much of
a risk. His mind was working furiously as he rode up
the busy street, his eyes shifting constantly from side
to side. The street was filled with people coming and
going in and out of the shops, but he had no confidence in the thought that it was too public for Joe Fox
to take a shot at him. His intuition told him to run
now, get the hell out of town, and keep riding. But the
thought of easy pickings at the isolated little bank on
the northeast side of town caused him to hesitate. The
temptation to really bankroll himself was too much to
pass up. His decision was made. He would hole up on
the creek bank, the same spot where he watched the
bank before. At just before closing time he would rob
it, and head for the mountains. He had to assume that
Joe Fox would check on the stable again, and Nate
would tell him that he had left town right away that
morning. *He won't know which way I went*, Starbeau
thought, *and if I'm lucky, he'll head out for Bozeman or
somewhere on the main road.* Satisfied then that he should
be able to avoid Joe Fox, he rode on out of town to
await closing time.

Joe rode up to the stable and dismounted, having
decided it wouldn't hurt to check with the owner to
make sure Starbeau hadn't ridden in early to stable his

horse. Nate Lewis was in one of the stalls near the back, raking out some wet hay. "Mornin'," Joe said.

Unaware that Joe had walked up behind him, Nate jumped like he had been struck. "Goddamn!" he exclaimed. "You scared the bejesus outta me!" The sight of the ominous-looking man in animal skins suddenly looming behind him did little to put his mind at ease even then.

"Sorry," Joe said. "I was in here before with two other fellers."

"Oh, I remember you," Nate replied without hesitation. *It ain't likely I'd forget*, he thought. "That feller you were lookin' for, the one you said was a friend of yours, he was here early this mornin', but he lit out when I told him you fellers asked about him."

"Don't reckon he said where he was goin'."

"He didn't say nothin', not a mumbly word," Nate responded, his eyes wide with excitement now that he was beginning to get the picture. "Didn't look like he was too eager to see you."

Joe paused for a moment to consider what he had just been told before saying, "Much obliged," and turning to go, leaving Nate scratching his head for the second time that morning.

There was a new set of problems now. Starbeau knew that he was being trailed. Maybe he hightailed it out of town right away, or maybe he was waiting in ambush somewhere, hoping to get a shot at Joe. Butte was a sizable city. There were many places to hide. *Maybe he ran and maybe he didn't*, Joe thought, *but I gotta be sure he ain't holed up here somewhere*. He decided he would have to search everyplace he reasonably could, hoping Starbeau was still in town, because he had no way of knowing which way he ran if that was the case. "Might as well start with the Miner's Chance," he muttered to the paint.

* * *

While Joe headed toward the saloon, Nate Lewis waited at the stable door, watching until the tall hunter was safely out of sight. Then he kicked his heels into the sides of his horse and left the stable at a gallop, headed for the sheriff's office. Upon reaching it, he burst into the office to find Deputy Jim Blackburn sitting at the desk. "Where's Pedersen?" he gasped.

"Sheriff Pedersen's gone fishin'," Blackburn replied. "He left me in charge. Whaddaya want, Nate?"

"There's just somethin' I think you oughta know," Nate started. "May be trouble and may not, but it sure looks like somebody's lookin' to kill somebody." He went on to tell Blackburn about the visitors to his stable. "That one that looks like an Injun, he looks like he ain't been told that all the wild Injuns has been run outta this valley."

"I expect he might be the same jasper that Tom Branch said came in the Copper King yesterday," the deputy said. "Ain't much I can do about it, if they ain't broke no laws yet. Tom said he didn't sell him no whiskey, so he ain't done nothin' yet."

"I'm just tellin' you that he was a pretty dangerous-lookin' feller. Thought you'd wanna know."

"I appreciate it, Nate. I'll have a little look around— see if I can find him—maybe find out what he's doin' in town—you know, just to let him know we've got an eye on him."

Shorty Wesson paused when the two men he was talking to at the bar were apparently distracted. He turned to follow their gaze to the front door and immediately understood what had caught their attention. "Well, forevermore," he whispered. "Would you look at that?" The three men stared openly at the stranger as he walked straight up to the bar. Shorty was about to tell him that he could not be served any alcohol, but Joe spoke first.

"Man, name of Starbeau, has he been in today?"

"Well, now," Shorty replied, "who wants to know?" This was the second time in as many days that some-one came in asking about Starbeau. Shorty felt a sense of obligation to protect his customers' privacy, and Starbeau was certainly a good customer.

Joe laid his rifle up on the bar in front of him. He was in no mood to bandy words with the bartender. "I do," he said. "Has he been in here today?" His tone was notice enough that he had no patience for evasive games.

The two patrons took a couple of steps back at the sight of the weapon resting dangerously close to them, fearful that the imposing stranger might be as wild as he appeared to be. Shorty found his tongue quickly as well. "No, mister, he ain't been in for a couple of days."

"He's got a room upstairs," Joe said, remembering what Shorty Wesson had told them before. "Maybe he's up there."

"I told you he ain't here. He wanted me to hold the room for him, but he ain't come back. It's just an empty room."

"What number?" Joe asked.

Shorty was beginning to get flustered by the brass of the strange rifleman. "Like I said, he ain't here."

Joe's hand tightened on the Winchester. "I ain't got time to waste with you," he threatened.

"Number seven, end of the hall," Shorty blurted. "But there ain't nobody in any of 'em right now."

"Much obliged," Joe said and headed for the stairs.

Bolting up the steps, three at a time, he almost col-lided with one of the ladies who worked the upper floor, a lusty woman of questionable age and obvious character. She stepped to the side to let him pass, gap-ing in her astonishment. "Where are you goin' in such a hurry, honey?" she called after him. When he ignored her, she shrugged and continued down the stairs. At the bottom, she found Shorty and the two patrons still staring at his back as he gained the top. "What's he lookin' for?" she asked. "If it's a woman, I'd take him on right now. It'd be like gettin' rode by a mountain lion."

"Trouble is what I expect," Shorty replied. "Go get the sheriff. Tell him there's a wild Indian on the warpath."

Upstairs, Joe worked his way down the hall, opening each door he passed. All the rooms were empty, just as Shorty had said. When he got to number seven, he paused a bit longer, making sure there was no evidence that Starbeau had checked out. There were two more rooms beyond seven. They were occupied by women with two beds in each room, and were obviously their living quarters. The guest rooms apparently served as their places of business. There was no one in number eight and three women in number nine, seated on the beds, involved in a spirited conversation that went dead silent when he opened the door. He hurriedly closed the door before there was time for comment.

Shorty had not lied. If Starbeau had been there before, he was long gone now. Considering the probability that the bartender might have sent for the law while he was searching the rooms, he went back in number seven again. After a quick look around again just in case he missed something on his earlier visit, he went to the window. As he had figured, there was a porch below on the first floor. Slipping his rifle strap over his shoulder, he opened the window and lowered himself out to arm's length. With his fingertips holding on to the windowsill, his feet were only about five feet from the porch roof. He dropped, landing on the shingled roof like a cat. Running across the wide roof, he made his way to the far front corner, where his horses were tied below. He rode off up the street as Jim Blackburn was running up the steps inside.

He had covered a good portion of Main Street before Blackburn caught up with him. Darting in and out of the saloons and stores, asking if anyone had seen a big man called Starbeau, his trail was not hard for Blackburn to follow, for there were startled folks coming out of the buildings behind him to gape at him as he proceeded along the street.

When he came out of the Cup and Saucer, Blackburn was waiting for him. "Hold on there, mister," the deputy ordered. "Just what in the hell do you think you're doin'?"

Joe stopped and studied the lawman for a few moments before replying. "Mindin' my own business, I reckon."

"Maybe you better come with me," Jim said.

"Why?" Joe asked. "Where are you goin'?"

"Why?" Jim echoed, perplexed. "Because I'm the law in this town, that's why. Maybe you'd better hand over that rifle, too."

"I haven't broken any of your laws," Joe insisted. "Is it against the law to look for someone?" When Blackburn foundered for a moment, unsure whether he was involved with a lunatic or not, Joe continued. "I'll not hand my rifle over to you or any man. Now go about your business and let me go about mine."

"Mister," Jim said, silently cursing the sheriff for going fishing this week, "you look and talk like a white man. But dressed up like an Injun like that, you're upsettin' the folks around here. Just what are you aimin' to do?"

"I told you, I'm lookin' for someone, and if you don't mind, I'm in a hurry."

Blackburn was not satisfied to let it go at that. "What are you plannin' to do when you find him?"

Before Joe could answer, a man came charging down the street on foot, yelling at the top of his lungs. "The bank!" he yelled. "Somebody robbed the bank! Wallace Tolbert's been shot!"

There was no time for Deputy Jim Blackburn to deal with a lunatic dressed like a Blackfoot warrior. He immediately ran to intercept the citizen spreading the alarm. "Where?" he yelled. "Which bank?"

The excited man stopped when he saw it was the deputy. Panting for breath, he said, "Miner's Bank! Mr. Tolbert's shot dead, I think. Marci Jessop's hurt. She got cracked on the head!"

"All right," Blackburn responded. "Run on over to Doc Murphy's. Tell him what you told me." Forgetting Joe, he started running toward the corner.

Joe climbed on his horse and followed along behind the deputy. He had a strong hunch that Starbeau might have had something to do with the bank holdup. If he guessed right, he might be able to pick up his trail.

When he arrived at the bank, right on Blackburn's heels, there was already a small crowd of spectators gathered. He dismounted and walked to a window on the side of the building where he could see and hear what was going on inside. He saw a body lying face-down on the floor, and a young woman sitting on the floor with her back against the wall. She was bleeding from a scalp wound and the blood had left a scarlet trail down her neck and stained her collar and blouse. Another woman was at her side, trying to comfort her.

"All right," Jim Blackburn ordered when he walked in, "all you folks go on outside. There ain't nothin' for you to see in here." The half dozen or so who had come inside to gawk slowly shuffled toward the door. Some of them, as Joe had done, found a window to peer through. "You can stay, Mrs. Stancil," the deputy said to the woman comforting Marci Jessop. "The rest of you, get on outside."

Turning his attention to the wounded girl, Blackburn said, "I've already sent for Doc Murphy, Marci. He oughta be here pretty quick." He glanced around him before continuing, taking in the signs of damage to the cage and counter before questioning Marci. "Tell me what happened, Marci. How many were there?"

With her head aching as if her skull was broken, the girl did her best to keep from crying as she answered Blackburn's questions. "There was only one man," she managed. "He kicked the front door open just as Mr. Tolbert was locking it and said to give him the money in the vault. He told me not to scream, but I couldn't help it, I was so scared, and that's when he hit me. I don't know what it was he hit me with—the rifle he was holding, I guess. I didn't remember anything for a few minutes, I reckon. The next thing I do remember was hearing a gunshot." She started to tear up again. "That's when he shot Mr. Tolbert."

"What did he look like?" Blackburn asked.

"He was big, a great big man."

"You think you would recognize him if you saw him again?"

"Yes. I didn't see his face. He had a bandana tied around his face, but I'd recognize him. He looked like a big bear."

The deputy paused for a few moments, trying to think of what else he should ask. "Which way did he go after he left the bank?" he finally asked.

"I don't know," Marci said. "I couldn't see where he went. I was too scared."

Unable to think of anything else to ask her at the moment, Blackburn stepped aside when Doc Murphy walked in. While the doctor examined the wound in Marci's scalp, the deputy pondered his next move, wishing anew that the sheriff wasn't out of town. He decided that the thing to do was to form a posse to go after the bank robber. He just wished that he knew in

which direction to start. He needed a tracker, and that
meant Burt Conroy. He'd send somebody to fetch Burt.

While Blackburn was trying to get his priorities in
order, Joe had already seen all he needed to know.
There could be little doubt that the man who had
robbed the bank and killed the owner was Starbeau.
While more spectators showed up as word spread
about the brazen daylight robbery, Joe led his horses in
front of the bank building and looked around him to
get the lay of the land. Drawn to the crime at the bank,
few of the spectators cast more than a curious glance
in his direction as he stood looking across the road at
the grove of trees and what appeared to be a creek beyond. It seemed to be the logical place to start scouting, so leading his horses, he walked slowly across the
road, holding to a line between the front door of the
bank and a small opening in the trees.

As he walked, he searched the ground around him.
Soon he found what he had anticipated. On the other
side of the road, he saw the clear boot prints of a very
large man, telling him that Starbeau had left his horses
and gone to the bank on foot. For Joe's natural eye, it
was not difficult to piece the picture together. There
were many tracks on the bank of the creek, some older
than others, but all recent. Starbeau had evidently spent
some time there before this day. It was just a matter of
finding the tracks that led away from the creek, and he
thought he had found them until he stopped to consider. The trail led back toward town, which didn't
make sense. But the hoofprints looked fresh, and that
was what almost led him on the wrong trail. They had
to have been made earlier that morning. He told himself that he wasn't giving Starbeau much credit for
being more careful than that.

Back on the creek bank, he searched more closely
until he found a print in a rocky slide next to the wa-

ter, and he knew that Starbeau had ridden into the creek, hoping not to leave tracks. He hadn't bothered to hide his footprints when he ran from the bank, but from this point on, he was intent upon leaving no trail at all. He was almost successful. Joe searched the banks of the creek carefully, upstream and down, on both sides, with no sign of exit from the water. After spending the biggest part of what was left of the afternoon scouring the bank, he had a stroke of luck. There were several places along the creek where rocks protruded down to the water. He had considered them all as possible points of exit, but found no tracks beyond them. As the afternoon light started to fade away, something caught his eye. It was not a hoofprint, merely a slash in the dirt at the edge of a flat rock some sixty yards upstream from the point where Starbeau had entered the water. On closer inspection, he decided it was possibly made when a hoof missed solid footing on the rock and slipped off the edge, scraping a small scar in the bank. It wasn't much to go on, but there wasn't anything else, so he paused to take a look at the possible lines of escape. There were only two that seemed reasonable choices to Joe. Starbeau could have continued on down the narrow valley, following the creek, or he could have ridden down a heavily wooded draw that would eventually lead to a line of low mountains covered with pines and spruce. He looked toward the hills and the tall forest of lodgepole pines on the lower slopes and thought, *That's where I'd head if I was trying to lose someone following me.*

The decision made, he went at once to verify his hunch while there was still enough light to look for sign. A small game trail led up the center of the draw where a dense stand of fir trees was already turning the scant daylight still filtering through the branches into night. This would be the obvious path to take if one was in a hurry, so he led his horses along the trail while he carefully searched for a hoofprint that would tell him he was on the right track.

In the rapidly fading light, he could not come up with a single print. He was reluctant to blame it on the lack of light, for he felt he should have been able to see some prints left by two horses even if it was almost dark. Had he guessed wrong? Maybe Starbeau chose to follow the creek south, after all, with the intention of taking the least obvious escape route. Joe pondered the possibility for a moment. It didn't make sense. If Starbeau followed the creek, it would lead him back to the south end of town. *And that sure as hell doesn't make sense*, he thought. He wondered then if he had been mistaken about the slash in the creek bank by the rock. Maybe it wasn't made by a horse's hoof at all, but misinterpreted because of a lack of solid sign. Now he was frustrated with himself. Starbeau wasn't smart enough to ride off leaving no trail to follow. Already hours behind Starbeau, Joe decided he had no choice but to make camp for the night and pick up the trail in the morning. He had to find some sign that told him he was on the right track, knowing that if he continued on hunches and intuition alone, there was a very good possibility that he would end up wandering aimlessly through the Montana mountains.

He went back to the creek to make his camp where there was water for the horses and a little grass for grazing. After building a fire, he settled in with some coffee and deer jerky for his supper. Thoughts turned from the man he hunted to the last night he had camped in the cottonwoods near the Clark's Fork River. He could still feel the touch of her body close to his, and her arms locked tightly around his neck. Usually when thoughts of Callie came to him, he tried to quickly dispense with them, fearful of letting his mind wander impossible trails. But on this night he permitted the thoughts to linger as he openly considered the possibility that the slender young girl had a deeper feeling for him beyond that of her rescuer. He had nothing to offer a woman that one would consider a promising future. He was at home in the forest, as deep in the mountains as he could get. He knew nothing of tilling the soil or raising farm animals. His ways were the way of the bow and rifle. He grunted in disgust. "Why do I care, anyway? She is gone now, gone to Oregon, and I've got a job to do here." He decided to put thoughts of Callie out of his mind, but it was a long time before she actually released his mind and let him sleep.

Under the same full moon, Callie lay awake, her mind filled with a plethora of thoughts and questions that lacked satisfactory answers. Since she had been returned to her friends and family, her days had been restless and uncertain. Although her parents and their friends told her that she was not to blame for what had happened to her, still she could not escape the curious glances from the other members of the congregation. Most of them found it extremely hard to look directly into her face when talking to her, as if her disfigured cheeks and jaw displayed the mark of the devil. There was only one person who looked into her eyes, seeing past the scars to her soul, and he was gone from her life forever. She wished now that she had told him she loved him. It may have reviled him, but she knew he would have been kind enough not to show it. She had waited all her young life to tell some special someone that she loved him, and she knew now that the opportunity would never come.

Tomorrow the congregation would bid farewell to the Missoula Valley, and begin the long journey to the Oregon country and the Willamette Valley, God willing. It was to be an arduous journey with many mountains to cross, and when they reached the Willamette, she would be a world apart from the one person she trusted above all others. She sighed and pulled her blanket up over her shoulders. Tomorrow was going to be a difficult day, but even in her young years, she knew that life didn't give a person many choices.

Chapter 15

As soon as it was light enough to see, he was saddled up and back on the game trail that led up the wooded draw. The only sign he could discover were tracks he had left the night before, but he was still not ready to abandon the trail. Leaving his horses to wait for him on the game trail, he climbed up through the fir trees on the side of the draw, knowing the tracks were there— he just had to find them. About seventy-five feet up the steep slope, he came upon them. Due to the steepness of the side of the draw, Starbeau had been unsuccessful in hiding his tracks and might have found it useless to even try. For they were distinct in the soft topsoil of the fir forest floor, leaving long slashes in the steepest places as the horses slipped and stumbled. *He couldn't make any progress up here*, Joe thought. *He's bound to have come back to the trail at the bottom.* Without wasting any more time on the side of the draw, Joe scrambled back to the bottom to retrieve his horses. Stepping up on the paint, he followed the game trail up the draw, and eventually he came to a point where two shod horses came down from the side and struck the trail where it fanned out at the base of a mountain.

It was easy to picture the hulking fugitive as he had woven his way up through the forest of firs and lodgepole pines, riding around large outcroppings of rock, as he climbed higher and higher. The careless trail of hoofprints and broken branches testified to the reckless pace he set for his horses in an attempt to put as much distance as possible between himself and anyone following him. Once Joe reached the shoulder of the mountain, he found the trail had leveled out and led around it toward the east slope. From there, it started descending toward a narrow valley to the north. It was Joe's guess that Starbeau had no specific direction in mind, but was simply running, hoping to disappear in the wilderness. Reaching the bottom of the mountain, Joe came upon a wide stream that had been hidden from the mountaintop by a thick canopy of trees.

Taking advantage of the opportunity to once again disguise his trail, Starbeau had ridden into the stream, causing Joe to slow down and carefully walk the paint up the stream, searching for tracks leaving the water. Already losing time due to the necessity to quit the trail the night before, he could only grumble over further delay in running Starbeau to ground. He followed the stream for over a quarter mile, scanning both banks intensely with no sign of tracks. With reluctance, and a generous portion of impatience, he turned his horse around and retraced his steps, grudgingly admitting that the belligerent bully had outsmarted him and reversed his direction in the stream. Sure enough, he had ridden no more than two hundred yards past the point where Starbeau had first entered the stream when he saw the tracks leaving the water. Starbeau had made no attempt to hide them—two sets of prints clearly led across a soft bank and across the valley toward the neighboring mountain.

Joe nudged the paint with his heels and the horse immediately reared up on his hind legs and screamed at almost the same time a shot rang out. Taken completely by surprise, Joe almost came out of the saddle. In rapid succession, two more shots ripped into the wounded horse, one in the withers, and one in the neck—both shots intended for his master. Joe just managed to pull his rifle and tumble from the saddle as the paint went down. He rolled over behind a tree, cocked his rifle and scanned the slope above him, trying to pinpoint the source of the rifle fire. There was nothing to be seen but the dense forest that covered the side of the mountain. Every sound in the valley went silent with the exception of the pitiful whimpering of the paint, causing Joe to feel sick in his gut to have ridden blindly into an ambush that took the life of his horse.

The dying horse made an attempt to get on its feet, but failed. Feeling as though he had caused the death of a close friend, Joe sadly rolled over on his side and aimed his rifle at the paint's head. Pulling the trigger, he instantly ended the horse's suffering. As soon as he fired, his shot was answered by a series of shots from the ridge above him, the bullets snapping through the branches of the pines and ricocheting off the rocky streambed. *Dammit*, he thought, still furious with himself for his carelessness, for he had assumed that Starbeau was at least a half day ahead of him. *He knows where I am, but I still don't know where he is.*

He looked for his packhorse and saw the black Indian pony about twenty yards away, standing in a small opening in the trees. "Come here, boy," he called and whistled. But the horse stood there and pawed the ground with its hoof, apparently confused. Joe tried calling it several times more with the same result. *Damn hard head*, he thought. *I'm going to have to go to him. I wonder just how good Starbeau has me pinpointed.* To test it, he slid over toward the opposite side of the tree and started to peer around the trunk. Another shot

immediately rang out from above, causing him to duck
back behind the tree trunk. He tried once more to call
the horse and was met with the same result. His concern was that the horse was an easy target, standing in
the open, and if he didn't get it to move, he was going
to be on foot. There was a lull in the shooting so he
figured Starbeau was reloading. Knowing he could not
afford to remain pinned down behind the tree, he didn't
take time to think about it. Leaping to his feet, he made
a run for the stream behind him. Running as hard as
he could go, he almost reached the edge of the stream
before Starbeau peppered the ground at his heels with
rifle fire. Diving the final few feet, he landed beneath
the bank as .44 slugs zipped over his head. Intent upon
working his way up around the deadly ambush, he
crawled a dozen yards down the stream until he gained
enough solid cover to make another try for the packhorse.

"Damn the stinkin' luck," Starbeau fumed, "Joe Fox."
How, he wondered, had the relentless tracker gotten
on his trail? "Well, don't make no difference now. This
is as far as he's goin'." He crawled over to the other
side of the boulder he had used as a shield in hopes
of getting a clear shot. "The son of a bitch," he complained, cursing Joe for his success in finding cover.
He was gripped by a moment of panic when he could
no longer see where he was. *The son of a bitch is like a
damn snake in the bushes*, he thought, and he was furious for having missed his opportunity to kill him. He
should have been more patient, he told himself, and
waited until the relentless hunter had ridden out into
the center of the clearing. But as soon as he had seen
the head of the paint horse emerge from the bushes
by the stream, he had pulled the trigger. And now the
dangerous half-breed had escaped into the tall pines.

He strained to scan the trees below the ridge. As

yet, there had been no return fire from Joe Fox, just that one shot to finish the paint, which meant he had not spotted Starbeau behind the boulder. Or did it? Starbeau had to consider the possibility that he had been spotted, and Joe Fox was stalking him, maybe making his way up the ridge even now. *Let the damn half-breed come*, Starbeau thought. *It'll be his day to go to hell*. The thought, designed to bolster his courage, had a hollow ring, however, as he was anxiously aware of the nervous sweating in the palms of his hands. "Damn him!" he muttered, remembering the cold merciless eyes that had gazed down at him after he had shot him in the shoulder. And the thought entered his mind that running might be the wiser of his alternatives. At that moment, Joe's black packhorse walked slowly across the clearing below, and Starbeau saw his best option. He brought his rifle up to his shoulder, took careful aim, and pumped three shots into the unfortunate horse, dropping it in the middle of the clearing.

He wasted no time after firing the shots, and ran up the ridge to where his horses were tied. Stumbling drunkenly, as if the devil himself were on his heels, he got a foot in the stirrup and swung his leg over while still fumbling to put his rifle in the saddle scabbard. Kicking the horse repeatedly, he left the ridge at a gallop, crashing through the sparse underbrush, oblivious to the pine limbs that slapped at his face and arms. Down the other side of the ridge he plunged, his horses struggling at breakneck speed to maintain their footing on the uneven slope. His rational mind tried to reason that it was impossible for the relentless hunter to have climbed the other side of the slope in the time he had taken to flee. Even so, he could feel a tingle in the center of his shoulder blades where a bullet might find him at any second.

Starbeau did not let up on his weary horses until reaching the bottom of the mountain, where he was

sure he had put enough distance behind him to rest
them. With his confidence partially restored, he convinced himself that he had taken the sensible route. *If
it was a fight in the open,* he told himself, *it would be a
different thing. But that bastard is as much at home in the
woods as a wolf.* He consoled himself on his decision to
run, saying it was the smart thing to do. *And Max Starbeau ain't never been no damn dummy.* Another thought
caused him to chuckle. *He'll play hell catching up to me
on foot.* His mind completely at ease now with the sure
feeling that he had seen the last of Joe Fox, he climbed
up in the saddle again and walked his horses toward a
narrow canyon between the two mountains facing him.

Separated from his prey by a mountain, Joe was of
another thought. The hunt was not over, merely de-
layed. He recognized the difficulty of catching a man
on horseback while he traveled on foot, but there was
no doubt in his mind that he would eventually track
Starbeau down.

Joe had never located Starbeau's position on the ridge
until after his packhorse was shot, but he managed to
get a glimpse of two horses as they crashed through
the pines, heading for the shoulder of the mountain.
By that time, the range was too far to waste a cartridge, hoping for a lucky shot. He was certain that he
was no longer in danger of getting shot himself, and to
prove it, he walked out into the opening to fetch the
few things from his saddlebags he would need to take
with him. With a mind to travel as light as possible,
he made a backpack with his blanket, and filled it with
cartridges, jerky, flint and steel, and after some delib-
eration, his coffeepot. Pausing then to take one last
sorrowful look at the faithful paint pony, he strapped
his bow and quiver on his shoulder, picked up his rifle, and started up the slope of the ridge toward the
spot where he had last glimpsed Starbeau.

Reaching the boulder that had been Starbeau's shield, he paused only for a second to notice the empty .44 shells lying on the ground before proceeding on toward the spot in the trees where he thought he had seen the fleeing man's horses. He reached the place where the bushwhacker had tied his two horses, and from that point on there was little trouble to follow the trail up toward the shoulder of the mountain.

There were no more sorrowful thoughts over the loss of his horse. His life had been in kinship with the wild creatures of the mountains, where death was but a part of living, and something to be expected, often in random acts of fate. So he was not prone to waste time regretting bad luck. He was on foot, his enemy was on horseback, and it would take a little more time to track him. But track him he would. He pulled his bow off his shoulder, and with it in one hand and his rifle in the other, he set out at a steady jog.

Like a man possessed, Starbeau drove his horses relentlessly, not certain of his way, but with the thought that the town of Helena was somewhere to his north. Finally, when he reached a river that seemed to have carved its way between two steep mountains, he was forced to rest his weary horses for fear he would otherwise be on foot. After a short rest, he started out again, following the river, for the mountains on each side of it seemed too formidable a climb. He pushed the weary mounts onward until darkness threatened to make the travel too treacherous to continue.

He was about to pick a place to camp when a flicker of light through the trees ahead caught his eye. He pulled his horse to a halt and dismounted, pulling his rifle out as he stepped down. The prospect of riding up on a party of Indians did not appeal to him at the present time. He decided to proceed on foot until he could determine just who he had happened upon. But before taking another step, he paused again when he heard a strange noise from the direction of the fire. At first he thought it the mournful buzzing of some insect, or other night creature. A few moments more of the strange twanging sound, and he realized what he was hearing. Grinning, he muttered, "It's a Jew's harp, by damn! And it ain't likely no damn Injun." His spirits lifted now with thoughts of the possibility of hot food and coffee, courtesy of a friendly stranger, he led his horses toward the sound.

Rounding a bend of the river, he saw the campfire, and stopped to assess the situation before making his presence known. It looked like two men, white men as he had figured, one of them was sitting beside the fire with the simple instrument held against his lips and proving fairly handy in stroking a lively ditty. The other was on his feet, dancing a jig to the sound of the homely rhythm. Starbeau's grin grew wider.

"Hello the camp," he called out as he approached the camp. His greeting caused an abrupt halt to the music, as both men scrambled to reach for weapons. "Saw your fire," Starbeau yelled. "I was hopin' that was coffee I smelled. Ain't nobody but me. Didn't mean to scare you."

"Well, come on in a little closer, so we can get a look atcha," the man who had been dancing called back.

Starbeau advanced a few yards closer. "Lemme tell you, I'm mighty glad to see you boys," he exclaimed, practicing his best tone of friendliness. "I ain't ashamed to tell you I'm as lost as a whore in church." He kept a wide smile on his face as he glanced around the camp, noticing the packs and tools near the fire and the horses hobbled near the river. Bringing his attention back to the two men, he said, "My name's Starbeau. I'm on my way to Helena, but I reckon I got off the trail somewhere back yonder."

The two men exchanged glances, then relaxed. "Well, Starbeau, come on in. There's a little coffee left in the pot. My name's Barney Cox." He nodded toward the other man. "He's Will Forney." Forney nodded, and they both looked the big man over as he led his horses into the firelight.

"You can put them horses over by our'n if you want," Forney said. "They look pretty wore out."

"They are wore out," Starbeau said. "I got jumped by some Injuns about ten or twelve miles back that way. Had to run for it."

"Injuns?" Cox exclaimed. "We ain't seen no Injuns around this part of the river since we've been here and there ain't been no talk of any. Awful close to Helena. Most of the Flatheads has moved farther north. Ain't that right, Will?"

"That's right," Will replied. "I don't reckon you've et, have you?"

"Well, for a fact, I ain't," Starbeau replied, "but I wouldn't put you boys out. I've got some bacon in my packs. I'd just appreciate borrowing some of your fire to cook it—maybe cook a little extra if you fellers are still hungry."

Feeling no further need to exercise caution, Barney insisted, "No need to get your grub out. We ain't put our salt pork away yet and the pan's still on the edge of the fire. You go ahead and take care of your horses. They look like they're needin' to get to some grass."

"That's mighty neighborly of you," Starbeau replied, and led his horses over to the riverbank with the others.

Will waited until Starbeau was out of earshot before asking, "Whaddaya think, Barney?"

Barney paused to watch Starbeau for a moment. "I don't know. I reckon he's all right. He's a big son of a bitch, though, ain't he?" He picked up a slab of salt pork and sliced off several thick strips and dropped them in the pan to fry. "He sure is hard on his horses," he commented.

"You say you're headin' to Helena?" Will asked when Starbeau returned and sat down by the fire.

"That's a fact," Starbeau replied. "First light, I'll be on my way."

"Well, if you're gonna keep followin' this river, you ain't never gonna get to Helena," Will said.

Starbeau chuckled. "I told you I was lost. I ain't ever been there before, and I was guessin' that this river might run toward it."

"What you need to do is ride up this river about two miles, till you strike a cross canyon. Follow that canyon north. It'll lead to a valley, and take you right to Helena, but you're still two good days away."

"Well, I'll tell you," Starbeau said, in an attempt to sound sincere, "I do appreciate your help. I feel like I oughta pay you boys a little somethin' for all your help."

"No such thing," Barney replied. "Glad we could help."

Starbeau finished his coffee and bacon and settled back to let it digest. "You know, I've got a bottle of good rye whiskey in my pack. Maybe you fellers would like a little drink."

Barney and Will looked at each other and grinned. "Well, now, that don't sound like a bad idea," Barney said.

The dregs of coffee in the tin cups were replaced with a generous shot of whiskey, a little more in the two partners' cups than Starbeau poured for himself. The talk got more and more casual as the level of whiskey in the bottle dropped, until Starbeau asked what the two of them were doing camped out on the river. A slight pause in the conversation occurred then before Will answered. "Nothin', we're just doin' some huntin'."

Starbeau chuckled. "I seen them picks and shovels over by your packs. What was you huntin'? Gophers?"

There was a long moment of silence then as the partners looked nervously at each other. "We're goin' after elk," Will said. "We always carry some tools with us just in case we need to dig a cave in the riverbank and cache the meat." He knew it was a poor answer, but his mind wasn't quick enough to come up with a better explanation.

"Well," Starbeau said, laughing, "don't make no difference to me, but it looks like you ain't been too lucky so far, or you wouldn't be eatin' pork."

"I reckon that's right," Barney said as he and Will tried to laugh convincingly.

At Starbeau's insistence, they finished the bottle and the burly visitor announced that he was having trouble keeping his eyes open. "I'm turnin' in," he said. "I think I drank too much."

"You ain't the only one," Barney said, shaking his head in an effort to scatter the cobwebs that had gathered in his brain. "Whoa!" he exclaimed when he rose to his feet to stand a bit unsteady for a few moments. "I ain't had that much to drink in a long time."

Experiencing similar problems, Will struggled to his feet and stood laughing at Barney, who was listing a little to one side. "Ain't we a fine pair?" He took a few stumbling steps out of the firelight to relieve himself. Barney stumbled after him and they stood elbow to elbow, both men rocking slowly back and forth, from one foot to the other, emptying their bladders.

Starbeau grinned approvingly and joined them after a few seconds to share their camaraderie in the sheer joy of urinating openly under a starry nighttime sky.

Unlike his two hosts, he was exaggerating his state of drunkenness, however, for he had purposefully spilled a great deal of his on the ground. Finishing with a series of pulsating squirts, the three said good night and retired to their blankets, Barney and Will to surrender almost immediately to their slumber, Starbeau to lie awake, listening for the steady drone of snores that would tell him the camp was his to do with as he wished.

Before taking notice of the picks and shovels, he might have been content to pass the night with the two partners, partake of their generosity, and get directions to Helena. But in his mind, the tools meant digging in the ground for something more interesting than making a hole to cache meat. With the money he stole from Bradley Lindstrom and the thirty-five hundred he had just netted in the bank holdup, he felt he was on a definite winning streak. These boys were hiding something, he felt real sure about that. He figured it was not by chance that they were camped where a fairly busy stream emptied into the river, and he was betting a bottle of good rye whiskey that there was a sluice box not far up that stream.

When the snoring had reached a steady pitch, Starbeau crawled out of his blanket and went to the packs, pausing only a moment to peer down at the sleeping men. *They ain't going nowhere for a while,* he thought, and proceeded to tear open all the packs lying off to one side of the fire. Strewing clothes and utensils about him, he emptied them, finding two small pouches of gold dust. Estimating the two were equally weighted, it was easy to assume that these pouches represented the equal split between the partners. It wasn't much, about fifty dollars' worth, he estimated, unless the pouches were just for show and the real haul was hidden somewhere. That made sense to Starbeau, and he was determined to find the stash.

He pulled a flaming piece of firewood from the fire to use as a torch, and looked around the camp, trying to spot something—a rock, a log, something out of place that might signal a hiding place. He gave up after a few minutes, finding it impossible in the dark. Their gold cache could be any place, in the camp, in the river, the stream. He decided to quit wasting his time. Returning to stand over the sleeping men again, he gazed down at them, making a decision. After a second, he decided that Barney would be the most likely to talk, so he straddled Will and bent low over him, tapping him lightly on his head with the barrel of his pistol. He could have done the job simply without warning, but he preferred to see Will's face when he realized he was about to die. Will, however, was too deep in his drunken sleep to be aroused by the gentle tapping, so Starbeau took the canteen lying beside him and sloshed water on his face. Will immediately came to, sputtering and blinking until opening his eyes wide to stare in confusion at the pistol barrel almost resting on his forehead, and the grinning face of Starbeau above it. Stricken dumb with a horrible paralysis at first, Will started to react, but the pistol went off in his face before he could move.

In no particular hurry, Starbeau moved over then to straddle Barney, who was turning sleepily over on his back, shaken awake by the shot. In the next second, he exhaled forcefully as Starbeau settled his massive weight upon his chest, pushing the air from his lungs. Wheezing noisily as he gasped to get his breath again, Barney tried to rise, confused by the weight that pinned him to the ground, only then realizing what was happening to him.

"Wake up, sleepyhead," Starbeau taunted, the malicious grin in place again. "You got some talkin' to do."

"I'll be damned . . . ," Barney responded and tried to free himself, but found he was helpless under the huge bulk of Starbeau. "Get the hell offa me!" he demanded, then called out for help. "Will! Will!"

"You want Will?" Starbeau mocked. He grabbed a handful of Barney's hair and jerked his head around so he could see his partner's corpse lying near the edge of the firelight, his lifeless eyes reflecting the flames from the campfire. "There he is. I asked him real nice where you boys hid the rest of that gold dust, but he didn't wanna tell me." He jerked Barney's head back so that he could look directly into his eyes. "Now I'm gonna ask you where that dust is."

"There ain't no dust!" Barney cried. "Swear to God there ain't!"

"Now, Barney, you ain't showin' a helluva lot of sense. I figured you'd be smarter than your partner over there. At least he didn't try to tell me there wasn't no gold. I reckon he figured it'd be better to be dead than part with a little bit of dust. Is it worth it to you? I'll tell you what I'll do. Hell, I ain't a greedy man. I'll just take Will's half of the dust, and go on my way. You'll be just as rich as you woulda been. It'll just be me and you partners, instead of you and Will. You do that and I won't have no reason to kill you. Whaddaya say, partner?"

There were no options for Barney Cox to consider. He might as well have a grizzly bear seated on his chest, his arms pinned under Starbeau's knees, his rifle out of reach of his fingertips. He was a doomed man, and smart enough to know that Starbeau was not likely to spare his life if he told him where they had hidden their take from the sluice box. But he knew for sure there was no question of it if he refused to tell. It was a straw thrown to a drowning man. He had no choice but to grasp it. "All right," he said. "I'll show you if you'll promise you won't kill me."

"Hell, yes," Starbeau responded, "I promise." He released him then and picked up his rifle. "You won't mind if I hold on to both rifles till I get my gold, will you?" he asked as if there were any question. "Why, this might be the best partnership you was ever in," he said while cocking Barney's rifle repeatedly until he had ejected all the cartridges and dropped the empty rifle on the ground. "We might wanna team up permanent-like," he went on, both men knowing it was a lie.

Barney got to his feet, his mind a roaring tornado inside his skull, desperately trying to see some way out of his situation, as he dutifully led Starbeau to a boulder the size of a haystack that protruded out over the edge of the water. His hands would not stop shaking and there seemed to be no feeling at all in his legs below his knees. Though he tried as hard as he could to think of some salvation, nothing presented itself except simply running for his life after he showed Starbeau the gold. Maybe the menacing brute would be satisfied and would let him live. A cold numbness spread up his fingertips and into his arms as he pointed to a spot at the base of the boulder.

"Well, dig it outta there, man," Starbeau exclaimed impatiently. "Let's see how well you boys was doin'."

"I need a shovel," Barney replied.

"That ground don't look too hard to me right there," Starbeau said. "I expect you can just dig that out with your hands. Besides, you get hold of a shovel, you might start gettin' crazy ideas about takin' a swing at me. Now, let's get at it."

Barney's hopes sank even deeper. Using a shovel as a weapon was the only plan he could think of in this desperate moment. With Starbeau's rifle leveled at him, he dropped to his knees and began raking away the loose dirt with his hands, praying for God to somehow come to his aid. After only a matter of ten minutes or so, he uncovered a pouch that appeared to be considerably heavier than those found in the packs. "Hot damn!" Starbeau exclaimed when he caught sight of it. "Lemme see that!" Seeing this was his only chance to escape with his life, Barney tossed the pouch toward the edge of the bank. When Starbeau quickly reacted and jumped to keep the pouch from falling in the river, Barney scrambled up from beside the boulder and ran for the woods. Starbeau snatched the pouch from the edge of the bank, then calmly turned and cut Barney down with two shots in his back.

Without bothering to confirm Barney's death, Starbeau went to the packs and picked up a shovel, then returned to dig in the hole Barney had already started. He immediately uncovered a pouch similar to the first and kept digging. Soon he was digging in solid dirt and roots, and he knew the two pouches were all there were. "I reckon that's all the elk meat there is in that cache," he said, laughing at his joke.

Since there were still several hours until sunup, he took his new treasure over by the fire to examine it. What had started out as a questionable day had turned out to be a great one. He had no idea how much his newly gained gold was worth, but he estimated that it was considerable. He was a wealthy man. In addition to this fact was the accumulation of two extra horses to sell, and the satisfaction that he had left Joe Fox far behind him. By the time the bothersome tracker reached Helena, if he followed him that far, Starbeau would be long gone—too long to leave a trail.

After retying the gold pouches, he searched the bodies, starting with that of Will Forney. He found nothing of value, and started to drag it away from the fire circle when he remembered something. Fishing around in Will's vest pockets, he found what he was looking for, the Jew's harp. Smiling broadly, he placed the simple instrument against his lips and with a meaty finger, flipped the spring a few times, producing a series of sharp twangs that was no kin to music of any form. But the irritating noise pleased him, and he kept it up for a while until tiring of it. Dropping the harp in his pocket, he dragged Will's corpse away.

When he went to search Barney's body, he found the man still alive, although paralyzed from a bullet in his spine. When he rolled him over, Barney screamed with the pain, causing Starbeau to start. "Damn," he questioned, "ain't you dead yet?"

Unable to move, but fully aware of the pain throughout his body, the mortally wounded man begged Starbeau to finish him. "Hell," Starbeau responded, "you'll die before long—ain't no sense in wastin' another cartridge." He pulled the Jew's harp from his pocket. "Here, I'll play you a little tune to cheer you up." He taunted the dying man with a few minutes' worth of tortured sounds from the instrument. Pleased with his new toy, he then left Barney with the comforting words that either buzzards or wolves would eventually come along and put him out of his misery. The mournful nonmusical sounds could be heard through the forest as the evil man strolled back to the campfire. He threw a few more limbs on the fire, then turned in to get a little sleep before starting out for Helena in the morning. It would take him two more days, but he was no longer in a hurry.

Chapter 16

Maintaining a steady pace between walking and running, Joe Fox, the adopted son of a Blackfoot warrior, tirelessly ground out mile after mile. Efficiently utilizing the combination of strength and willpower that resulted from years of roaming the highest mountains in the Rockies, he constantly gained on his prey. As he scaled the steep slopes and made his way through forest thick with fir and spruce, he seldom stopped for rest, and only occasionally for food. Such was the determination of Joe Fox.

In mountainous country, he never conceded advantage to a man on horseback, knowing that the horse required longer rest periods than he. Once he reached the valley where Starbeau had followed the river, however, he grudgingly surrendered the advantage to the horse. To make up for it, once it appeared that Starbeau was going to continue to follow the river, he pushed on after nightfall, even though it meant he would be unable to read sign. He didn't know if Starbeau really knew where he was going or not, but he figured he could stay with the river for a long time before he reached a cross canyon where he would be forced to wait for daylight to see if Starbeau turned north to Helena or continued following the river.

Daylight found him still some two miles or more from the cross canyon, but prints he discovered along the riverbank told him that he was still on Starbeau's trail. Rounding a bend in the river, he paused to sniff the wind, for he thought he detected the smell of smoke. Slipping his bow back on his shoulder in order to use both hands on his rifle, he moved cautiously forward, alert for an ambush. It seemed unlikely that Starbeau would have lingered in this place, but Joe could now see that there was a camp of some sort a few hundred feet ahead.

Moving even closer, he saw the source of the smoke on the wind, the dying ashes of a fire, but there was no one about, and no horses that he could see. Then he noticed what appeared to be someone sleeping on the far side of the smoking coals. So he knelt where he was for a while, watching for someone else to enter the scene. While he waited, he noticed the open packs and clothing and supplies scattered upon the ground. Someone had evidently raided the camp, he decided, and he might be waiting for a corpse to move. So he rose to his feet, and with his rifle ready to fire, walked slowly into the abandoned camp.

As he had suspected, the man was dead, shot in the face at point-blank range. *Looks like some of Starbeau's work*, he thought. Planning only a quick look around, he spotted another body beyond a huge boulder by the river's edge. This one was lying in a puddle of blood, and Joe was about to turn away when the eyelids flickered open. The man stared with dull eyes at Joe for a few seconds before begging, "Finish me off."

Surprised, Joe knelt beside the man to do what he could for him, but discovered right away that there was no hope for the unfortunate soul as the pitiable eyes searched his and repeated his whispered request. Joe knew there was no use in speaking words of encouragement. The wounded man knew there was no hope for him, and he was just taking a painfully long time to die. "Who did this?" Joe asked. "Starbeau?" The man nodded painfully, and Joe asked, "Do you know where he's headed?"

Barney slowly nodded again and rasped, "Helena," then begged once more, "Finish it." Understanding, Joe nodded solemnly in response and Barney whispered, "God bless you." Rising to his feet, Joe moved behind him, so he could not see the pistol when he pulled it from his belt. One shot in the back of his head finally laid Barney Cox to rest, easing his dread of still being alive when the vultures arrived to feast on his bones. Joe glanced up to see a couple of buzzards already starting to circle. Wasting no more time, he kicked some dirt on the smoldering campfire and started back on Starbeau's trail, knowing that he was now less than a half day behind the murderer.

Departing the camp, he found the trail even easier to follow, for Starbeau now had four horses leaving tracks. His earnest desire was to overtake the cruel killer before he reached the city of Helena. The thought of his frustration when trying to make sense of the many buildings and people in Butte was still fresh in his mind. His experience in the bustling city also showed him that his appearance prohibited him from moving about unnoticed. The law had almost caused him to lose Starbeau's trail when the deputy stepped in to question him. In view of these factors, Joe decided to gamble on the accuracy of Barney Cox's statement that Helena was Starbeau's destination. Instead of continuing to follow Starbeau's tracks upriver to the cross canyon, he decided to strike out across the mountains with the hope of cutting the killer off before he reached the broad valley and Helena.

He took the first opportunity he came upon to ford

the river and then made his way once again up through the lodgepole pines, using a distant peak as his point of reference, pushing even harder than he had before coming upon the two miners. Gliding doggedly along the many game trails, he chewed a strip of deer jerky when he was hungry while still maintaining his pace. Moving with the soft tread of a mountain lion, he emerged from a stand of spruce trees near the top of a high ridge to startle a buck and two does nibbling at some low plants at the edge of a high meadow. As they bolted away into the forest, he never bothered to think about what an easy shot it would have been for fresh meat. Thoughts of Callie lay heavy on his mind, ever increasing the closer he came to overtaking the brute that caused her so much pain and shame. He would always carry the guilt that none of Callie's torment would have happened if he had killed Starbeau when he first had the chance.

The frightened deer that just bolted caused him to remember the look in Callie's eyes when she had turned to leave his camp on that last night. She would be on her way to the Oregon country now. Hopefully, she would be able to forget this terrible period of her life. Had he thought it appropriate, he might have told her that he would always carry her in his heart. He could not help her to forget, but he could erase the monster that had defiled her from the face of the earth. He had hunted and killed before, man and beast, but he had never before felt the fire in his veins like this except once when he rode against the Crows to avenge the deaths of his mother and father.

He continued on through the day until darkness forced him to stop, the steep mountainsides being too treacherous to travel in the blackness of the thick forest. Coming to a stream near the bottom of a slope, he dropped down exhausted, to quench his thirst and to rest. With thoughts of Callie still on his mind, he fell asleep nonetheless, his body demanding rest, having given all that it could.

Starbeau squinted his eyes against the afternoon sun in an effort to get a better look at the house ahead. Built on a gentle rise beside a creek, it was the first sign of civilization he had come to in the wide valley. He smiled, feeling satisfied that Helena couldn't be far away now. It would be a good time to rest and water his horses, he thought, and maybe get a hot meal for himself. After turning his horses toward the water, he took a long look at the little frame house and the barn and corral behind it. It had the look of a well-run farm. The house was painted and the barn was in good repair. He suddenly took a new interest in the farm when he spied a young girl of about thirteen or fourteen walking from the barn to the house. She paused a few moments when she spotted the man and four horses approaching the creek.

"Good day to ya, little miss," Starbeau called out in his friendliest tone. "I'll just water my horses in the creek, and if your pa don't mind, I'll let 'em rest a spell before I go on to Helena."

"Pa won't mind," the girl replied as she reached the corner of the front porch.

Starbeau stepped down from the saddle and walked closer to the house while the horses drank. "That's mighty neighborly of you," he said. "Is your daddy in the house?"

"No, sir," the girl replied, slightly surprised to see the size of the stranger when he stepped down on the ground. "He took the wagon into town for supplies."

"Is that a fact?" Starbeau responded, the situation becoming more interesting by the moment. Before he could ask any more questions, the door opened and a woman came out on the porch, having heard voices and wondering who her daughter was talking to.

"If you're looking for my husband," Mary Lester said, "he won't be back for a couple of hours or so." She frowned as she looked past him to the horses drinking at the creek. "You must be the man he was talking to about the horses. He wasn't expecting you until tomorrow."

Quick to realize an opportunity when it was freely presented to him, he replied, "Yes, ma'am, I reckon one of us musta got our days mixed up." He glanced at the girl and winked, wondering whether she remembered that he had told her he was just stopping to rest before going on to Helena. She expressed nothing more than a slight frown of confusion. "Well, I sure hate it that I missed him," Starbeau went on.

"Me, too," Mary said. "I know he's needing a couple of horses. He'll hate it he missed you." There was an awkward moment of silence then as he waited for her to remember her manners. "Would you like to sit on the porch for a while and have a cup of coffee? I've got some cold buttermilk Janie can fetch from the creek. I ain't started supper yet, but there's some cold biscuits left from dinner."

"Why, thank you, ma'am. That sure would set good right now. I ain't had much but salt pork lately." He stepped up on the porch to tower over the woman, his eyes roaming over her from head to toe. She looked not a lot different from thousands of frontier women, overworked and prematurely gray, her eyes reflecting the weary look of hard summers and cold winters. If she had been the only choice, he would have been interested. But since she was not, Starbeau decided he preferred the daughter. He turned to glance at the young girl as she walked down to the creek to fetch the buttermilk from the spring box.

Already startled by the frightening appearance of the man up close, Mary instantly felt uneasy about the way his dark eyes followed her daughter. "I don't want to waste your time, Mr. . . ." She paused to let him introduce himself. When he failed to do so, she continued. "I'm sure Paul will come to see you tomorrow."

"Ain't nobody else here? Just you and the girl?" he asked.

"Well," she hesitated, "not right at this moment, but we have a couple of neighbor men that help out— oughta be here at any minute."

Now that there's a lie, he thought as a smile spread wide across his face. "I ain't in no hurry. Maybe I'll wait till your hired hands get here. Maybe they'll wanta look at them horses." He went over to the two chairs at the end of the porch and sat down. "That buttermilk oughta taste real good." It pleased him that she was showing signs of caution. He enjoyed intimidating people, especially women.

She stood for a moment, wishing she had not offered him food and coffee, undecided as to what she should do. It might be that she was giving in to needless fears, but the man had the look of a predator, like a wolf sizing up a lamb. *Oh, Lord*, she prayed, *please let me be wrong about this man.* "I'll go in and see about the coffee," she finally said, thinking of the shotgun over the fireplace.

Janie returned from the creek carrying a large gallon jug. "I'll help Mama," she said as she passed him on the porch and went directly into the house.

"You do that," he replied, a mischievous grin upon his face.

Inside, she startled her mother, who was lifting the shotgun down from the fireplace and almost dropped it when Janie walked in. "Mama, what's wrong?" Janie whispered.

"I don't know," Mary said. "I just wish your daddy was here." She wasn't sure that she wasn't just letting her imagination run wild, and she didn't want to scare the girl if this foreboding feeling of danger was nothing more than baseless fears.

"Mama," Janie whispered, "when he rode up, he said he just wanted to rest his horses and then he was going on to Helena. He didn't say anything about coming to see Daddy."

Trying hard to control her feeling of panic, Mary propped the shotgun against a kitchen chair. Straining to keep her voice calm, she said, "Let's just give him some of that buttermilk and a couple of biscuits, and maybe he'll get out of here."

"I hope you wasn't gonna make coffee with that shotgun." The voice came from the open doorway as Starbeau stepped inside and stood leering at the two captive females.

Not sure how much he had heard before he walked in, Mary tried to pull her shattered nerves together. "I was just getting it out of my way," she said. She snatched the jug of buttermilk from her daughter. "Janie, run out to the barn and see if we've got any fresh eggs. I'll pour a cup of buttermilk for our guest." She poured a cup of the milk, spilling a good portion as she tried to steady her trembling hand. When her daughter hesitated, confused by her mother's instructions, Mary spoke again in a voice as calm as she could manage. "Go on, child. Do as I told you."

Impassioned by the naked fear in the woman's eyes, Starbeau, his evil grin a constant fixture, took a step to block the girl's way. "I bet you already fetched them eggs this mornin', didn't you, little gal?" He grabbed her arm and pulled her with him to the table. "You stay here with me and your mama, and we'll have us a time like you ain't never seen before." Still holding Janie by the arm, he picked up the cup of buttermilk and drained the whole thing. Laughing, he smacked his lips loudly. "Ain't much better'n a cold cup of buttermilk," he roared. "But I know somethin' better. Ain't that right, Mama?"

Desperate, Mary grabbed for the shotgun, but Starbeau kicked it out of her reach, and with his free hand, clutched her around the throat. With mother and daughter trapped in steel-like grips, he backed Mary up against the kitchen wall, dragging Janie along with him, oblivious to her screaming and fighting. Clamping down tighter and tighter on the entrapped woman's throat, he grinned in her face as she fought for air.

Dangling like a rag doll, Mary Lester began losing consciousness as the air was shut off from her brain. Her life began spinning before her mind's eye; images of her husband, her family, friends from her childhood flashed before her. As she slid deeper into a dark abyss, the last image she remembered was that of a savage warrior.

Suddenly Starbeau released her and grunted as if something had struck him and knocked the wind from his lungs. As she slid down the wall to collapse on the floor, the cruel brute grunted a second time and staggered toward the table, a fire-hot pain searing his lungs and gut. Confused and in excruciating pain, he didn't resist when Janie pulled free of his grasp. Clutching a chair to keep from falling, he turned to face the avenging spirit standing in the doorway, the bowstring fully drawn. "Joe Fox!" he said with a gasp a split second before the final arrow was released and driven deep into his stomach.

Only then realizing what had happened to him, he looked down in shock at the deadly shaft buried in his gut, and his fear of the unknown seized his terrified mind. Suddenly, he vomited a vile mixture of blood and buttermilk, then fell to the floor, pulling the chair over on top of himself.

Still terrified, unsure what her fate was now at the hands of this new demon, Janie ran to her mother's side while Joe Fox grabbed Starbeau's ankles and dragged the huge corpse out the front door, across the porch, and off on the ground, breaking the two arrow shafts in Starbeau's back when he landed. He stood looking down at the corpse for a few moments. One each in the back for Bradley and Nancy Lindstrom, he thought, and the one unbroken shaft for Callie. Then he went back inside to check on Mary Lester.

He found her sitting up with her back against the wall, her daughter by her side. The two of them stared in uncertain fright at the formidable spirit dressed in animal skins. A sob of relief escaped from Mary's throat when he asked, "Are you all right, ma'am?"

It was a few moments more before she was able to get up, with the help of Joe and her daughter, and sit in a chair. "Who was that monster?" she managed, though her throat was hoarse and painful.

"He's the devil, ma'am," Joe answered, "and I've been chasin' him for a long time. As soon as I round up those horses, I'll drag him away from here." He waited while she and Janie explained that they thought he was a man who was supposed to bring two horses for her husband. Joe politely remained until they had finished relating the entire incident, even though he was eager to be on his way. "Yes, ma'am," he said when they were finished, and took his leave.

"Hold it right there! You take another step and I'll blow your head off." Joe had little choice but to stop. The man holding the rifle aimed at his head looked determined enough to do as he had threatened.

"No, Paul!" Mary cried from the doorway. "He saved our lives!"

Baffled by the scene that had met him when he returned from town, Paul Lester was at least relieved to see his wife and daughter safe. "What the hell happened here?" he exclaimed. "Who's that?" he asked, pointing to the body lying in his front yard.

"That's the devil," Janie said, repeating Joe's words. "And he was gonna kill Mama and me till he came along." She pointed at Joe.

Joe waited again through the relating of the incident and longer, since Paul pressed for a more detailed account of who Starbeau had been. "I reckon I might oughta go tell the sheriff about it," Paul said.

"I wouldn't bother," Joe said. "Just dump him in the ground somewhere. Ain't nobody gonna come lookin' for Starbeau. Your wife said you need two horses, so I'm leavin' two of those by the creek. I'm takin' the other two, since he killed my two horses. And I'm takin' the stuff in those packs. It's stuff he stole from some other folks."

"Mister," Paul said, shaking his head solemnly, "I don't know how I can ever thank you enough for saving my family."

Joe nodded. "I'm just glad I got here when I did."

When he turned to leave, Mary said, "God bless you, Joe Fox."

"Thank you, ma'am," he replied. It was the second time in as many days that he had been blessed, once for taking a life, and once for saving two.

Glad that he didn't have to go into the town of Helena, he left the saddle on Starbeau's big bay gelding and chose a spirited little sorrel that had belonged to one of the miners Starbeau had murdered. He took his pick of their two saddles. He didn't want a horse or saddle that might remind him of the ruthless killer and the misery he had caused for someone he held dear to his heart. With a wave of his hand to the Lester family, he led the packhorse back down the valley.

Chapter 17

It was good to be in the mountains again with no sense of urgency to get anyplace. He still had tasks to perform, but he decided he would do them at his leisure. He took time to hunt, and time to dry the meat. He had plenty of cartridges, thanks to Starbeau's packs, but he still hunted with his bow to conserve his supply of ammunition. He felt that he was home again, alone again, where he was before he encountered Malcolm Lindstrom and Pete Watson. It seemed a longer time ago than the few months it had been. He still thought about Callie, and hoped that she had managed to put her ordeal behind her. He would continue to think about her for a while, but like everything else in the mountains, he told himself, those thoughts would fade with the seasons.

Sheriff Lon Pedersen sat at his desk, reading the newspaper. His deputy, Jim Blackburn, stood looking out the front window, one foot propped on a wooden cartridge box. Things were back to normal in the sheriff's office, although Jim suspected that Pedersen still left most of the blame for the bank robbery and murder of Wallace Tolbert at his feet. A posse had scoured the mountains all around Butte with no results until they finally admitted it useless to continue. Jim argued that there was little he could have done to prevent the hold-up, and his best tracker came up empty on finding a trail to follow. He figured Pedersen was equally to blame for having gone fishing, although he didn't voice it to his boss.

"Well, I'll be damned," Blackburn muttered when a rider leading a packhorse pulled up to the hitching post and dismounted. When Pedersen looked up from his paper, Blackburn went on. "It's that crazy son of a bitch that looks like a wild Injun. I told you about him—came ridin' through town scarin' the hell outta everybody." This garnered Pedersen's interest, and the sheriff put down his paper, got up, and came to the window. "The only reason I didn't lock him up was a feller came running down the street hollerin' about the bank being robbed and Tolbert shot," Blackburn continued. "I didn't have time to mess with no fool half-breed or whatever he is."

"You figure he had anything to do with the bank holdup?" Pedersen asked.

"I don't see how he could," the deputy replied. "Like I said, he was talkin' to me when it happened."

"Well, let's see what he wants." Pedersen went to the door and opened it just as Joe Fox was untying a large cotton sack from one of the packs.

"You didn't learn much the last time you came through this town, did you?" Jim Blackburn blurted when he joined Pedersen at the door. "You're lucky I didn't lock you up then."

Joe did not answer right away, just gazed at Blackburn for a few seconds, as if deciding whether or not to bother. He finished untying the sack before speaking. "You the sheriff?" he asked Pedersen. When the sheriff nodded, Joe said, "I got somethin' here to give you."

"All right," Pedersen replied, "come on inside."

"All the same to you," Joe responded, "I'll just give it to you out here." Glancing at Blackburn, he said, "You folks are too quick to wanna put people in that jail and not let 'em out." Holding his rifle in one hand, he tossed the sack on the steps. "That's all my business here. I'll be goin' now."

"Wait a minute," Pedersen responded. "What's in it?" He was beginning to share Blackburn's opinion of the strange mountain man.

"The money Starbeau stole from the bank," Joe answered.

"The hell you say," Pedersen exclaimed, and reached for the sack. Peering inside, he asked, "Is it all there?"

"I don't know," was the stoic response.

"How much is in here?"

Again, "I don't know."

"You don't know?" Pedersen exclaimed, hardly believing. "Didn't you count it?"

"No."

"Why?"

Becoming impatient with the word game, Joe said, "Because it didn't belong to me, so it didn't make any difference how much there was."

Pedersen could hardly believe his ears. Then a more important question came to mind. "Where's the man who stole it? What did you say his name was?"

"Starbeau," Joe said. "He's dead."

It was obvious that the sheriff wanted more details than Joe was inclined to offer, but the adopted son of a Blackfoot warrior was eager to leave the busy town and return to the mountains. He didn't feel it necessary to explain that he had not counted the entire sack of money, but he *had* counted out two hundred and fifty dollars that he felt belonged to Callie's people in the mule train. He was not certain there would ever be an opportunity to return their money, but he would hold it for them in case he decided to see the Oregon country for himself. There was also the matter of the sacks of gold dust he assumed had been stolen from the two miners Starbeau killed. He hadn't decided what to do about that.

His talking done, he grabbed the saddle horn with one hand, and with his rifle in the other, stepped up in the saddle. Backing his horse away from the hitching post as if expecting the lawmen to try to stop him, he suddenly turned the sorrel and was away at a gallop.

"Hey! Hold on there!" Blackburn yelled.

"Let him go," Pedersen said. "Hell, he didn't rob the bank. I don't think we'll see him around here again."

Grace Templeton stood in the door of her husband's store, watching the slender young woman bending over a large iron pot, stirring the clothes with a paddle. After a few moments, she turned to her husband. "Horace, I think this is a mistake."

"What is?" Horace replied.

"Letting that child stay here with us. Every time I look at her it breaks my heart."

Horace Templeton walked over to stand behind his wife. "Well, I don't know . . . ," he began. "She's a good worker, and she sure don't eat much. I didn't think she was all that much trouble."

"I declare, Horace, you don't even know what I'm talking about, do you?" When her husband responded with a mystified look, she just shook her head. "Men," she uttered, exasperated.

For a fact, Horace didn't know what his wife was complaining about. The young lady really wasn't much trouble. She seemed content to live in a corner of the back storeroom and she was a genuine help with the chores. Besides, what choice did a Christian family have? She refused to go on to Oregon with her own family, and they were about to give up their dream of finding a new place with friends and family already waiting for them until Grace said Callie could stay with them.

Luke and Jenny Preston, the only family from the congregation that had decided to settle in the Missoula Valley, had extended an invitation to the girl to stay with them. But Callie declined, saying she would work for her room and board with the Templetons. The two Flynn brothers had volunteered to stay to help Preston build his cabin, planning to rejoin the congregation in Oregon when the cabin was finished. "Seems to me everythin' worked out all right," Horace commented. "Callie's gettin' along just fine, as far as I can see."

Grace favored her husband with a look of astonishment. "I declare, you really can't see what's happening right before your eyes, can you?"

"What?" he demanded, impatiently.

"She's dying of a broken heart," Grace declared. "Maybe not so much as you'd notice right away. But she's telling herself that he's gonna come for her one day."

"Who?"

"Joe Fox, that's who. The poor child hides that pitiful scarred-up face from everybody that comes around here—taking those long walks by the river at night—and it ain't been that long since those Indians raided this place."

Horace was struck dumb for a second. "You think she's really waitin' for Joe Fox?" He found that hard to believe. "Hell, Joe Fox is somewhere so far back in the mountains . . . I doubt we'll ever see him around these parts again."

"And that's why that poor child is dying of a broken heart," Grace said.

"Well, I reckon she's welcome to stay here as long as she wants," he said, and went back to the barrel of molasses he had been in the process of opening before his wife started the troublesome discussion.

"She's too young to be giving up on her life," Grace continued, still watching Callie. "The best thing for her is to go back to her folks. I'm gonna talk to her about it. Luke Preston has almost finished his cabin, so the two Flynn boys will be heading to Oregon pretty soon. Maybe I can persuade Callie to go with them. She needs family, and we can't give her that."

As if sensing that she was the subject of someone's conversation, Callie paused and straightened up to ease the strain on her back. She had in fact stopped turning away from the stares of strangers and regulars alike who came to the trading post. She had learned to ignore the pitying stares as well as the rude, curious gawks, and keep her head held high. She could have told Grace that, although she watched the valley road every day for Joe's return, she did not expect it. They had said their good-byes, and gone their separate ways. The hardest part had been trying to explain to her mother and father why she just couldn't go to Oregon with them. She felt that if she had remained with the congregation, the stigma of her brutal assault would go with her, forever alive in their minds. Here in this valley, she was just the woman with the scarred face. She knew that she could not stay with the Templetons forever, but maybe God would show her a sign before long, and she would know what to do. She brought her mind back to the wash. *Better get these out of the pot and hung up if they're going to dry before dark,* she thought.

The evenings were getting warm enough now to be quite pleasant for a walk along the river. Callie hurried to help Grace clean up the supper dishes so she would have time to walk before it became too dark. She knew it worried Grace and Horace if she stayed out after dark.

Taking a light wrap for her shoulders, she left the house behind the trading post, and turned away from the valley road. In a melancholy sense of mind, she decided to walk down by the old line of caves where she and her family had spent the winter. It had been some time now since she had visited the caves. Horace had warned her that there was no telling what manner of vermin or animals might have taken up residence there since they were vacated. She wasn't concerned.

Walking down the line of dark holes in the bluffs, she counted the openings until she came to her family's cave. She stood staring into the dark entrance for a long time, thoughts of a happier time filling her mind. Remembering a night that seemed long ago, she climbed over the top of the cave and stood gazing out toward the stand of cottonwoods across the clearing— where he had made his camp. There was nothing there now but the lonely darkness. She closed her eyes and pictured him, dressed in animal skins, his hair in two long braids, like an Indian, tall and straight as he walked toward her with long fluid strides. It brought a smile to her face.

She opened her eyes to find the vision still in her mind. Blinking rapidly to clear her senses, she thought at first that she was dreaming. Then her eyes began to fill with tears of joy, for she realized that it was no dream. It was him, striding toward her, leading two horses behind him. She didn't wait any longer, but ran to him, desperate to capture the dream before it could fade away.

He caught her in his arms and kissed her scarred face again and again while she clung to him as if afraid he might slip away. "I've come to take you home," he said, "our home. That is, if you'll have me."

"I'll live anywhere as long as it's with you, Joe Fox," she answered, "even if it's in a tent."

Thinking of the sacks of gold dust in his saddle-bags, he said, "I think we'll do a little better than that."

With her heart threatening to burst with joy, she squeezed him tighter still and whispered, "How did you know I'd wait for you here?"

"I didn't," he said. "I was on my way to Oregon."